TRAGIC

A CRYPTID HORROR THRILLER

BY EDWARD J. MCFADDEN III

SEVERED**PRESS**

TRAGIC

Copyright © 2023 by Edward J. McFadden III

WWW.SEVEREDPRESS.COM

This novel is a work of fiction. Names, characters, places and incidents are the product of the author's imagination, or are used fictitiously.

Any resemblance to actual events, locales or persons, living or dead, is purely coincidental.

ISBN: 978-1-922861-73-3

"Come what come may, time and the hour run through the roughest day."
— William Shakespeare

1

Borderland Pass, I-49, Ozark Mountains, 4:51 PM CST, March 12th, 2021

The COVID pandemic set Carter Renfrow free.

He relished no longer having to wear a disguise to go to the supermarket, and he didn't miss the constant fear of being recognized by some random citizen. Carter loved being able to see his kids again, even if it was from afar, and that simple act gave purpose to his lost life. The incident had taken so much from him, his freedom—his entire life, but then he'd gotten lucky. When the world locked its doors for a year he disappeared, and the pandemic normalized the use of medical masks, and with them came anonymity.

The wind roared as I-49 knifed through the western edge of the Ozark Mountains. Darkness pressed in on the highway, the thump of the Ford passing over expansion joints creating an upbeat tempo that was keeping Carter awake. His eyelids drooped, and shadows danced at the periphery of his vision, amorphous fingers of fog massaging the road and blending into the creeping dusk, the glow of the setting sun angling through narrow breaks in the dark clouds like dying spotlights. White oaks with dead leaves clinging to their branches and shortleaf pines packed the sides of the road, the underbrush buried in a blanket of snow that stretched to the interstate's shoulder, the gray forms of the rolling mountains fading beyond the wash of the car's headlights.

Carter had been driving for six hours, and his neck ached. Tommy's away game in West Fork was the following day at 11 AM, and he wanted to get a good night's sleep so he could get up early and reconnoiter the location. He also hoped to catch a glimpse of Katie, but his daughter didn't go out much these days, and he doubted she'd make the trip. Debra would surely be there, but his wife no longer factored into his plans. When the cops came for him, she'd left him for dead, and that's exactly how he planned to keep things.

The windshield clouded, and Carter turned on the defroster and cracked the windows. Cold air leaked into the white Taurus, and he turned on the radio, silky jazz filling the car. Thick clouds of fog billowed across the road, and no red taillights pierced the gloom ahead. Carter glanced in the rearview mirror, his brown eyes streaked with red, the stubble of his crew cut like bristles on a hairbrush. No headlights cut through the fog behind him, so Carter eased off the gas pedal, the un-scratchable itch of unfounded worry churning his stomach. He lifted his beer from a cupholder and took a pull, the alcohol and wheat-flavored effervescence dulling his angst.

He leaned against the window, a dull pain massaging his neck. As darkness settled on the highway, Carter went through his mental catalogue, reliving the past two years, hoping something would change, but he knew better than most what happened when he did the same things but expected different results.

Carter tapped the Ford's wheel in rhythm with the jazz as he thought of the good times when his kids were young, and all his horizons were sunny. The memories were a mental elixir, and they brought him back to a time when he had a job teaching high schoolers about history and the world hiding from a disease was fiction. Before the incident. He slumped in his seat, his eyelids falling to half-mast, weariness leaking through him, the sound of the radio dying away.

Beep. Beep. Beep. Sharp alarm chimes blared from the car radio.

Carter shook his head, blinked, sat up straight, put down the beer, and gripped the wheel with both hands. Visibility had dropped to fifty yards, the whiteness ahead thicker than the deepest night.

Beep. Beep. Beep. A female computer voice said, "This is an NWS Severe Weather Update. Scattered whiteouts have been reported on I-49 north of Winslow. Reduce speed and use extreme caution."

Pinpricks of red appeared in the gloom ahead, and Carter pressed on the brake.

Beep. Beep. Beep. The message repeated.

Dense fog obscured the road and the horizon disappeared, the windshield a blank white canvas. Red taillights appeared out of the whiteness, the booms of collisions, and the sound of crunching metal carrying over the interstate.

Carter jumped on the Ford's brake, but it was too late.

The Taurus rear-ended a black sedan. Plastic cracked, metal crunched, and rubber screamed as Carter was thrown forward, then pushed back as an airbag exploded and pinned him to the seat. Air rushed from his lungs and tiny pinpricks of light danced before his fading vision. The radio fell silent as the Ford came to a rocking halt and stalled out. Pain pierced Carter's chest as the seatbelt dug into his shoulder, and his ears rang like he'd been knocked in the head with a two-by-four.

Vehicles were strewn haphazardly across the road and its shoulders, red taillights piercing the whiteness, headlights casting deep elongated shadows over the chaos. The accident scene extended into whiteness, and the interior lights of cars blossomed in the haze as people got out of their vehicles.

Carter glanced at the glovebox where he kept his Heckler & Koch VP9, but decided to leave it where it was. When the cops arrived, he had to be gone. He considered abandoning the rental car and fleeing into the surrounding forest, but the cold wind pressing into the Ford from the cracked-open windows convinced him otherwise. But the police were probably already on their way and w—

A spark of light caught Carter's eye and he glanced at the rearview mirror.

Headlights appeared in the whiteness, two glowing reptilian-like eyes bearing down on the Taurus.

Carter jerked on the Ford's steering wheel, but the car was stalled and there was no place to go anyway.

The impact jarred Carter's bones and rattled his teeth as he was pulled against his seatbelt, his head still ringing like an alarm bell. Plastic cracked, metal twisted, and the rear window shattered as the Ford's trunk caved in, tiny shards of square glass spraying the inside of the car. Wind gusted through the opening, thick fog curling around the vehicle like ghosts.

The roar of a tractor-trailer's horn blared like a klaxon. More lights in the rearview.

Carter reached to unbuckle his seatbelt but froze. Jumping from the vehicle would only put him in a worse position. Inside the protective shell of the Taurus, he had a chance. Out on the road, amidst the remains of car bumper pool, he'd be crushed like a bug.

The semi roared past the Taurus in the right lane, and the Ford rocked from the force of its passage.

Carter pressed his eyes shut.

An explosion of rending metal, breaking glass, and shrieking brakes rose above the ringing in Carter's head. He opened his eyes and saw another car fly by in the right lane and smash into the eighteen-wheeler, the small blue car disappearing beneath the truck's massive trailer.

Ahead, flames licked the growing darkness, and Carter's nerves danced just beneath his skin, sweat dripping down his forehead and back. A gust of wind tore away the whiteness and invisible spiders crawled down Carter's spine as he stared at the rows of smashed cars on the road ahead. Vehicles of every color, size, and make were scattered about, smoke and flames rising from many of them.

He needed to get out of the line of fire. Carter twisted the ignition key and got nothing but faint tapping through the echo of the bell tolling in his head. Moisture migrated from his mouth to his armpits as total helplessness clutched him. He'd felt that way before the incident, and his skin crawled, heat washing over him as more headlights appeared in the rearview mirror.

The pop of a bumper smacking a bumper, and the car wedged in the Taurus's trunk lurched forward. Metal tore and glass exploded as a wail of pain pierced the chaos, the cry of a person in great pain or suffering immense sorrow.

Everything was still for a heartbeat, the wind bitching and yelling. Thick clouds of frozen mist rolled across the road as the cold air condensed the fog and blended into the surrounding snow-blanketed mountain valley known as Borderland Pass.

Airbrakes chirped and the staggering screech of rubber gripping slick concrete carried over the interstate as headlights bright as the sun illuminated the horrific scene.

A semi rammed the carnage like a snowplow. The *womp* of a deafening explosion and the car lodged in the Taurus's trunk vibrated like a tuning fork as it was pressed forward. An eruption of flying glass and metal engulfed Carter as the Ford was lifted from the ground and pushed aside like a leaf.

Carter's stomach dropped out, pain lancing his back and neck as the Taurus flipped and landed on its side wedged between an upside-down car and a box trailer. The upside-down vehicle was still sliding, and for an instant Carter saw a woman's face through the broken windshield, felt the raw terror in her eyes, then she was gone, her car sliding off the road.

He wiggled his fingers and toes. The seatbelt tore into his neck, but he didn't dare release it. The belt had already saved his life twice, and as he stared into the angled rearview, he saw more headlights blooming beyond the white-shrouded wreckage.

With each impact came the jarring vibration of contact, followed by the shifting of the pile, and the ensuing squeaks and pops as the destruction tightened and settled. Carter wanted to do something, help those that were hurt, help himself, but he lay frozen, his body pressed against the Ford's driver's side door. His mind strayed to the police again. When they arrived, every person involved would be cataloged and questioned, and if he didn't have the right answers—even if he did—he could end up in jail by day's end.

No sirens wailed, and Carter remembered where he was. Borderland Pass cut across a desolate section of I-49, and there was nothing around except trees, rolling mountains, and the people and animals who dared to call the place home. It could take hours for rescue services to arrive given the growing darkness, weather, and location. When they did arrive an army of medics would be required, in addition to every tow truck in Arkansas, and it could take days to untangle the mess.

Something stung Carter's right eye and he reached up to find a thin stream of blood leaking from a cut on his forehead. He hadn't even felt the blow, but that wasn't surprising. Every muscle in his body ached like he'd run a marathon, and his head still rang like the noon bell.

The thumps and vibrations continued, but as the impacts got further away from Carter's position the Ford didn't shift, and his spine stopped shrieking with each impact. The Taurus was crammed into the destruction, and the interstate had become a junkyard, all the cars compacted into a semi-solid chunk.

There was yelling and screaming, but he couldn't see anything except the inside of the Taurus, the mashed-up metal in the rearview, and the scattered desolation of the vehicles before him. He felt like a piece of tuna in a can, and the thought of food made his stomach grumble. He'd planned on eating when he reached the motel, but now he'd have to rely on a bag of chips and the remaining four beers. Carter licked blood from his lips. What would happen if there was an infant in one of the piled-up cars? An elderly person that needed medication or constant care?

Carter rolled his shoulders, the seatbelt biting his neck. None of that was his problem because if his fellow crash victims discovered who he was they'd string him up like a posse that's caught a bank robber. He glanced at the medical mask wedged into the crack where the windshield met the dashboard, and his thoughts strayed to the black neck gaiter wrapped around the H&K in the glovebox.

The Ford creaked as it moved slightly. Another loud thump echoed through the pass, and Carter figured another truck had joined the pileup. How many cars would be crushed before the road was closed? How many people stranded? Carter recalled news stories about massive multi-car pileups, and he knew that more than a hundred vehicles had been involved in some of them.

A chunk of ice formed in his stomach as Carter reached for his burner phone which had been thrown across the car and lay at his feet wedged under the gas pedal. He couldn't reach it, and once again he considered snapping out of his seatbelt.

The booms of impacts had stopped, and no vibrations ran through the Taurus. Carter's heart pounded as he listened hard, filtering out the crying wind, and cataloging each scream and call for help. He heard no more collisions.

Fog peppered with specks of ice wafted into the Ford, the cold pricking Carter's face and pushing up goosebumps. A woman wailed, ranting about her baby. Someone needed to help her baby. Cries of pain, shouts for assistance, and the hiss of punctured radiators carried over the desolation, the air thick with the scent of gasoline, antifreeze, and smoke.

Carter snapped out of his seatbelt and tried to stand, using the car door for support. The Taurus shifted and rocked, and Carter stopped moving. With the vehicle on its side, and the front and rear windows filled with metal, his only option, if he wanted out, was the passenger side door. Assuming it wasn't smashed permanently shut, he could climb out. He reached down and grabbed his phone, pocketed it, and stood.

Broken glass crackled beneath his feet as Carter grabbed the passenger seatbelt and used it to pull himself onto the transmission column. He peered up at the churning whiteness through the shattered window, and then glanced at the glovebox, then back up at the blinding whiteness.

He had no clue what awaited him out there and given his luck he didn't want to take any chances. Carter searched the front seat and found his gloves and hat. He zipped his winter jacket, snapped open the glove compartment, and pulled free the H&K. He unwrapped it and pulled the black neck gaiter over his head, covering his face from the nose down, and then put on his hat and gloves. Then he chambered a round, wedged the pistol into the small of his back, and forced open the Taurus's door.

2

The car door was crushed, and Carter had a hard time forcing it open. With the vehicle on its side and him perched on the transmission column, he had little leverage. The VP9 bit his back as he struggled and pushed, sweat forming on his face beneath his mask, the creak and whine of shifting metal rising above the whistling wind. After several minutes of struggle, he was able to release the lock and get the door open. Getting through it was another matter.

Using the passenger seat headrest as a step, he slithered partway out. With his legs dangling in the car, and the door pressing on his back, Carter army crawled free.

Cold wind bit his face, the car shifting and swaying under his weight as he pushed to his knees. The whiteout had thinned, but not much, and thick fog still settled over the valley.

Borderland Pass was packed with destroyed cars. Apocalyptic devastation stretched into shadowy flame-dappled whiteness, filling the road and its shoulder with a chaotic mess of SUVs, cars, box trucks, campers, and tractor-trailers. The sound of human suffering and panic carried on the breeze, and headlight beams cut through the growing darkness, forming large bright clouds in the whiteness.

An eighteen-wheeler was wedged against the Taurus, and the front half of a small blue car was buried under the truck's trailer, its rear-end sticking out, red taillights blinking intermittently. Behind the blue car, a van and a pickup were jammed together as if they were one vehicle. The driver of the van was slumped over the steering wheel, and Carter didn't see the driver of the pickup.

Someone was yelling, and Carter realized his ears were still ringing and he rubbed his temples. A woman was shrieking, her panicked cries like sandpaper on Carter's brain.

"Help! Please. Anyone, please help."

Carter's first instinct was to call for an ambulance and he pulled his phone free. No signal. Not surprising. He was in the middle of nowhere, in a valley at two thousand feet, and then there was the growing storm. He put the phone away and searched for the source of the plea.

A black Honda was half in the Ford's trunk, and behind that, there were two flipped-over cars and a motorhome that now had a car inside it. People crawled and fought from the wreckage, their faces bloody, but Carter didn't see anyone calling for help.

Nothing moved ahead, and Carter thought the cries for help might be coming from the trailer of the eighteen-wheeler next to the Taurus.

He inched down the side of the Ford on his hands and knees like a kid afraid to stand up on a balance beam, the destroyed car shifting beneath him. When Carter reached the trunk he climbed down to the road, though touching feet to cement wasn't possible given the knot of vehicles and debris that covered the interstate.

The calls for help got louder and Carter worked his way around to the rear of the semi, where he found a woman hovering over a man strapped in the driver's seat of a blue Nissan embedded in the back of the trailer.

"Hello?" he called, ears still chiming dully.

The woman stopped wailing and turned, her brown face smeared with blood, dark eyes frenzied, her long black hair disheveled.

Carter peered through the blown-out back window of the Nissan as he considered how to get the woman out of the vehicle. The car had plowed into the back of the semi, and its front end was wedged beneath the truck's trailer. Carter had no intentions of climbing through the thin rear window, so he used the blue car's bumper to hoist himself onto the roof, and he crawled to the front of the vehicle.

There was nothing left forward of the dashboard except squeezed metal, the engine crushed and smoking, a trickle of antifreeze dripping onto the frozen road. The rear doors of the trailer were partly wedged open, and Carter pulled his phone and tapped the light app.

His breath caught in his throat as he stared into the dark tunnel of the trailer. Corpses filled the gap, their light brown faces torn away, their crushed skulls dripping blood. A zap of static electricity ran through Carter, a wave of sorrow rolling through him.

The truck had been transporting people, and they had been standing freely in the trailer.

Carter slipped his phone away and dropped down into the Nissan's wreckage, using the dashboard for support.

The steering column was pushed back along with the rest of the front end, and though the airbag had deployed, the man behind the wheel was wedged between the steering wheel and the seat, which had broken from its mounts and was angled backward. Blood covered the man's face, and his chest was an open wound, guts spilling out around the steering wheel which was now part of his ribcage. It didn't take a doctor to see that the man was going to die, if he hadn't already.

The woman recovered and said, "Help me. Please!"

"Help you do what?" Carter said, his mask tickling his nose.

The woman's eyes narrowed, and pain creased her face, then softened.

"Sorry, it's just…" Carter had never been good at giving people bad news.

"We need to get him out of here," the woman said. "Can you help me? Please?"

Carter wanted to tell the woman to mask up. The last thing he needed was to catch COVID. Instead, he said, "I'm sure help is on the way." He heard no sirens, and with the fog, helicopters would be out of the question, but he saw no reason not to try and soothe the woman's pain.

She didn't buy what he was selling, and she said nothing, her face impassive.

"Listen, what's your name? Mine's…" He hesitated for the briefest instant as he remembered he couldn't give his real name. "Mine's Ray. Ray Destrie." He never used the same alias twice, and he'd gotten adept at making up names.

"Aniyah."

"Aniyah, if we move him, we could do more damage than good," Carter said. "Does he have a pulse? When was the last time he spoke? Or opened his eyes?" He hoped these subtle nudges would break the woman from the trance of shock. When she didn't answer, he added, "And even if we can get him out without hurting him further, where will we bring him? It's a disaster area out there."

Aniyah looked around as if trying to see through the walls of the semi's trailer, then her gaze fell back on her husband. The man's chest didn't rise and fall, and he made no sound. As if Carter's words had penetrated her daze, she reached out with a shaking hand and placed her index and middle fingers just to the side of her husband's Adam's apple. She held them there a long time, and when she finally pulled her hand away her face fell, and her shoulders slumped as the cruelty of acceptance tore a hole in her reality.

"You O.K.?" Carter asked. What a stupid question, but isn't that what you said when you were trying to show compassion?

She looked at him, tears welling in her eyes again.

"Let's get you out of there," he said.

With that, the dam broke, and Aniyah started to cry, a slow sob that grew into full-on hysterics. She wailed and babbled. Her life was over. What would she do without Harry? How would she live?

Carter knew she'd just been through a traumatic event, and lost her husband, all in ten minutes, and there would be time for mourning, but that time wasn't now. "Hey! Come on now. We need to help each other if we want to live."

"Help is on the way, right?" she said, worry lines creasing her face.

Carter said nothing.

"I can't leave him like this."

With his frustration growing at a pace he didn't understand—he'd just been knocked around also—he said, "Fine. Stay here. When the authorities arrive, I'll send them your way, but…" He trailed off. That not being able to tell people bad news thing again.

"But what?"

"But they'll most likely be more concerned with the living. Like you, you are alive, remember? Are you hurt?" Blood covered Aniyah's shirt, but it looked to be her deceased husband's. She wore slacks and heels, and it occurred to Carter that she'd need to bundle up and change her footwear.

Aniyah said nothing.

Carter started climbing out of the car.

"Wait," she screamed. "Don't leave me alone. Please."

"Do you have any other clothes you can put on?"

"My gym bag is in the trunk, but…" The trunk was a block of twisted metal, and the bag was encased in it.

"A jacket?"

She nodded.

"Pull it on and I'll help you out."

Aniyah stared at the corpse of her dead husband, bursts of crying and wails of pain still exploding from her in sporadic bursts. She reached over and closed her husband's eyes and mumbled a prayer, then made the sign of the cross.

Carter reached out to take Aniyah's hand and she said, "I don't know what I'm going to do without Harry." She gazed up at Carter, her brown eyes pleading for guidance and reassurance, but he had none to give. There were likely many people in need of assistance, and he was beginning to get frustrated. Aniyah could climb out on her own when she was ready. He pulled back his hand and her eyes grew wide.

"What is it, Ray?"

"If you want to live you need to put your grieving on the backburner," he said, the sounds of chaos growing around him. "There will be a time to mourn, and think about him, but right now you need to worry about yourself." He reached into the car again and this time she took his hand.

Carter hauled Aniyah out of the Nissan, and they climbed across the roof.

The whiteout was lifting as darkness leaked over the interstate, and visibility was a hundred yards. Carter felt like he was trapped in a cloud as he watched people mill about like lost ants as they crawled over smashed vehicles. The scent of gasoline, burnt rubber, and the astringent smell of antifreeze pervaded the air, and thick black and white smoke mixed with the fog as it twisted and wound through the wreckage.

Aniyah screamed.

Carter jerked his head around and followed her gaze, which was locked on a young man missing an arm, his head crushed, his legs twisted and broken. The corpse was pinned against the Nissan's rear bumper, and it looked like the guy had exploded through the windshield of the car behind Aniyah's.

"Guess he didn't have his seatbelt on," Carter said.

Aniyah looked at him like he had four heads, a look of disgust similar to his wife's.

Carter had spoken to nobody in the last two years other than strangers who were necessary for survival, and it struck him that what he'd said was incredibly insensitive, especially to a woman who had just seen her husband crunched. He said, "Sorry, again, I'm still a little dazed myself."

She nodded, smiled at him, and said, "Thanks for helping me out of there."

"No worries, well, you have worries, but... You're welcome." Suddenly it hit Carter how beautiful Aniyah was. Her face, though smeared with blood, had a distinct loveliness, her large brown eyes pools of warmth.

A vicious growl carried on the wind.

The palms of Carter's hands itched as a tremor of fear and worry buried into him like hungry maggots.

A gurgle, and the gnashing of teeth.

The wreckage behind the Nissan shifted, and there was a grunt and the rumble of exertion.

Aniyah cried out again, her voice cracking with horror.

The corpse of the young man was gone. A thick smear of blood trailed over the crushed white hood of a box truck and disappeared into a car that no longer had a roof.

"Wait here," Carter said, and Aniyah didn't protest.

He slid off the roof of the Nissan onto the wreckage of the vehicle behind it. The clang of metal, a random thumping, and a strange chuffing sound echoed over the road as Carter followed the trail of blood.

The driver of the box truck was dead, despite the seatbelt holding his corpse in place. The vehicle looked old and there were no airbags. Carter climbed over the truck's hood, being careful not to touch the blood slick, which was getting thicker.

A loud throaty groan of effort rose above the clanging and thumping, the wind, and the cries and yells of his fellow crash victims.

"Hello?" Carter said.

No response, and the clanging and thumping and grunting stopped.

Carter dropped between two wrecked cars and worked his way toward the shoulder of the road, following the blood trail. His heart hammered, his thoughts a chaotic sea of waves and whitecaps, conflicting ideas and facts. He had seen the corpse, right? He was following a trail of blood, wasn't he? Why? And who the hell would be dragging a body toward the woods when there were people who needed assistance?

The wind whistled and sang as it worked its way through the destruction, the wreckage like a surreal instrument, Carter's nerves jangling with each ghostly note. Someone yelled—sounded like a child, and he picked up his pace, dancing across a bumper and jumping onto the hood of a pickup that was only damaged on one side because it was on the shoulder of the road.

A young girl in a blue ski jacket wearing a white medical mask with Dora the Explorer on it, her blonde hair spilling out from beneath a white knit cap, stared into the forest at the edge of the interstate.

"Is everything O.K.?" Carter asked.

No response.

The corpse he was tracking lay strewn on the interstate's shoulder, thick bloody claw marks raking across what was left of the body's face and chest. Fingers of fog reached out from the dark tree line, mist lifting from the snow-covered underbrush.

Huge crimson footprints marred the dirty snow and trailed into the forest, and a bestial roar thundered over the desolation.

3

Borderland Pass, I-49, Ozark Mountains, 5:16 PM CST, March 12th, 2021

Darkness engulfed the destruction, dying headlight beams cutting through the fog, the chill wind sharp as a blade. The glow of flames flickered in the gloom, the whiteout surrendering to an army of thick stratocumulus clouds bursting from the western horizon. The air was ripe with the scents of gasoline, smoke, and despair.

Carter stood motionless, his eyes ranging over the tree line. An amorphous black shape glided just within the forest. A bear, maybe? He knew black bears crawled all over the Ozark Mountains, but they weren't very big or aggressive, and attacks were extremely rare. Still. What else would've dragged a corpse through the wreckage? The wind gusted, swirling the whiteness, and two yellow pinpricks of light pierced the darkness beneath the tree canopy.

A warm dread crept over Carter, the heat of terror and helplessness. His back ached, his stomach going sour. The two yellow orbs hung in the darkness eight feet above the ground. If the lights were the eyes of a black bear, it was a big one and it was standing on its hind legs.

He reached for the H&K, remembered the little girl was standing next to him, and instead pulled his phone and hit his light app. Carter aimed the weak light toward the woods, and the yellow pinpricks disappeared.

Carter's breath caught in his throat like a fishbone. Huge four-toed footprints in the soft snow formed double tracks like those of a bipedal creature, three-inch slices at the tip of each digit delineating claws. The tracks trailed away into the milky darkness. He pocketed his phone and dropped to a knee before the little girl, who hadn't taken her eyes off the forest where the eyes had been. He said, "What's your name, sweetie?"

The wind whispered and sighed as the young blonde looked at the tree line, then down at the ground. "Stacey. What's yours?" She brushed away a stray length of hair that had snaked out from beneath her white ski cap.

"Ca… Ray. Where's your mom and dad?"

Stacey pulled up her mask, her eyes ranging from the trees, to the corpse, then over her shoulder, but she said nothing.

"Are they still in the car?"

The kid nodded.

He wanted to ask the girl why her parents allowed her to wander around the accident scene by herself, but then he remembered her parents could be trapped in their car or dead. "Do you want to take me to them?"

Stacey shook her head no.

"Where's your car?"

The kid made no sign.

Carter took the girl's chin in his hand, and said, "Maybe I can help them. Just show me which car is yours. You don't need to go anywhere near it if you don't want to. O.K.?"

The glow returned to Stacey's eyes when Carter said "help them", and the kid nodded. "I'll show you, but that's it." She thrust out a pinky.

Carter wound his pinky around Stacey's, pushed to his feet, and said, "Deal."

The pair worked their way north along the shoulder of the road. Crying, shouts, and garbled conversations rose above the wind as flames licked the darkness, black smoke driving away the whiteness. As they walked, Carter said, "Stacey, did you see what dragged that body to the edge of the road?"

The girl stiffened as if recycling a bad memory.

"Well?" he pushed.

"Not really, I mean… I saw a shadow, but not… whatever took the dead man."

"A shadow?"

"A big one."

"Anything else?"

She hiked her shoulders. "Nothing except the blood."

Right. The blood.

"That's my car," Stacey said as she pointed. "The green one with the black roof."

As soon as he saw the crushed SUV Carter knew there was no way Stacey's parents were alive. The truck had rammed into a flatbed trailer, and the roof had been peeled back like a tuna can. What was left of the SUV was in the right lane, and the car next to it had a bloody corpse on its hood.

Stacey stared at the ground.

"Wait here, for me, O.K.?"

The kid nodded but didn't look up.

As Carter worked his way around and over the wreckage, he wondered if Stacey would ever be able to have a normal life. Regardless of whether her parents lived, she was scarred for life. He also knew kids had an amazing ability to forget, and maybe someday, years from now when all this had faded, she would be able to move on.

But probably not.

Carter spit up in his mask and gripped the jagged edge of the truck's crushed passenger side door. The interior of the SUV was splattered with blood, and the car's driver was male judging by the clothing drenched red. The man had been decapitated, and his head, its face crushed and deformed, lay between the man's legs in the footwell. A notched spinal column, muscle, gristle, and blood leaked from his jagged neck.

The woman sat crushed in her seatbelt, the front of her face peeled off, her white dress tie-dyed red and purple. Her head hung at an odd angle, her remaining eye staring at Carter. In the backseat, a child's booster seat was strapped in, and to Carter, the thing looked like it belonged in a jet fighter. The top of the child seat fell just below the height of the dashboard, which was why Stacey still had a head on her shoulders.

He scanned the backseat of the car and saw a teddy bear and baby doll dressed in a wedding gown-type dress. The white ruffles on the doll's dress had tiny dots of blood on them, so he left it where it was and grabbed the brown teddy bear. It was one of those things kids made themselves at birthday parties, and the bear wore a blue shirt with a T-rex on its front.

Carter avoided a knot of people and worked his way back to Stacey.

No sirens wailed, and Carter checked his watch. Though it felt like days had passed it had only been twenty-five minutes, and he figured the authorities were just getting mobilized. He glanced down at the teddy bear he carried. Carter was picking up strays at a precarious rate, and that was exactly what he didn't need. The suddenness of his predicament twisted and gnawed at him as he climbed over the wreckage.

He could just start walking and abandon the rental car, but... Was there anything in there that could tie the vehicle to him? He'd used his fake ID and credit card to rent the car, so if he abandoned the Ford eventually the rental company would get around to giving his information to the police, so he'd have to get a new set of documents. Not the end of the world, but it involved risks, and it would take time. He could strip the plates and scratch off the registration, but that would take time and would only slow down the inevitable.

Carter searched his memory. He had his meager bag of clothes, which had his DNA all over it, but DNA matches take time, and he didn't think an abandoned car in the middle of a hundred-car pileup would be a priority, but eventually...

He froze, one knee on the hood of a crushed SUV, the other on the oil-soaked pavement. How had he forgotten about his stash of money—the most important thing. It was hidden under the spare tire in the trunk. That settled it. He would need cash, especially if his credit card had to be tossed. Carter sighed and rolled his shoulders, a cloud of steam forming around his head. Maybe the accident had scrambled his eggs a bit more than he thought. He rolled his shoulders as he pushed up onto the truck's hood. Maybe going back wasn't all bad. He could get his stuff, hand the kid off to Aniyah, and make like a tree.

Carter found Stacey right where he'd left her, but she wasn't alone. A person wearing a neck gaiter decorated with a wicked mouth filled with sharp teeth stood over the girl. Carter slipped behind an overturned van and watched. Maybe this was his chance to hand off the girl, but something about the guy sent the mice scurrying up Carter's spine. He held a flashlight, the glow of fading headlights glinting off the guy's glasses.

Stacey stared up at the man, hands before her Dora mask like she would've been biting her nails were she not impeded. The guy was trying to talk the little girl into taking her mask off so he could see her face.

Starbursts of heat blossomed in Carter's chest, sweat dripping down his back despite the cold. He caressed the grip of the VP9, stepped from concealment, and said, "Hey, Stacey, everything O.K. over there? Look what I brought." He held out the teddy bear.

Stacey scurried to Carter's side and accepted the stuffed animal, her lips curling slightly.

"Howdy," said the new guy. "She your daughter?"

"At the moment," Carter said. "Can I help you with something?"

The guy laughed, an attempt to sound like a good old boy, but it was forced and even Stacey realized it. She stepped closer to Carter.

"Naw, all good. Name's Jed. I just saw her, and well, with that thing running around."

A red flag rose in Carter's head. "Thing?"

"You didn't see it?"

Carter said nothing.

"It was huge, black, and the way it moved..." The guy shook his head. "Like a fish through water. Like it was floating on air." Jed shook his head again. "I know that sounds crazy..."

"It? What was it?"

"Your guess is as good as mine, partner. I didn't get a good look, but I felt it, you know? Watching. Evaluating. It wasn't no bear."

Carter was getting a better vibe from Jed now that he'd talked to him. The man's jeans were ripped and dirty with mud, but otherwise, he looked fine. With the conversation over, Carter wanted to get back to his car and get on with it, but he was afraid if he left now Jed would follow him, and three's company but four's a crowd.

"How long you reckon we'll be out here? It's gonna get cold. I think that camper up there has a fire going." He pointed, but Carter didn't see any flames licking the darkness in the direction he pointed.

"I don't know," Carter said.

Stacey tugged on Carter's jeans. "Did you find my mom and dad? Can you help them?"

Carter glanced over at Jed, who was watching a thin trickle of green antifreeze run onto the shoulder of the road. Carter patted the kid on the head, and said, "No, sweetie, I can't."

"Are they dead?"

Jed coughed and snorted like he was fighting to hold back tears.

"Yes." Was all Carter could push out.

Stacey nodded as if this wasn't new information.

"Jed, I've got to go back to my vehicle," Carter said. "Where's yours?"

The man's eyes lifted along with his mask, the nightmarish mouth of teeth painted thereon moving up and down as he talked. "That red pickup over there, and before you say it, yes, it's Jed with the red."

The pickup didn't look that bad, but Carter did think it odd that a rosary of pink sunglasses hung from the rearview, and its bed was filled with painter's easels. The pickup had rear-ended a box truck, but it had a heavy grill-guard of black metal pipes that had protected the front end from the majority of the crash, and Carter saw the twisted form of a kingbird on an Oklahoma license plate.

A white compact car was under the pickup's bed, the red truck's rear wheels on the hood of the car's hood. The vehicles on either side pressed in on the pickup, but it looked drivable, not that it mattered. Based on what Carter had seen, they were somewhere in the middle of the devastation and the cars in this deep would probably take days to be recovered.

Carter felt the clock in his head ticking, and he pictured police and rescue personnel fighting through the darkness. He didn't have much time. "Why don't you see if you can find that fire you mentioned, and we'll meet you up there?"

Jed nodded, but with his mask, Carter couldn't tell how the man felt about it.

Carter didn't wait to find out. He put his hand gently on Stacey's shoulder and spun her thirty degrees so she was facing south. Then he started marching down the shoulder, pressing her before him. He cut into the destruction before they reached the dead body, and when he looked back Jed was watching them. Carter was careful to pick a route that came nowhere near Stacey's parents, and a knot of heat clogged his throat. He'd known this young girl for a few short minutes, yet he felt an overwhelming responsibility for her that was akin to what he felt for his own children. Stacey had her entire life before her. A life in which she would be the only survivor of her nuclear family.

Did Tommy and Katie even care that they didn't get to see their father? That people called him a criminal? That he was on the run?

Probably not, and shame washed over Carter as he lifted Stacey onto the hood of a blue sedan.

4

The faint *womp womp* of helicopter airfoils pounding the air carried faintly over Borderland Pass. It was far off, but the thumping was getting louder. Carter figured the bird would survey the damage, report back to command, and phones would be ringing all over Arkansas. "Won't be home for dinner, babe, me and the crew got a shit show to deal with. Don't wait up."

Aniyah sat atop Carter's rental, her feet hanging over the remains of the exhaust system like she was dangling her feet in a pool. She didn't look up when Carter approached. The woman had lost her husband, and the adrenaline of the accident and her survival were fading, her new reality smacking her in the face.

Carter and Stacey avoided the semi wedged next to the Ford, and worked their way around to the opposite side, where Carter hoisted Stacey onto a crushed hood before joining her.

"Aniyah," Carter said.

She looked down at him from her perch atop the Ford, her brow wrinkling with lack of recognition.

He hardly knew the woman, but the creases of pain that cut across her forehead and the dazed dullness of her eyes sent a wave of sorrow breaking through Carter. He said, "It's Ray. From… before."

As if she'd solved some riddle her face softened, and her big brown eyes grew wide. "Of course, I'm sorry. Who's your friend?"

Stacey shifted her little feet, the car hood popping as she wrapped her arms around Carter's legs.

"This here is Stacey," Carter said.

"Well, hello, Stacey," Aniyah said, her face brightening as if she didn't remember her husband was dead and she was sitting at the heart of a massive multicar pileup. Carter didn't know if Aniyah was a mother—maybe she just had a pet—but in his experience, every woman carried the 'care' gene to varying degrees, and there was no child a mother didn't want to nurture. That was the only reason humanity had survived as long as it had.

"Hi, my mom and dad are dead," Stacey said with a bluntness only children and homicide detectives are capable of.

Aniyah's face clouded, her eyes shifting toward her car and her dead husband. "I'm sorry to hear that, sweetie." She inched off the Ford onto the smashed hood Carter and Stacey stood on. Metal flexed and snapped as she held out her hand to the girl. "Do you need a hug?"

Stacey looked up at Carter, and he nodded.

While Aniyah was providing Stacey a comfort he couldn't, Carter vaulted up onto the Ford. The car teetered on its side as he gazed at the carnage and planned his next move. He had to get his money and backpack with his personals and clothing, but he didn't want to be too obvious about it. The bag would be easy, the money not so much. The Taurus's trunk was crunched like an accordion, but then he remembered the back seat went down and he might be able to gain access to the trunk that way.

Thick darkness settled over the interstate, overtaking the white, the pounding of the approaching helicopter rising above the wind. The bird's spotlight burned through the fading whiteness, a series of small fires and the glow of failing headlights pushing away the shadows that frolicked at the edges of the road.

Several cars down, along the western shoulder of the road, a group of ten or so people had formed. A dense patch of forest separated the northbound lanes from the south, but Carter couldn't tell if there were cars rolling on the other side of the interstate. Most likely that side of the highway was a mess just like the two northbound lanes. Borderlands Pass didn't discriminate.

"Are you guys hungry?" Carter asked.

Aniyah and Stacey both wagged their heads.

"I'm going to go over to that group and see if anyone knows anything, but first I'll grab whatever I have to eat from my car." He knew he had a few beers left along with a bag of chips, but food was food, and it would buy him some time.

Getting back into the Ford was easier than getting out. He slithered through the passenger side door and climbed into the backseat. His pack was in the footwell behind the driver's seat. He pulled it free and put the chips and beers in it and slipped his phone into his back pocket. The latch holding the rear seats in place was jammed shut, but he was able to work it open after jerking on it several times.

The roar of the helicopter was like thunder now, the darkness peeling away.

Carter looked around, but he was fully hidden by his destroyed vehicle as he pulled free his sack of cash and stuffed it in a side pocket of his pack. With that done, he wormed his way out of the Ford and rejoined Aniyah and Stacey.

A searchlight panned over the wreckage as the copter glided past. People waved and cried out for help, but the Army green bird didn't pause. It crept slowly down the interstate, gliding above the median strip, fog curling up from the trees, the rotor wash stirring the fallen snow, ash, and sparks.

When the copter had passed, Carter broke out the chips and offered Aniyah a beer.

"I don't drink, but…" She held out a hand and Carter opened the beer and handed it to her. He had no water, but he guessed in a pinch they could melt snow. Aniyah took a long pull off the beer, her face twisting. "I'll never get what folks find appetizing about this stuff." She looked at the can like it was filled with poison, and in a way, Carter knew that's exactly what the stuff was. Alcohol was useful, but far from healthy, though he knew beer was an exception to that rule. In addition to alcohol, beer provided many of the nutrients in bread and had served as a main food source for the cradle of civilization thousands of years ago, hence the saying "beer is food."

"They're not so bad." Carter popped a beer for himself. He didn't really want it, but he was starving, and he wanted to leave the chips for Stacey.

"Did you find anything… else out there other than this flower?" Aniyah said as she stroked Stacey's hair.

"Yeah," he said. "The corpse was abandoned on the shoulder of the road. Stacey here found it."

Aniyah's eyes filled with grief, her face reforming into a mask of sorrow, worry, and fear. "I'm so sorry to hear that. Is ther—"

A furious growl and sharp guttural tapping echoed over the scene. Then an earsplitting wolf howl hyena laugh, followed by a primal scream of pain.

Carter stopped drinking his beer, Stacey froze with her hand in the potato chip bag, and Aniyah covered her mouth with the palm of her hand.

The wind hollered and argued, shadows billowing from the tree line along the road, fog flowing and cresting over the wreckage like whitewater on a storm-swept sea.

Carter pulled Aniyah to the side, Stacey watching like a hawk, and told her what he'd seen—the dark absence of shifting nothingness, and what Jed had told him.

"None of that makes sense," Aniyah said.

Carter looked around and lifted his hands in the universal sign of "what are you gonna do?" He pulled on his pack, and said, "I'm going to head over to that little group and see if anyone knows anything."

"What could they know?" Aniyah asked.

"Maybe one of the truckers has a working radio? I don't know. Be right back." A stab of guilt knifed through Carter's stomach and climbed up his spine. "It's warmer in the car. Why don't you climb back in there and wait?"

Aniyah's brow wrinkled, her spider senses kicking in. "Is it really a good idea to split up?"

"Is it a good idea for…" Carter jerked a thumb toward Stacey, "…For her to hear what will be discussed over there?"

Anguish tore at Aniyah's features, but she nodded.

Carter worked his way over destroyed vehicles until he reached the shoulder of the road, where he paused and listened. There were several voices just beneath the chattering wind, but he couldn't make out what they were saying.

The knot of survivors had grown, and perhaps twenty people huddled in the darkness. Two voices rose above the others, a man and a woman, and Carter positioned himself at the edge of the group so he could hear what was being said. He looked over his shoulder and saw Aniyah and Stacey watching him from atop the Ford. So much for staying warm in the car.

"I think we should go," said the male voice. "There's strength in numbers and how far can it be? A half a mile?"

"Who cares how far it is? Moving around will just make things more difficult. Rescue workers will be here to get us out of here soon. They probably already made arrangements at a hotel for all of us."

"Yeah, and my car insurance isn't going to go up," said a third voice.

"Maybe we should vote," said yet another voice, and Carter had to restrain a chuckle.

"Well, I'm hiking out of here," said the first male voice. "Anyone who wants to come with me saddle up. Those who are staying are welcome to use what's left of my camper for shelter." He pointed at a huge camper trailer several vehicles south. The thing looked untouched in the darkness, but as Carter stared, he saw that the engine compartment had the trunk of a car in it, and the camper had been rear-ended, but the main cabin looked intact.

The group started to break up, some folks to gather supplies as the owner of the camper led a line of people to his doorstep. Carter eased into the shadows of the tree line. If he was going to run, now was the time, but guilt tore at his instincts. Moms might nurture, but fathers felt the often-overwhelming pressure and need to provide and protect. He couldn't see Aniyah and Stacey from where he hid, but he sensed their fear and disappointment, the horror of his betrayal.

"Shit," he said, and headed back to the Ford. He'd get his strays setup in the camper where they'd be safe, then say he had to take a leak and slip away. The clock was ticking, but still no sirens tore away the stillness, the pounding of the survey copter a faint thumping that blended with the drumming of his heart.

Light snow began to fall, cyclones spinning over the destroyed cars, cycling in and out of the forest. The wind picked up, pushing through the pass, the darkness growing deeper as thick clouds settled overhead, the moon a distant memory.

When Carter got back to Aniyah he explained his plan—minus the peeing and betrayal, —and she and Stacey wasted no time jumping off the Ford. Carter was happy to see Stacey was clinging to Aniyah's leg, and not his. A sting of disappointment pierced his relief. It was good the girl was bonding with Aniyah, and maybe their chance meeting would provide healing for them both, each having withstood great losses on this day.

It made Carter think of his own daughter, and a thin smile slid over his face. He and Katie had a special bond, as Debra did with Tommy.

His smile slid away as he remembered a trip to Mouseland when the kids where young, and Carter's stomach churned with the memory like it was yesterday. Everything Debra did, every word she said, affected Katie at her delicate age, and even with the majesty of Mouseland surrounding the family Debra just couldn't give the kid a break.

Tommy stood back and smiled as he sucked it all in like the prodigal son.

Carter had lashed out at his son without thinking, "What are you smiling at, dipshit?"

The boy looked up at him with wide eyes.

Debra broke off her berating of Katie midsentence and locked her eyes on Carter like he'd just picked a lollipop off the ground and licked it.

"What did he do?" Debra fired off.

"I don't like his attitude," Carter said. "And what's your problem? We're in the happiest place on Earth?" Carter's nerves hadn't stopped jangling since he got off the plane.

Katie moved in beside her father and Tommy took up position behind his mother as the two titans of the family squared off, the jingle and whine of It's A Small World blaring in the background. It wasn't the family's finest moment, but he saw how similar he and his daughter were, and he felt ashamed that he'd been unable to bond with his son. And when Katie had—

A guttural clicking sound carried over the wreckage, followed by a wolf-like howl crossed with the shrieking of a hyena. The wail snapped Carter from his musings and tore away any hope or rationalization that what Carter had seen was a bear or other animal of the woods. No, whatever was making that sound was something else altogether.

"What was that?" Aniyah said. "I've never heard no bear yawk like that before."

"Me either," Carter said. "Let's hurry."

As they climbed over cars and trucks to get to the camper it started to snow in earnest, thick fluffy flakes the size of a thumbnail. The snow swirled and spun, the wind hollering, the tips of Carter's fingers stinging with cold.

A line of six people waited outside the camper as the rig's owner ushered those staying behind inside his mobile casa. People were climbing over a crushed green sports car and were then lifted through the top portion of the camper door with the help of people inside. When the trio arrived, there were only two people ahead of them and Carter hoisted Aniyah and Stacey onto the green car.

"I'm going to hang out here," Carter said. "Keep an eye on things."

Aniyah didn't meet his eye.

"No, Ray," Stacey wailed. "I need you. Please don't leave me."

"I'm not leaving," he lied. "I'll be right out here."

Stacey planted her feet and lifted her chin with a determination reserved for those who still believe the world is flexible. "I need you with us."

Carter's heart melted. Nobody had needed him in so long that he'd forgotten how it felt.

The owner of the camper was a big man who wore an N95, jeans, and a t-shirt that read "Better Dead than Red." He held out his paw to Stacey. "Don't be afraid, darling. I don't bite. My name's Roger." The guy looked up and upon seeing Carter, a middle-aged white man, and Aniyah, a young African American woman, his brow wrinkled. "You her parents?"

"No," Aniyah said. "They've…"

"They're dead," Stacey said.

Carter couldn't help but smile. He recalled when the family dog, Porkchop, died. He and Debra had been so worried about how Katie and Tommy would take it. PC was part of the family, their friend. The reality that both children began asking for a new dog the day after Porkchop died showed him the innocence of children, and their resilience in the face of sorrow and danger because they hadn't been beaten down by the world. Stacey had been beaten down, a flower stepped on by the wild animal of fate, but she'd bounced right back up.

"Are you coming?" Stacey said, her eyes locked on Carter.

He was no more immune to Stacey's request than he'd been to his own kids, both of whom had gotten him to do things he'd never imagined he'd do. "Yup, I'm coming," Carter said, and he climbed on the green car, its hood popping and shrieking under his weight.

5

Borderland Pass, I-49, Ozark Mountains, 5:33 PM CST, March 12th, 2021

The distant warble of sirens was Carter's cue to leave. He was packed in the camper with twelve other people, darkness pressing into the tin can through the curtained windows. Carter was off to the side, pressed into a small space between a storage closet and a bathroom made for miniature people that stank like a truck stop commode.

Aniyah had masked-up and was making the rounds, getting to know the others, and Stacey was playing with her teddy bear and a girl a bit younger than her. With everyone masked, faces were a mystery, but the tension in the trailer was palpable, and easily seen in the haggard eyes and wrinkled foreheads of his fellow survivors.

Waiting was the worst. A watched pot never boils, and Carter's skin crawled with tension. He needed to move, to be away from all these people. He wasn't claustrophobic, and he'd never been antisocial, but the pandemic and being on the run had changed how he felt about humanity. The chatter of people created a buzz in his head that ratcheted up his anger to a point that required him to consciously control his building rage every moment of his life. He'd taken to doing breathing exercises, deep in, deep out. Deep in, dee-

"Hey, you wouldn't happen to have a smoke, would you? I'm jonesing." The guy wore an N95 over his mouth and nose, but his bloodshot eyes and black eye sockets marked the guy as a boozer… or worse.

Carter knew the smart answer was a simple no, but with his internal clock running at double time and his nerves stretched to their limit, he said, "Do I look like I smoke?"

The eyes above the white mask narrowed, but the short balding man moved on to his next victim, a woman that looked so scared Carter felt for her. The woman's hands were shaking and she gripped a phone like it was rosary beads.

Anger welled in Carter, a suffocating heat, the urge to pound the guy to dust. Big breath in, big breath out.

"Hey, honey, you wouldn't happen to—"

Carter put a hand on the guy's shoulder, spun him around, and said, "Back off. Even if she has one, you're not smoking in here. Look around, dipshit." Now everyone was watching, and Carter felt his stomach go sour. So much for flying under the radar. Now he really did need to pee.

"Who the hell are you? Her dad?" the guy said.

Silence fell, the wind hollering, the camper creaking and popping.

Carter made a show of rolling his shoulders and cracking his neck. It had been years since he'd been in a physical fight, but at the moment he wanted nothing more than to take out two years of frustration and injustice on this insolent little asshole and the price be dammed. Carter laughed, his best I've got nothing to lose cackle, took a step toward the man, and said, "I'm not sure you want to go there. You see, you're a—"

A growl-bark, and the camper rocked violently as if shoved by King Kong.

"What the hell is out there?" shrieked a woman who cradled an infant in her arms.

"Quiet," Carter said, index finger in the air the way his mother used to when she was scolding him.

Sniffing, like the largest dog in history was exploring beneath the camper. Grunts, a low rhythmic clicking that sounded like something big gargling. A roar thundered through the trailer and the camper rocked on its springs.

Carter reached for the Glock but pulled back his hand. Not yet.

The cigarette guy screamed, his eyes shifting to the floor in embarrassment.

Stillness broken only by the tinkle of the wind working its way beneath the camper's aluminum facade.

The trailer rocked and almost tipped over as a chuffing and growling drove away the arguing wind. Something huge threw itself at the camper and it pitched back and forth on its springs. The clang of snapping metal rang over the clamor as the hitch assembly broke free, and the camper listed sharply.

Everyone adjusted their positions with the shifts and leans of the trailer, attempting to utilize their weight to keep the camper from tipping over. This real-life amusement park ride continued for thirty seconds, the shrieks of his companions and the grunts and growls of the beast stabbing Carter's brain and stoking his growing fury.

The trailer rolled, and the world spun, cracking wood, tearing steel, rushing air, and the crunch of metal biting metal filling the camper. Windows shattered, cabinets opened, and plates and glasses tumbled free, breaking and cracking as they bounced around.

Carter was tossed like trash; he crashed into another person, and they both smashed into the refrigerator. He saw Aniyah reaching out for Stacey, but the kid was thrown across the cabin only to be plucked from the air by an older man who'd been sitting at the dining table. People were flung around as the smell of human waste wafted through the trailer, and Carter felt the putrid scent catch in his throat.

The waste tank was leaking.

A massive rending of metal as the floor of the trailer, which was now the ceiling, crunched and bent, steel flexing, wood snapping. With a squeal akin to a wailing infant, four black curved claws pierced the side of the camper, tearing away wood and aluminum.

Carter braced himself, instinctively taking hold of the person he'd slammed into. She smelt faintly of flowers and onions.

Huffing, clicks, moans, and the claws pulled free. Grinding sounds, then a deep vibration as the camper rocked back and forth. Then the stillness of snow peppering aluminum as the wind serenaded the darkness.

A loud bark and the camper flexed and popped as the beast jumped off, the mangled trailer ringing like a bell.

Carter covered his ears, considered praying, but thought better of it. Instead, he let go of the woman he was shielding and used a shelf in the storage closet to hoist himself up so he could see out the side window. He peered through yellow and green curtains that looked like they'd arrived in a time capsule from the seventies.

Darkness shrouded the interstate, the faint glow of flames leaking through the blackness. Snow billowed and swirled, but nothing moved.

Somebody screamed.

Where moments before darkness speckled with white had filled the window, now eyes peered through the broken glass and torn screen.

Dark eyelids slipped over black eyes, yellow corneas appearing and disappearing as the massive beast blinked. The creature shifted its head, and for an instant, all Carter saw were bloody teeth, the beast's mouth open in a toothy grin. The thing threw its head back, roared, and disappeared, the aluminum alloy siding on the trailer humming and snapping as it flexed.

Carter's sigh of relief was so full he wondered how long he'd been holding it. The tips of his fingers and the bottoms of his feet tingled, his palms sweating, his lower back a battleground of pain, stress, and knotted muscles.

Someone gagged, the stench of human waste wafting through the overturned camper. Brown sludge oozed down the paneled wall next to the refrigerator, the nasty flow of liquified shit collecting around Carter's feet.

"I have to get out of here!" yelled a woman close to the crap waterfall.

"Easy now," Carter said. "Don't let a little smell get you killed." Truth was that was the understatement of the century. His hackles were on full alert, and his throat ached under the strain of holding back his gag reflex.

Someone puked, and the crowd broke into a cacophony of yelling, cries of disgust, and gagging, followed by a painful-sounding retch.

The panicking woman pounded on the upside-down closed door, her hand grasping the handle.

Carter laid a gentle hand on her arm. "I wouldn't do that."

The woman, middle-aged with pale skin and frizzy red hair and a field of freckles creating a map on her forehead, hesitated, one hand on the door handle, the other covering her mask.

Nobody spoke as the wind trilled and bitched, the camper groaning and popping. A minute bled away... two... three...

"I think it's gone," said the redhead, who then promptly threw up. Puke oozed from beneath the folds of her medical mask, thin streams of light brown viscus fluid leaking down the woman's neck. She shook her head like a suffering dog, puke spraying the wall and the front of Carter's jacket.

Carter stepped back, covering his face with his arm as if warding off a blow.

The woman pushed open the camper door and it fell back on its hinges and slapped against the side of the camper as Red disappeared into the white-speckled darkness of the thickening storm.

Everyone started yelling and screaming at once, the cacophony of humanity in panic mode beyond Carter's capacity to process. Two folks tried to wriggle their way through the group toward the door, the stay or go argument over. Sirens wailed in the distance, but no daggers of red or white knifed through the blackness.

A gust of freezing wind grabbed the camper door and slammed it closed.

Two others joined the folks looking to escape the confines of the trailer, and Carter's heart dropped when he saw one of the people was a woman with an infant. He didn't give a shit about much—his family—but Carter's heart went out to the child. The infant couldn't make its own decisions and would certainly die out in the cold. But it wasn't his business or his concern. Shit, his own family wasn't his business anymore. But still...

The group looking to leave was led by a man with a gray beard, and the guy could've passed for Santa had it not been for his black Navy jacket. When Santa reached the closed door Carter moved out of his way. If this guy wanted out, more power to him, though Carter's stomach churned with the knowledge that it was the wrong decision.

Santa pushed out of the camper and closed the door behind him.

The clock in Carter's head was winding down to double zero, and he tried to get Aniyah's attention. She'd taken up position in a forward bunkbed, her eyes locked on Stacey who sat huddled with her new friend. All he had to do was slip out behind big Santa.

Instead, Carter put out an arm and stopped the woman with the infant as she tried to follow Santa. "Listen, you don't know me, but I—"

"Don't touch me and get out of my way." The woman was frantic.

Carter took a breath, the stench of human waste so strong it was hard to speak without gagging. He reminded himself he was a masked stranger, and she was a mother with a young baby who had just been in a massive multicar accident and was still hours away from rescue. "Look, I don't want to touch you. It's just, it's really—"

"I don't care! Get out of my way!" She looked over her shoulder at the gawking crowd for support.

There are times in life when minding one's own business is the unwritten rule. People walked by assaults in progress on the streets and didn't dare help with a medical emergency for fear of being sued. Yet, still, as a parent... Carter couldn't let it go. Infants have no advocate, but apparently on this day, at this moment, he was this child's advocate.

Carter gripped the woman's arm and shook her. "Polite time is over. If you take your child out into that storm with no sign of rescue the baby will die. Dead. On you, because you didn't listen to reason. I know you're scared, and the smell..." He waved a hand. "We're all scared and sick, but you have to think of your child."

She stared at him, her mouth opening, then closing.

"Are you hearing me?"

Blank eyes stared at him as wind worked its way through every crack and hollow in the camper.

"I'm not letting you take your baby out there," Carter said. "We can—"

A gunshot pierced the night, and Carter and everyone in the camper fell still, except the infant, who began to cry.

6

The echo of the gunshot hung in the still air, and Carter's stomach crawled with unease. He felt the VP9 in the small of his back and an overwhelming urge to draw down and rush from the camper washed over him, the prickly fingers of worry and fear tickling his neck and spine. He heard only the breathing of his fellow crash victims, the wailing of the infant, the brush of the wind, and the tinkle of snow.

There were no further gunshots, and Carter settled down, relaxing his tensed muscles, and swallowing the turd stuck in his throat. From far off came the muffled cries of someone calling through a bullhorn, and with each muddled word the clock in Carter's head sped up. Darkness pressed into the trailer, cellphone lights illuminating the camper like a funhouse, and people gagged and dry heaved, the stench of puke and shit an eyewatering aroma.

The gunshot told Carter the beast was most likely gone, or dead. Large or small, there's little defense against a bullet, and he figured it was safe to go outside. He tried to get Aniyah's attention. She was tending to Stacey, who was crying along with the child she'd been playing with. That young girl didn't appear to have parents with her, either.

After staring at Aniyah like she was naked for over a minute, the woman's radar finally kicked in and she looked in his direction. The deep welcoming pools that had been her eyes were red and half closed, her forehead a roadmap, perspiration running through the creases like tiny rivers.

Carter licked his lips. He had to lie. There was no other option. She and the kid would be better off without him. He pointed at himself, toward the door, then at the floor in a 'be right back, you stay here' gesture.

Aniyah nodded, then looked at her feet.

Carter had only known the woman half an hour, yet he sensed she knew he wouldn't be coming back. He waved, but she made no sign as he slipped out the door.

Out on the interstate chaos reigned. People shouted and fought, snow came down sideways as the wind tore up the pass, and visibility was thirty feet. Folks argued, their masks moving up and down with speech, but Carter couldn't hear what they were saying.

Flames licked the white-speckled darkness, and swirls of smoke danced over the devastation. Carter drew the H&K and held it at his side as he eased along the side of the camper. He hoped Aniyah, Stacey, and the others would stay where they were until real help arrived despite the stench. He couldn't help them. Carter could hardly help himself.

"Yo," came a voice from the darkness. "You alright?"

Carter scanned the wreckage and found Jed standing atop the hood of a white minivan. He had a rifle in his hands now, and he still wore the evil grin mask, but he'd added a camouflage jacket that looked brand new, a black knit cap, and gloves. He looked like he'd just crawled out of an outdoor catalog. Carter raised a hand. "Still alive. That you who fired the shot?"

Jed nodded.

"Why? You hungry for varmint?" Carter winced. He should've left out that last part. Damn, he wasn't used to being around people.

Jed cackled, his mask shifting up and down. "I ain't hungry."

"What then?"

Jed waved him over.

The storm raged and showed no signs of easing. The whiteout had lifted, but visibility was fifty feet in the swirling white, the tar-like darkness filling every empty space and suffocating the road.

Carter adjusted his mask, put away the H&K, and climbed onto the roof of the green sports car packed against the camper's side. As he eased down into the mass of vehicle ruins yelling and screaming filtered through the snowy night. The wind sang as Carter crawled across the green hood toward Jed, but the big man ducked behind an overturned van.

The voices of the combatants rang over the interstate. Carter reminded himself what he'd learned out on the road over the last two years, living between the cracks of civilization: people were assholes, and would kill for almost nothing. The fight he overheard now made him want to put a chunk of lead alloy into the foreheads of both fighters. He rolled his shoulders, cracked his neck, and reminded himself he wasn't the asshole whisperer.

But the rage… He had to control the rage, that part of himself he hadn't known existed. It had been buried deep… until the incident forced it from the shadows.

"You're an asshole, man. I found it, so it's mine," came a voice that sounded like a drunk Jack Nicholson.

"I've got a kid. An injured wife. I need it," came a second voice, a light, weak appeal that sounded like a mouse pleading with a lion.

"Do I look like I give a shit?"

Carter worked his way around the green sports car to the end of the overturned van Jed hid behind. Snow pelted his face, the wind working its way into his collar, his heart thumping.

"Give it to me."

"Go melt snow, you freak," said phantom Jack.

"Piss off!" The mouse was now a cat.

When Carter reached Jed's side he said, "What the hell is going on?"

Jed pointed the rifle, his wicked grin mask unmoving.

Two men stood atop a smashed Jeep Laredo, the forest green metal crackling as the two men circled each other. One guy was tall and wore a long deerskin jacket and a cowboy hat, the other a blue ski jacket, jeans, and a black knit cap with an orange tiger on the front.

The Bengals fan held a bottle of water.

To Carter's surprise, it was the cowboy that sounded like the cat. "Hand it over. My kid needs it."

"So do I," yelled Bengals Boy.

Before the pandemic, there'd been an extended blackout, and Carter recalled the fights that broke out at gas stations and supermarkets. Shit, at the Apple Store. Three lost meals to anarchy, and add to that the accident and the storm, and what's left is a toxic stew of humanity bubbling over and looking to place blame for a situation that could only be laid at the feet of Mother Nature. Yet, it was snowing water, there was snow packed in the forest's undergrowth all along the highway, and these two dipshits were fighting over twelve ounces of processed H_2O. Man feeding on man, and it had only taken forty minutes.

The combatants squared off, metal flexing and shrieking. Cowboy tried to snatch the water, but the smaller man was too fast.

The air sizzled with tension, and Carter considered drawing the VP9 and putting a stop to the insanity, and yet... Let the morons fight, and while they pummeled each other, he'd slip away.

Jed had the rifle, but like Carter, he watched the insanity, his eyes aglow, snow accumulating on his head and shoulders.

Forcing Bengals Boy left, Cowboy dodged right, and his hand shot out and grabbed the water from the smaller man.

"You shit!" Bengals Boy dove forward, wrapping his arms around Cowboy's legs and driving him back.

Cowboy reeled, stepping back to the edge of the car's roof. The two men struggled on the brink like Gollum and Frodo at the edge of the precipice inside Mount Doom.

Jed laughed, and Carter's stomach twisted. Carter had tried to shed his initial evaluation of Jed, but that laugh, the pleasure the man was taking in the pathetic scene playing out before them made Carter wonder if perhaps his first read had been the right one.

"I... Will... Kill... You..." said Cowboy as he struggled to keep his footing on the car's roof.

Snow swirled and the wind howled and argued. Bengals Boy tore free, his left arm coming around and delivering a roundhouse punch that caught Cowboy on the bridge of his nose.

Cowboy staggered back, his arms out for balance, and he dropped the bottle of water. It hit the car's roof and exploded, water running down the side of the wrecked car.

With a wail of anger, Bengals Boy attacked. He threw himself forward and both men tumbled off the roof and smashed onto the hood of the next car over. The men clutched at each other, punching and yelling as they rolled around, a bloody corpse hunched over the destroyed car's steering wheel.

A gunshot rang out, and Carter covered his ears. Jed's rifle was pointed at the dark snow-swept sky, the thin curl of white smoke twisting from the gun's barrel blowing away in the wind, the scent of cordite replacing the stench of shit stuck in his nostrils. Carter's ears rang, and he rubbed his temples.

The two fighters were frozen. Bengals Boy had Cowboy in a headlock, and the guy's Stetson had been knocked off, but both men stared through the wreckage at something Carter couldn't see.

Jed inched out from behind the overturned van. "You two shitheels done?" he said, and Carter almost laughed.

Harsh growling, chuffs, and sniffing carried above the wind.

Cowboy's gaze shifted to Jed. "This isn't any of your concern," he said.

"Yeah," said Bengals Boy.

Both men turned their attention back to the eastern shoulder of the road, which Carter couldn't see because of the crumbled pile of metal blocking his view.

Jed saw Carter and his eyes went wide, his mask stretching as he lifted his eyebrows. "You believe this shit?"

"I do," Carter said.

"You morons do realize the water is gone because you two are too stupid to live?" Jed said. "You know that, right?"

That seemed to drive a nail in the dispute's coffin, and as Bengals Boy let Cowboy out of the headlock both men gazed east, Carter, Jed, and his gun forgotten or at least put on the backburner.

Jed jerked back the rifle's bolt, dropped a shell in the firing chamber, and slammed the bolt home. "What the hell are these fags looki—"

"Oh, shit," yelled Cowboy. Both men vaulted to their feet, gave up the fight, and jumped west, each disappearing into gaps in the wreckage.

A roar pierced the storm, a guttural wail part fury and part frustration. The cry died away, and loud sniffing blended into the screaming wind and the growing calls of the bullhorn.

Jed chuckled, the wicked grin on his mask moving up and down.

Carter said, "I don't think they're running from you."

The shriek of metal scraping over metal rang over the interstate, and Carter noticed a pattern. Shriek, tap, tap, shriek, and mixed throughout bending and popping metal.

"Does that sound like footfalls on metal to you?" Carter asked.

"No."

"What is it then?"

Jed put the stock of the rifle to his shoulder and eased into the gap between the van and the car crushed against it. There wasn't much space, but Jed dropped to a knee and snaked around a chunk of trash that looked to have once been a black Mini Cooper. Blood and antifreeze ran from the block of metal and plastic.

Carter glanced over his shoulder at the camper where Aniyah and Stacey hid. The trailer's door was still closed. It was the perfect time to slip away. The tree line was dark, the traveling group had moved on, and no one walked along the shoulder of the road.

Jed's rifle barked, and he yelled, "What in Christ's name…"

Carter surged forward, squeezing around demolished vehicles and scurrying over car hoods. Even as he ran toward the commotion, he asked himself what the hell he was doing, and when he arrived at Jed's side he was panting and mentally berating himself for acting so impulsively.

Jed stared at him, eyes wide, and in those eyes Carter saw… recognition? Fear?

"What? What did you see?"

"I… I'm not sure," Jed said, but for some reason, Carter thought the man was lying. Jed's index finger inched toward his mouth, and he added, "Your mask."

His mask had slipped down, and he quickly pulled it back into position. Had the man recognized him? Carter said, "What the hell are you shooting at?"

"Let's go see. Partner."

7

Carter followed Jed as he wove between demolished cars, climbed over snow-covered chunks of fused metal, and avoided any vehicle that had occupants inside it. Jed had reached his stray quota also. Carter kept his eyes straight ahead, the horrors in many of the vehicles an unnecessary sight. He wasn't afraid of blood, nor did it make him sick, but he'd seen enough entrails and crushed skulls for one day. No people wandered about, everyone was either holed up or had begun the trek either north or south to meet the rescue workers. Red spinning lights cut through the snow to the north, and Carter estimated emergency personnel would arrive on the scene within the next ten minutes and he needed to be gone.

Jed stopped, planted his feet, and used the hood of a destroyed Mustang to brace the rifle.

The wind pushed snow over the interstate, and most of the vehicles were dusted like powdered donuts. Carter positioned himself behind Jed and stared over the man's shoulder, getting the bead of what he was aiming at, and his breath caught.

A young woman with long straw hair sat on the front bumper of an old VW van. The vehicle was on the eastern shoulder, and it appeared to have avoided a serious collision only to be rear-ended by an SUV that was buried halfway into the van's interior. The woman smoked, the orange speck of her burner glowing through the dark whiteness.

Carter opened his mouth to speak, to ask why Jed was aiming the rifle at the woman, but he realized she wasn't Jed's target at all.

A shape deeper than night, like a total absence of light, glided from the trees toward the smoking woman, who appeared unaware of the approaching menace.

"What are you waiting for?" Carter hissed.

"Shut it," Jed said. "I want to make sure… Just shut it and let me do my thing."

Carter reached for the VP9, his fingers curling around its grip.

Ahead on the road, an explosion rocked the night, and a growing orange ball of fire with a halo of black smoke pushed up into the blackness, sparks dancing like fireflies in the snow. Screaming and yelling, and the muffled calls of bullhorns were coming from both directions now, and to the north, the sirens and lights of emergency response vehicles grew close.

Jed ignored the growing commotion, his eyes locked on the dark shape emerging from the forest.

Carter shifted on his feet as he struggled to see through the snow and gloom. The palms of his hands itched and sweat dripped down his back despite the cold that was working its way through his jacket and pants into his bones like radiation.

"I think..." Jed pressed his eye to the scope atop the rifle, "I've got a Maglite in my back pocket. Grab it."

Anger welled in Carter. It had been a long time since he'd taken orders—from anyone, let alone a stranger. Still, Carter's stomach tightened as he bent and retrieved the flashlight. Worry pain filled his chest with heat, the growing calls of the bullhorns sending zaps of nervous energy racing up and down his spine, thoughts of a jail cell tickling his nerves.

Snow and ice pellets surged over the interstate, the scent of burnt rubber and gasoline filling the air. The remnants of the explosion shone to the north, an orange glow within the field of white, tendrils of dark smoke writhing within like giant monstrous shadows.

The woman finished her smoke, dropped it to the ground, and put it out with a twist of her foot. The target of her focus removed, she appeared to notice the shadowy silhouette easing from the woods toward her for the first time. She bounced to her feet, her head jerking east toward the forest.

"Light it up," Jed mumbled through his wicked grin mask.

"What? Light wh—"

"Are you dense? You're seeing what I'm seeing, yes? Light the thing up. Now!"

Carter aimed the flashlight and turned it on.

Harsh light cut through the snowy darkness, the snow swirling, the scene revealed in garish black and white as the creature stepped into the cone of light.

The woman screamed, her gloved hands going to her face, but she didn't run.

Carter's neck tightened, and terror rooted him to the ground, a scream of horror stuck in his throat.

The creature looked like a cat crossed with a bear, and it was bigger than a grizzly but smaller than an elephant. Its black, shaggy coat was dusted white with snow, and the beast moved with the fluidity of water, separating from the shadows of the forest like a building storm. It walked on its hind legs, two large muscular arms hanging by its sides, the glint of curved claws at the ends of its digits. A long snout tainted red with blood protruded from its head below glowing yellow eyes that were locked on the young woman.

"Shoot it," Carter said, then he remembered the H&K, and he drew it.

"Not yet. I want to see what it does," Jed said.

"See what it does?" Carter flipped off the safety with his thumb, depressed the firing safety, and fired the H&K, the shot ringing out like an alarm bell.

Jed pulled back but didn't fire.

Carter's shot went high and wide, missing the beast by two feet.

The creature dropped onto all fours and slipped into the wreckage before Carter squeezed off another round.

Jed bristled, all fury and frustration. "Now you scared it off."

"You think?" Carter pointed the flashlight.

Through the tangle of vehicles and snow Carter saw the creature leap onto the hood of a white pickup, its yellow eyes burning through the white-speckled darkness. The thing howled, an odd bellow that sounded like a cross between a wolf, an elk call, and the cackle of a hyena. Patches of nasty mange covered the beast's neck and shoulders, its dog-like nose blowing jets of smokey condensation.

Huge jaws hung open, dark drool leaking through broken teeth, two thick fangs hanging over bloody black lips. The beast's dark fur was covered in snow, and shadows nestled within the cords of muscle that knotted the creature's appendages.

The monster's huge head swiveled, eyes like searchlights, and Carter felt the cold fingers of fear squeezing his stomach and pounding his lower back.

With the smoothness of a snake, the creature eased back, shook its head, and stood on its hind legs. In the gloom, the beast looked fifteen feet tall. It roared again, teeth displayed, saliva dripping from its mouth, eyes aglow, claws outstretched and searching for flesh.

Carter brought up the VP9 and tried to sight the creature through the crushed cars, but let the gun fall to his side. He was an O.K. shot, but even James Bond couldn't hit the beast with that many obstacles in the way, not without a magic bullet that could make turns.

"Where'd you get that?" Jed asked, eyeing the H&K.

A fire ignited in Carter's stomach, and he almost told Jed it was none of his goddamn business, but why fight with the man? What purpose would that serve? "The guy who owns the camper Aniyah and the kid are hiding in had several guns. He said I could use this one."

"That's an expensive weapon," Jed said, his tone dripping with disbelief. "He just gave it to you?"

"Loaned," Carter said.

"You look like you know how to handle it," Jed said. "I don't know many city folk that know how to fire a—"

The wail of the creature cut Jed short. It jumped from the hood of the car onto its roof, a blur of black fur dusted white. Metal flexed and plastic cracked as the creature moved through the wreckage, and Carter's thoughts strayed back to the smoker. He said, "Come on. We've got to…" What? What did he have to do? Kill it? Could he? Carter looked down at the VP9 and decided he could. "We've got to stop that thing before it hurts someone."

Jed said, "I think that time has passed."

"We can't just sit here and do nothing. We have to kill it," Carter said. He was aware of what he was saying, and though the word 'kill' left a bad taste in his mouth, a responsibility grew in him, a sense that it was up to him to right the wrong, defend the innocent against evil. But he wasn't a superhero. He was barely a man anymore.

"Kill it?" Jed said. "Why would I want to do that? It's an Ozark Howler."

With Jed's words still hanging in the frigid air, a scream carried over the interstate, the call of a woman in pain. "Help! Hel… pppppppp."

Carter's mouth grew dry, heat spreading over his cheeks, pain twisting his neck. If he had hit the beast when he'd had the chance…

Jed stood, eased out of his hiding spot, and scrambled toward the commotion.

An Ozark Howler? Somewhere in the back of Carter's brain, the memory of a television show fought to break through years of callus, a documentary about… what was it?

He looked over his shoulder and nothing moved to the south, but to the north red daggers of light fought through the dying snow. He had to slip away, but the scream. If the beast killed the woman, it would be partly on him. He'd missed his shot, and now he was the only one around with a gun, other than Jed, who had a rifle that was one notch up from a musket.

For the second time, he ignored the counsel of the rational side of his brain which had been screaming for him to get the hell out of Dodge since moments after the crash. Because that primal part of his brain, that annoying, self-righteous, overconfident, angry part, the part that drove him to do things he'd later come to regret, had far more control than he wanted to admit. Despite knowing this, and his commitment and constant vigilance not to get involved in things that weren't his business, he held the VP9 in a doublehanded grip as he moved through the wreckage, his head buzzing with rage.

Ozark Howler… where… It had something to do with Bigfoot, and the show had something about Yeti—that was it. He'd seen a documentary about cryptids, creatures of legend for which there exists no real proof of their existence. Carter pushed down a laugh—he had proof, and now he understood Jed's reluctance to kill the beast. The creature would be worth something alive or dead. What did it matter to him, anyway? People living below the radar didn't champion the existence of mythical creatures.

Another scream of pain accompanied by loud gurgling and huffing, followed by the slap and rip of meat being torn from bone.

Jed fired, the rifle shot carrying over the road and echoing through the hollowed-out cars. "Shit!" Jed yelled, and when Carter arrived at his side, he was loading another bullet into the rifle.

"Where is it?" Carter said as he gazed past Jed toward the forest.

The blonde girl was shaking as she pointed at a crushed car. "It found the body in that car... It had something in its mouth," she forced out.

Blood speckled the snow crimson and footprints with four clawed digits led back into the heart of the accident wreckage.

Carter raised the H&K and panned it around. He heard the huffing of the beast, and the crack of a snapping bone peeled over the road.

"Please stay in your vehicle," came a male voice over a bullhorn. "We will come to you. Please stay in your vehicle. Help will arrive shortly." Carter saw spinning red lights creeping along the shoulder of the road to the south, the rhythmic chirp of sirens rising above the wind.

A cacophony of rending metal, breaking plastic, and shattering glass, accompanied by heavy footfalls as the Howler crawled across the accident scene, the stump of a bloody arm hanging from its jaws.

Carter shifted his position, aimed the VP9, but there were too many obstructions, and the risk of a ricochet was too high.

The beast pulled the arm from its mouth, three-inch claws digging into flesh, blood dripping from the creature's fangs. Then the Ozark Howler lived up to its namesake and threw back its massive head and wailed, the sharp cry ending in a staccato chuckle-like bark that climbed down Carter's spine like a tarantula.

Jed dropped, rolled, and disappeared under a flattened Corvette.

Sniffing... Metal popped like a gunshot as the beast pounced onto the roof of the car next to Carter, and he dove into a destroyed vehicle to avoid being crushed. He stretched across the car's front seat, twisted onto his back, and aimed the H&K at the smashed-out window.

Snow blew into the car, and a thin layer of white settled on Carter as he waited, VP9 sighted. Emergency workers were close now, he heard their voices, the sound of saws as people were cut from their vehicles. The car he hid in shifted.

Carter wormed out onto the frozen payment and crawled into the maelstrom of twisted metal.

8

Deep breaths like the inhaling and exhaling of the sea. Loud wheezing and taps and gasps, the flex of metal, and the pop of plastic. Carter snaked between two cars and army crawled under an SUV that was basically intact. The cement was frigid, and he felt the cold working its way through his clothes like acid, reaching for his bones. The sharp scents of gasoline and antifreeze came and went with the gusting wind. He held the VP9 before him like he was crawling through an enemy tunnel, his back muscles spasming with pain. Dull spotlights shone through the darkness and storm of white, the calls of the bullhorns close.

Jed was nowhere to be seen.

Glass shattered and metal folded, the shrill screech of claws raking over steel echoing over the devastation. The Ozark Howler was on the move.

Ahead, a maze of crushed cars, frozen concrete, and rubber tires bathed in a pulsating red glow filled his field of vision. He was boxed in by wrecks on both sides. Carter rolled onto his side to relieve the pressure on his lower back, and closed his eyes, taking shallow breaths, filtering out the push of the wind and the cacophony of the rescue.

He saw himself denying emergency care as he directed medical staff to the shit camper, where Aniyah, Stacey, and the others waited, as far as he knew. Then he'd be handed off to a police officer... but maybe not. He figured police and rescue would be stretched beyond their capacity, and it would take time for the staties and other backup agencies to arrive on the scene.

The snowfall had diminished to a flurry, and soon helicopters would arrive to haul people to hospitals. In his mind's eye, he saw buses waiting to transport survivors to hotels. Would they ask for ID in the chaos? And if they did, why wouldn't they accept his fake driver's license? It was well done, and would only turn up fake if it was run through the system, and why would they be doing that?

Why take the chance? Carter's muscles tensed, the sound of rending metal and cracking glass getting closer.

Two furry black tree trunks appeared ahead as the beast squeezed between the SUV Carter hid under and the vehicle before it. Sniffing and chuffing. There wasn't enough space for the Howler to drop to all fours and stick its nose under the car, so Carter stayed where he was, the H&K in a double-handed grip as he aimed at the legs.

Carter held that position, his side going cold, his arms aching from keeping the gun rock steady.

The beast mounted the crushed bumper of the car in front of Carter, and a deafening explosion of metal, glass, and plastic rocked the SUV he hid under as the Howler climbed over the wreckage.

It was time to move. Back or forward were the only options, so Carter flipped back onto his stomach and inched his way back the way he'd come. The cold road pulled at his jacket, lifting it, and for an instant, the bare skin of his stomach scraped over concrete.

He reached the rear of the SUV and hesitated. The beast had gone still, and only the faint mumble of emergency workers, sirens, and the wind could be heard. Carter was hesitant to finish his crawl because his legs would be exposed, and he couldn't see if the beast was waiting to pounce on any morsel that revealed itself.

Change of plans. Forward was always better than back, so he crawled across the slick road again, through a puddle of antifreeze, until he was positioned below the crunched front bumper, where he paused, staring up at the snow-filled sky, the glow of flashlights and spinning emergency lights frolicking in the darkness.

Ahead, five feet away on the road in a gap between the SUV and the car before it, sat a cracked side view mirror. In its reflection, he saw cracked blue plastic and a dark patch speckled white.

The SUV shifted slightly, the creak of steel resounding over the road.

He reached out for the mirror, his arm a snake and his hand its head. Carter came up a foot short, and he jerked his hand back.

Wind, yelling voices, and cries of joy.

Carter pressed forward until his head was inches from being exposed, and he stretched, reaching out for the mirror.

A murderous roar and a baseball mitt-sized paw raked through the gap between cars, the air before Carter's eyes shimmering with its passage as it missed his arm by inches. Broken glass pricked his palm as he wrapped his fingers around the mirror and pulled his hand back. Like a dog digging for a bone, the Howler dug in the gap between the crushed vehicles, grunting with exertion, its ragged breathing streaming into the gap, its claws raking over metal.

Carter angled the mirror so he could see what was happening, and the broken image of the beast filled the splintered mirror.

The Howler's yellow eyes peered down into the gap, the creature's cat-like ears straight and stiff as the beast listened for its prey. Cords of muscle rippled beneath black fur, and when the Howler saw the mirror the beast screamed and doubled its efforts, the SUV shaking under the creature's assault.

Carter backed away, positioning himself beneath the center of the SUV, the VP9 in one hand, the mirror in the other.

A chorus of snapping plastic, twisting rubber, and breaking glass filled the world as the beast leaped onto the SUV's roof. The truck's springs popped and sang, its shocks collapsing and breaking as the SUV sagged on its suspension. The space between the exhaust system and the road was cut in half, and Carter scrambled backward, the engine of the SUV thumping to the frozen road.

Carter used one of the SUV's flat tires for leverage and pushed off, turning himself around. But his foot slipped, and for a horrifying instant, he was wedged beneath the rear axle in the fetal position, his legs tucked to his chest, arms at his sides as he squirmed and twisted.

When he was turned around, head facing the rear of the car, he paused and inched out his hand, angling the mirror so he could see a portion of the SUV's roof. Nothing but darkness, the glow of emergency lights, and snow as fine as ash.

He stuffed the VP9 into the small of his back, gripped the SUV's rear bumper, and tossed the mirror to his right as far as he could. It hit a fender with a clang and fell to the road.

The beast shrieked, its hyena-like laugh carrying over the interstate.

Carter surged forward and hit his head, an earsplitting ring driving out all other sounds, but he didn't stop. Using the bumper for leverage, he pressed to his feet between the two crushed cars and pulled the H&K in one smooth motion.

The SUV sagged behind him, the suspension giving out as the Howler crawled to the edge of the SUV's roof, the momentary distraction of the mirror pelting metal giving the creature pause. The Howler swiped its massive paw at Carter, and the air between his head and the beast's mitt grew hot.

Carter dove left and slammed into the quarter panel of a red pickup, and as he bounced off the snow-coated steel, his mind spun to Jed and red. He dove between two destroyed cars and hit the road hard, the air rushing from his lungs, but that probably saved his life.

The beast pounced, shards of glass and pieces of plastic raining down on Carter as snow speckled his face. Darkness washed over him as the beast straddled the two vehicles he hid between.

Carter rolled under the car next to him and kept moving, steadily making his way east, a fresh trickle of blood streaming down his forehead.

"Over here!" someone yelled. Emergency personnel worked their way through the destruction, flashlight beams pushing away the darkness, shadows dancing just beyond their reach.

The pounding crunch of heavy footfalls crushing metal rang over the road, but Carter didn't look back. He pressed to his feet and dodged right, slamming into the green roof of an overturned van, and sliding along its length until he reached its end. His lungs burned, his eyes cinders, his stomach a painful knot, cold piercing the tips of his fingers and toes. He considered stopping and standing his ground. The Howler was big, but not bigger than 9MM full metal jacket parabellums. And yet...

A piece of fender whizzed by his head, and Carter's ear buzzed because the object had come so close. He dropped to his hands and knees in an attempt to disappear in the wreckage, but didn't stop moving.

The beast wasn't fooled. It came on, a roiling knot of fur and teeth, its powerful legs pushing aside debris, its chuffing and snorting carrying on the wind.

The shoulder of the road loomed, the black smudge of the tree line beyond. Only two rows of mangled vehicles left, and he didn't dare slow. Carter stuffed the VP9 in his jacket. Firing the weapon was no longer an option with law enforcement and emergency personnel on the scene. Even if the authorities thought his killing of the beast was justified, he was carrying an unlicensed handgun and that would lead to a series of questions that would put him behind bars for a very long time.

Carter doubled his pace, his jeans tearing on the concrete, his lungs bitching and complaining. Thoughts of entering the forest didn't ease his fears or worries. The Ozark Mountains were the Howler's territory, and he had only one extra clip of ammo and no food or other supplies except the cash and extra clothing in his pack. Did he want to be in the woods with the beast, in the dark? Alone? Maybe he could shake the beast and walk through the wreckage and slip by the emergency workers coming up from the south. That could—

The subcompact Carter slithered under rocked on its springs, and all four of its tires exploded, the car dropping as Carter rolled out from beneath it. He vaulted to his feet and ran, weaving around one last car before breaking for the shoulder of the road.

A gurgle and the Ozark Howler screeched, its laughing bark carrying over the highway. The emergency bullhorns fell silent, and a volley of flashlight beams were redirected toward the sound.

Carter spared a glance over his shoulder as he ran, his feet slipping and sliding on the frozen pavement.

The cat-like beast crouched atop a car, its black coat slick with moisture, its yellow eyes aglow. It was staring at him, its fangs and four-inch claws driving Carter on.

Jed peered out from beneath a ruined truck, the white teeth of his wicked grin mask glowing in the darkness.

9

Borderland Pass, Ozark Mountains, 5:59 PM CST, March 12th, 2021

Carter hit the snow-covered grass strip that separated the wilderness from the shoulder of the interstate **at** a full run. The snowbanks at the edge of the highway were slick with new-fallen snow and below that, a thin coating of ice crackled and snapped as he threw himself toward the forest. He slid, arms out for balance, the H&K slipping deeper into the crack of his ass. Steel drainage grating marked the end of the snowdrift-covered grass and the start of a scree pile that tumbled from the woods. Gray stones ranging in size from a boulder to a pebble plunged down the embankment like frozen water, every rock slick with ice and a potential ankle breaker.

Wind pushed snow into his eyes as it swirled and eddied, the dark wall beyond the tree line oozing fog. Stray flashlights and headlight beams shimmered in the white, the world colored in garish grays. Rocks tumbled and cracked as Carter scrambled up the incline, losing his footing as he reached out and clawed at slick stones. He didn't dare look back because he didn't need to. Carter felt the pressure of the Howler, heard its footfalls and ragged breaths of exertion, and sensed its hatred, its need.

Another thin stretch of snowdrift-covered grass then the cover of the trees. Carter entered a thicket of full evergreens, their branches laden with snow. The underbrush was an intertwined knot of twisted pricker vines and dead vegetation that tugged and tore at his clothes as Carter threw himself into the forest, sinking into the accumulated snow.

The darkness grew deeper, the sounds of the interstate falling away as he slipped around evergreens, his movements erratic as he stepped in holes, tripped over dead branches and vegetation, and ran into boulders. Branches whipped his head, the tiny knife-like needles of the evergreens slashing at his face.

Carter's heart pumped like a steam engine, the ringing in his head getting louder and driving out all other sounds. He'd been running for his life for two years, yet hiding in hotels and flying under the radar seemed luxurious compared to his current situation.

The evergreens fell away and were replaced by tall shortleaf pines and white oaks with dead leaves clinging to their branches. Blackness filled the woods, and tree trunks appeared in his path out of the inky soup like wraiths. Carter considered pulling Jed's Maglite, but decided to give the Howler a light to follow wasn't the smartest move. It was bad enough he was leaving clear tracks in the snow that even Stacey could follow, but that couldn't be helped.

His mind wandered as the wind stroked the trees, the squeal and whine bringing back a memory of his daughter's first orchestra concert.

Katie had sat broken and weeping outside the music room, her head in her hands, her violin case on the floor beside her. Carter's heart had hurt. Kids could be so damn cruel, and as he'd watched his daughter cry, the heat of failure spread through him. He'd never felt so hopeless, and in that moment, he would have done anything to make his little girl feel better.

Competition was competition and he didn't believe in participation trophies, but seeing his daughter weep made him think maybe that was just an old-fashioned stupid idea. She'd missed one note, and the ensuing shriek had caused gentle laughter throughout the auditorium.

Carter wrapped his arm around Katie and pulled her tight. "You did great, sweetie. Want some ice cream?" The universal problem solver.

She paused in her crying to give him a look of frustration that was a little too like Debra's for his liking. "Dad, you've got ears."

"Yup, and they hurt thanks to you."

That got a smile.

"It's your very first show. What did you think? You would be a pro first time out of the gate?"

Katie stopped crying and Carter hugged her.

He called up that memory often, and he could still smell her flowery perfume, the chemical scent of her hairspray. If she were with him now, he'd apologize for everything.

Cracking branches, the crunch of compressing snow, and grunts snapped him from his reverie. The beast was so close he imagined its hot breath on his neck and felt its cold stare. He couldn't shake the unease that had burrowed into him when the Howler had fixed its yellow eyes on him. It was more than pure fury, rage, and an instinct to hunt and kill prey. No, there was more in those eyes. An intelligence. A knowing. A knowledge that told all other living things this was the Ozark Howler's land, and anyone not invited best move on.

He reached a thick stand of oaks that were packed so tight together for an instant Carter thought it was a wall constructed from logs. A row of chickadees sat in a line on a sagging tree branch beneath the cover of a snow-covered evergreen, cooing softly in the blackness. Carter traversed the line of trees, his thoughts straying to why the birds hadn't scattered. He slowed, sucking for air, his ragged breathing echoing through the forest.

A large gray boulder covered in snow and frozen moss rose from the forest floor like a monument, and Carter hid behind it as he peered back the way he'd come.

Fog swirled from his passage, and pricker vines and tree saplings protruded from a layer of fog that hung five feet above the ground, the thin vegetation like tentacles searching for prey. The wind whispered and sighed through the tree canopy, the commotion on the interstate a distant rumble. Nothing moved in the tangle of trees and underbrush. The snow had stopped, but with the thick black clouds and creeping darkness, visibility was still limited. Again, he considered pulling the flashlight, but he didn't want to give away his position.

He pulled down his neck gaiter as he looked around, surveying his position, perspiration dripping down his chin and freezing. With the moon shrouded, determining direction was difficult. The rumble of the interstate was east, but he hadn't taken a straight path through the woods—quite the opposite. Carter reached for his cell phone. Even without a signal, his compass app would work.

Panic filled him as he padded his jacket and plunged his hands into his jeans pockets. "Shit. Shit. Shiiitttt!!!!" he squawked. In his scramble to escape the Howler, he'd lost his phone which he now remembered he'd put in his back pocket. Not a huge problem—it was a burner—but now he had no way to communicate with the outside world, signal or not.

The clicking, stuttering laugh-like howl of the Ozark Howler echoed through the woods.

Carter drew the VP9, which still had a bullet chambered and was ready to fire. He struggled to see through the fog and darkness, but he saw no movement. Trees scraped and tapped, the wind playing the forest like a wooden flute. The gun was cold in his hand, despite the glove, and his stomach grumbled. He had no food, and the pinecones hanging from the shortleaf pines turned to fruit in his mind's eye as he imagined food. And he could use a drink. He'd never been a big boozer, but recent events required a dulling mechanism, and there was nothing more effective and available than good old whiskey. Carter tasted it on his lips and felt the warmth and the burn.

A howl pierced the night, not a hyena's laugh, but the growl of a beast frustrated with chasing down prey when there was plenty more waiting on the interstate. The creature was too big to survive on roadkill, and the intelligence it showed told Carter the creature was smart enough to know it couldn't go back up to the highway tonight. Shoot, Carter felt the same way. Who would blame a trigger-happy cop who shot someone accidentally after stumbling upon a fifteen-foot monster with four-inch fangs and razor-sharp claws?

No, despite the dangers it was he that needed to get back to the road, but which way? North or south? He could use the cover of the forest until he was beyond the accident scene, and then just blend in. He had his pack and cash was king. He'd have no problems laying low and getting himself a new identity because he still had all his contacts. A new burner, a few calls, some cash payments, and he'd be back in business. He'd miss Tommy's game, but what could he do? Life kept testing him, and the hits just kept on coming.

That was a message he'd drilled into his children, especially his son. The shit never ends until they plant you in the ground.

Tommy hadn't wanted to play baseball. It had crushed Carter because he'd played his entire life and was a huge fan of the game. To hear his son say he didn't want to play because he didn't think he would be good sent a wave of failure crashing over Carter. This was his fault.

So, he'd campaigned, and Tommy agreed to play, only to be crushed with disappointment in his very first game.

It was a perfect storm, the game on the line, when Tommy had come to the plate. Carter's nerves had danced, and he wrung his hands as he watched his son tap home plate with his bat the way he'd taught him.

Tommy took three brave strokes but came nowhere near the ball. The boy had been crushed, but even Carter had known that delicate moment wasn't a time for swing criticism.

After the game, in the car, Carter listened to his son say he wanted to quit, how he was no good, but Carter had worked with the boy every day thereafter, and by the kid's third game he was knocking singles into left field and as a teenager baseball was his son's go-to game.

He smiled as he recycled the memory and trudged south. There'd been no sign of the Howler, the wind, and cooing nightbirds the only sounds. He stepped from cover, listening hard for the highway, which without cars trundling along its length was nothing but a faint murmur that could barely be heard.

Snow crunched beneath his feet as his boots broke through the thin layer of verglas below the freshly fallen snow, his feet sinking into the winter's accumulation. He might as well be leaving signposts behind him, but he saw no solution. He couldn't swing from trees or fly, so he'd have to be careful, maybe create a few false trails by backtracking on his footsteps. Time was of the essence, however, and spending the night out in the woods, in the cold, didn't appeal to him, Ozark Howler or not. Perhaps he could start a fire, but like the flashlight, that would be like sending up a flare to the beast or anyone searching the woods.

Tree branches creaked and cracked as the wind gusted, dusty snow swirling, and Carter caught the scent of burning rubber, gasoline, and pine. The mix of smells was oddly pleasant, the pine giving the scent a candle-ish quality. He was making so much noise he stopped walking, mice racing up and down his spine, sweat dripping down his back, the chill of night leeching into his limbs through his jacket and gloves.

Carter felt the unnerving pressure of being watched, and he dropped to a knee, the H&K at the ready. His mouth was so dry it hurt, and he snatched up a broken piece of verglas from a footprint and put the dirty ice in his mouth. Cold water trickled down his throat as he gently sucked on the shard, relief flooding through him like he was drinking a glass of wine after he'd just crossed the desert.

The forest whispered and sighed, the thin shortleaf pines swaying, their needles clicking like millions of cockroaches scuttling over glass. He grabbed another shard of ice and got to his feet, his skin crawling. The rational side of his brain told him it was time to run, but Carter stood his ground as he gazed into the forest, the coating of snow aflame from the faint glare of the moonlight and starlight fighting through the glowing clouds.

Carter didn't see the Howler, so he continued south, sucking on his ice, his mouth cold, throat raw. The small amount of water was invigorating, and he felt the tension draining from his muscles, the pain in his stomach easing. Trudging through the snow was difficult work, and the snow was working its way into the cuffs of his jeans and filling his boots. Carter considered making snowshoes from evergreen branches, but instead dropped to a knee, tucked his pant cuffs into his boots, and tied the boots tight.

The scent of rot... no, spoiled meat... and the rusty tang of blood carried on the wind. Dead leaves tinkled, and a low growl carried through the trees.

A feeling of being watched washed over Carter and rooted his feet to the forest floor, his heart thumping, pain settling in his lower back.

To his right, two yellow pinpricks appeared in the stygian darkness. They hovered fifteen feet from the ground, and Carter went cold as the Howler x-rayed him.

The creature was forty feet away and running would only serve to spur the Howler on. He spread his legs, braced himself, and brought up the VP9. Trees and underbrush filled the space between Carter and the beast and hitting the creature would be pure luck given the distance, obstructions, and Carter's abilities as a marksman. The sound of the gunshot no longer concerned him. He was far enough from the interstate that even if the shot was heard, the authorities had more pressing issues than investigating a good old boy hunting out of season in the middle of a blizzard.

The wind gathered up snow and tiny cyclones danced through the trees on a blanket of mist that lifted from the snowpack. Like the smoke of a magician, the beast disappeared behind a puff of fog.

When the swirling snow cleared, the Ozark Howler was gone.

Nervous energy coursed through Carter, pain leaking to his extremities. He let the H&K fall to his side, his eyes locked on the empty patch of blackness where the beast had been. Trees swayed, the undergrowth rattling and creaking, a wave of bending vegetation heading in his direction as chuffing and grunts echoed through the forest.

Carter ran, and tree branches lashed his face and thorny vines tore at his clothes as he threw himself blindly through the woods, panic filling him, his mouth dry as paper again. He heard the murmur of the road and ran toward it, darkness pressing in on him as he stumbled through the underbrush, winding around tree trunks and through thickets of evergreens.

The distant static of cars filled the night, Carter's head buzzing as he ran. There was no way the interstate was open, but I-49 had tributaries and side roads, and with the highway closed there was bound to be traffic on roads that rarely saw more than farm vehicles. With the warmth of hope driving him forward, he plunged deeper into the forest, following the sound of the road. At a minimum he could walk to a hotel, at best someone might even give him a ride.

Carter pocketed the VP9 when he reached a large boulder that stretched across the face of a hillock, the static of the road beyond. The stone was coated in verglas, which was covered in snow, and it was difficult for Carter to find purchase as he climbed. His feet slipped, and he was forced to put out his hand to break his fall. Pain arced through his wrists as he crawled on his hands and knees, gripping the slick rock as he slowly inched his way to the pinnacle of the hill.

Panting, lungs stinging with pain, Carter clambered onto the top of the boulder, and hope fled as fast as it had arrived.

It wasn't a road Carter heard, but a river.

10

Carter scrambled down off the boulder, the ground between the stone and the riverbank a nightmarish field of frozen devil grass—tall icicles with green cores rising from the snowpack like surreal spikes. The grass tinkled and snapped as he made his way to the river's edge, the murmur of water flowing over dark ice-covered stones filling the shallow river valley.

Opaque sheets of cracked ice ran from the rocks into the gurgling water.

He tested the ice sheet and it spidered and cracked, so he headed south, following the line of the river until he reached a set of rapids that didn't have an ice sheet covering its flow. Carter pulled off his gloves and dropped to his knees, cold stinging his fingers as he cupped his hands and scooped water into his dry mouth. Chill river water spilled down his chin onto his jacket, but Carter didn't care. The water was ice cold, and though it chilled his core, it refreshed and reinvigorated him.

Sleep pulled at his eyelids as he pushed to his feet, dried his hands on his jacket, and pulled his gloves back on, which was no easy feat with his hands damp.

The wind had died down, and a gentle breeze pushed through the Ozarks, the crackle of dead leaves, the snap and pop of tree branches, and the soothing sound of water rushing over stones carrying through the forest.

There were no signs of the Howler, so Carter continued to trek upstream, stepping on rocks when he could to minimize footprints and hide his passage. The Howler was intelligent, but smart enough to follow footprints? Probably not. His scent was a different matter altogether. Could the beast track his scent with the ground covered in snow? He didn't think so, and if it could, the snow would certainly make it more difficult.

Carter scanned the river's edge ahead, looking for a shallow place to cross. The last thing he wanted to do was get wet. The cold would kill him, but getting wet to the knees might be worth it if trekking through the river water would knock the Howler off his scent.

No crossing opportunity presented itself. The river got wider and deeper as he walked, shadows tracing his every movement, darkness and fog slithering around trees and rising from the ground like wraiths as the night deepened. He didn't have a watch because he was used to having his phone, but Carter knew it was getting late. If he didn't find his way out of the forest soon it was going to be a long, cold night.

He considered climbing a tree to get his bearings, but with everything covered in snow and ice, it was too much of a risk. The rolling mountain peaks of the Ozarks were varied and spread out, so climbing to a peak wouldn't be very productive.

The river widened further and ended in a sinkhole surrounded by evergreens dusted with snow. Steep rock walls encircled an iced-over pond, and a thin crystallin waterfall was frozen still as it fell into the sinkhole. The tongue of ice sparkled like a wall of diamonds in the darkness, and Carter paused to gaze at its beauty.

His mouth was dry again from the exertion of trekking through foot-deep snow, so he scooped up some of the white stuff, made a tight ball the size of a quarter, and popped it in his mouth.

The ridgeline around the sinkhole was a mix of tumbled scree and evergreens that clung to the sliding earth, several of the trees almost horizontal as they jutted out over the hole.

Carter gave the edge of the depression a wide berth, and still almost fell twice, the slippery slope to the sinkhole's edge only feet away. He slowly worked his way around to the waterfall and climbed over a series of large snow-covered boulders at the frozen fall's base.

The dark maw of an opening leading behind the waterfall shone like a doorway to another universe, the black triangle standing out against the white. Carter's first thought was it was a bear's den, and a family of hibernating black bears slept therein. He stopped before the opening and sniffed, but he got none of the telltale rancid smells associated with bones, rotting meat, animal body odor, and stale air.

He reached into a pocket, pulled free Jed's Maglite, and turned it on. White light filled the opening and Carter felt the tension drain from him. There was no cave, no sleeping bears.

An escarpment of thick rock stuck from the cliff face, a portion of which had broken off at some point in the distant past creating a rock chamber. When the waterfall was flowing the rocks would be covered by cascading water, but now there was a narrow dark space behind the paused waterfall.

Carter stepped inside and shone the light around. He couldn't stand up straight because of the angled stone ceiling, but he could see out the opposite end of the crag. Stone angled away from the frozen falls and disappeared into a jagged, broken, step-like series of stones that led away into blackness.

The bark-like laugh of the Ozark Howler carried on the breeze, but it sounded far off.

He dropped his pack, perched the light atop a stone, and stowed the H&K. With a little work he could create a nice snow shelter where he could wait out the night. Things were always easier in daylight, and even though the Ozarks hadn't seen the sun in a month, it would be much easier to get his bearings in the half-light of a gray winter's day than in the pitch-black of night. And he had a feeling the Howler laid low during the day.

With the chill breeze working its way into his collar and the gap between his gloves and jacket, Carter dug with his gloved hands, slowly closing the entrance to the chamber. Snow leaked into his gloves, and it took the better part of twenty minutes, but when he was done there was a thick snowdrift blocking access to the crag.

Carter worked his way deeper into the stone crack, the chill of the frozen waterfall making the already cold air frigid. At the opposite end, Carter repeated the digging process, filling in the gap so the shelter was completely closed off to the outside world.

When all the hard work was done, he sucked on ice as he made a snow platform to sleep on, using the extra clothes in his pack to create a barrier between himself and his frozen bed. He had a lighter, and again he considered making a fire but decided against it. With the shelter sealed, heat was already building and the walls sparkled as the snow condensed.

He zipped his jacket up and pulled up his neck gaiter to preserve his body heat. It had felt good not to wear the mask, but the cold air had bitten his pale cheeks, the fresh air tickling his nose.

Carter climbed onto his makeshift bed and nestled into himself, pulling down his knit cap until it almost covered his eyes, the mask almost meeting its lower edge. Cold seeped up from the frozen snow, but his body and the ambient air were warming. A weariness like he'd never experienced before washed over him and Carter's eyelids drooped.

Thoughts of Jed and images of the Ozark Howler spun in a kaleidoscope as his mind raced through the events of the last few hours. His bumps and bruises protested, and his head filled with a gentle buzz. Blackness crept in around the edges of his vision, his hammering heart slowing, warmth spreading through him like alcohol. He closed his eyes, sleep tugging at his subconscious, and in that darkness, he saw a memory.

Car horns blared, metal clanged, whistles blew, and the chatter of humanity filled the city street. Tall buildings rose around him, and Carter stood on the sidewalk, people breaking around him. He was a rock in a stream, and as he stared forward into the crowd, all of whom were lost in their own worlds and paying him no attention, his eyes locked on the group of young men that were his quarry. They were laughing and joking, passing around a brown bag as they moved through the flowing knot of people like a snowplow. People avoided them, the throng parting like the little shits were Moses and the crowd the Red Sea.

The heat of anger and hatred filled Carter, and he reached into the pocket of his jacket and caressed the H&K VP9. He felt the overwhelming urge to draw down and start shooting. Collateral damage be damned. Yet, he knew what that would mean, and though his hands shook and his vision was tinged with the strain of anger, he pulled his hand free, leaving the gun where it was.

Carter saw his reflection in the glass façade of an office building, and he used it to watch the group of young men as they jaywalked across the street, car horns blaring. One of the shits lifted his middle finger, and another pounded a car hood, a thin cigarette hanging from his mouth, smoke billowing over the road.

He took a deep breath and reminded himself he wasn't the law, judge, or jury. Yet... His fingers tingled and his back spasmed as frustration tore through him. Carter turned away from the glass facade, went to the corner, and watched his prey cut down a side street while he waited for the Don't Walk sign to transition to Walk. His mind drifted as he watched the cars roll by, people with lives driving places they had to go to. All that had been taken from him, the bliss inherent in the daily grind that so many people complained about. He wished he could go back to a time when his biggest concern was figuring out new ways to teach kids about the past, but he didn't have a time machine. All he had was his anger and regrets.

A stiff breeze brought the smell of garbage and French fries, his nose itching, his back aching with stress. His prey turned down an alley, and when the sign switched to Walk, Carter hurried across the road and planted himself at the head of the alleyway. The strong scent of trash escaped the alley, and as Carter peered around the edge of a brick apartment building his stomach frothed with hatred, anger, and worry. What was he doing here? If a cop saw him stalking the kid, with a weapon in his possession, he'd be in deep trouble.

Despite the rational side of his brain arguing logic, Carter slipped into the alleyway, his hand in his pocket grasping the H&K. The sounds of the road and humanity died away, the smell of marijuana floating down the lane, clouds of white smoke hovering over the boys as they passed around the paper bag. The little shit was out on bail, partying, acting like everything was O.K. and nothing had happened.

"Who's this old turd?" said one of the kids when he saw Carter approaching. The acne covering his face rivaled poison ivy, and his bright brown eyes were glassy with wickedness.

All five of the turds turned to look at him, including Danny. The boy's hair was cut short—he'd just been in court—and his leather jacket made him look like a poser biker. The kid eyed him with recognition, but said nothing.

"What do you want, old man?" said another kid.

Carter's white-hot anger flamed hotter, his stomach burning, every muscle in his body tense. He slipped his hand into his pocket and gripped the VP9.

Danny got to his feet and came forward. As the leader of his little band, he was expected to be the alpha, which was one of the reasons the kid had ended up in jail. But they'd let him go, and Danny was drinking, having fun, his life back to normal. It wasn't fair, and he wouldn't let it stand.

"I'm talking to you, old man!" the kid repeated as Danny advanced, his lips turned up in a smile, his hands balled into fists.

Carter drew the H&K and held it out before him, single-handed, gangster style. He'd fired hundreds of practice rounds in the woods, and he'd gotten good with the weapon, but in the heat of the moment, rage painting his vision red, all his training and practice fled.

Danny backed away, hands out before him in the universal gesture that said, calm down, but Carter was gone, lost in a fantasy of anger where he'd put everything right. He screamed as he aimed the gun and pulled the trigger, the pop and crack of the weapon firing echoing through the narrow alleyway. Bullets peppered the kid and he fell back, dots of blood appearing on his shirt. Carter squeezed the trigger until the gun clicked empty, his throat stinging from his wail that never seemed to end.

Carter came awake with a start, the echo of a roar ringing in his head. Was it the Howler? Or was his mind still raddled by the nightmare, his nightly pennants?

The hiss of a snake made the question irrelevant.

11

Ozark Mountains, 2:19 AM CST, March 13th, 2021

With the incident still painted on the inside of his eyeballs, Carter climbed from sleep. As he opened his eyes he felt in his jacket for the flashlight, a faint rattle echoing through the snow shelter. Not the jangle of a rattlesnake, but the gentle swish-like vibration of copperhead tails.

Four sets of glowing eyes peered down at Carter from a crack where the rock ceiling met the mountainside.

Carter's fingers wrapped around the Maglite, and he pulled it free, but didn't turn it on. He searched his memory for anything he knew about copperheads and recalled his father's lecture when he was a boy. He'd seen a few in the wild as well as in captivity, and he knew copperheads weren't social snakes, and though they usually hunted alone, they often hibernated in communal dens and returned to the same den each year with the same roommates. They were poisonous, but attacks were rare, unless agitated or disturbed in their den. Like he was doing right now.

He didn't know if the beasts would get spooked if he turned on the light. Sweat dripped down his back, the wind singing and shuffling snow and ice, the faint tap and creak of tree branches blending with the gentle buzz of the snake's vibrating tails and the faint echo of their breaths.

Carter turned on the light.

The frozen waterfall and the two snowdrifts Carter had created to seal his shelter sparkled, and ice melted across the fallen wedge of rock that was the shelter's ceiling. From within the den four snakes peered down at Carter, red forked tongues lashing out as they smelled in three dimensions, picking up his scent.

Under the harsh Maglite the vipers glistened, heads lifting, wet eyes locked on Carter. The beasts were wound up in tight circles, like stored rope, their heads floating and swaying above dark brown bodies. Hourglass-shaped markings overlaid on light reddish-brown skin ran the length of the creatures. It was difficult to tell how large the snakes were, but they looked like full-grown adults. Despite their aggressive-looking postures, the creatures appeared content to stay where they were.

Without his phone, Carter had no way of knowing what time it was. He felt somewhat refreshed from his nap, but he didn't like the idea of continuing his trek out of the forest in the dark.

The gentle vibrating hum of the copperheads reminded him it wasn't his choice and sleepy time was up. It was time to move on whether he wanted to or not, darkness and Howler be damned. He dug his gloved hand into the snow and made himself an ice ball to suck on as he watched the snakes, replaying his father's hiking lecture from when he was a boy.

"Son, the eastern copperhead feeds on a variety of prey, and generally they're an ambush predator. Do you know what that means?"

Carter had nodded in understanding, but said, "Not really."

"I've seen copperheads hiding behind rocks, under bushes and other strategic positions, where they lay in wait for unsuspecting prey. Copperheads freeze instead of slithering away and rely on excellent camouflage. People are usually bitten because they go too close to them."

Like fifteen feet away in their den with a 300-lumen flashlight blazing.

There was always the H&K, but he left it in his jacket. He looked around for a stick, or a stone he could throw, but again thought better of disturbing the vipers. They weren't bothering him, and though he couldn't sleep with them watching him, that didn't mean he needed to agitate the beasts. He could stay awake until sunup and before he—

A broken bestial bark followed by a staccato laugh-howl scattered Carter's thoughts.

Pebbles tumbled and shards of ice slid as the copperheads uncoiled and slipped deeper into the mountainside.

Carter turned off the flashlight.

The call of the wind died away and silence filled the night, Carter's eyes constantly straying to the spot where the snakes had been. No eyes glowed from within the crack.

Sniffing and huffing carried into the shelter, and a dark shadow passed before the opaque frozen waterfall. The tinkle of cracking ice, the puff and sigh of shifting snow, loud grunts and coughs of exertion.

Carter's bed of snow chilled his back and knotted his muscles. Lethargy filled him, that debilitating weariness of getting just enough sleep to let one's body know more rest is needed. He stowed the light and slipped one of the backpack straps over his shoulder. Invisible ants covered his body, his mind conjuring images of the Ozark Howler standing just beyond the thin barrier of snow.

More digging, sniffing, and a pale pinpoint of gray light appeared in the snow wall at Carter's feet. He held his breath as he pulled the VP9.

The gray light disappeared as something black and glistening wet filled the gap and the darkness deepened.

Pale light seeped into the shelter as the hole in the snowdrift grew.

A yellow-rimmed eye filled the hole.

Sniffing, digging, and snow cascaded toward Carter. The glint of claws in the snow, faint moonglow, and starlight filtered through the growing gap. Did the beast smell him?

Carter glanced over his shoulder at the opposite end of the shelter. He couldn't see it in the darkness, but he knew there was another snowdrift sealing him in.

A loud roar pierced the night.

The upper portion of the snow wall caved in, and Carter rolled off his platform and landed on his back. He brought up the VP9 as an explosion of snow poured into the shelter, burying him to the waist.

Yellow eyes shone in the darkness as the beast dug, snow and ice flying, the Howler grumbling and snorting, its giant paws the size of shovel heads.

Carter fired twice into the cascading snow, and the 9MM rounds cracked into stone. He couldn't see the beast, and he swam through the snow toward the opposite end of the shelter as ragged breaths chased him, the scent of rust and body odor filling his nostrils like rotting meat.

A carnal scream.

Carter crawled and dug, his vision growing blurry, his food deprived muscles protesting.

The Ozark Howler barked and chuffed as it powered through the snow, sensing a meal, which was probably rare when most of the other animals were asleep or gone for the season.

A claw caught Carter's boot, and for a heartbeat, a vision of him being jerked backward into the flowing snow filled his mind. He struggled forward with renewed effort, the VP9 still in his hand, the cold steel biting his palm. He could turn and empty the gun, put the beast down here and now... or at least he could try. It was dark, he was in a confined space, on the move, with a rock ceiling and stone walls inches away. Ricochets were a real possibility and putting a bullet in the beast might just make it angrier.

The barrier wall wasn't thick, and he surged forward into the snowbank, tumbling through the loose snow onto the precipice behind the frozen waterfall. Carter tucked and rolled, coming to his feet, and slipping on slick stone. He thrust out his arms to steady himself and when he hit dry stone he lurched forward and fell.

With a shout of fury, the Howler heaved itself through the snow and swiped at him, the baseball-mitt-sized paw raking the air above Carter's head. The blow passed, the white glow of the pool in the sinkhole below spinning across Carter's field of vision. He vaulted to his feet, knee-deep snow tugging at his legs as he lunged toward the woods.

Visibility was twenty feet, the gray gloom of the wee hours shrouding the world in darkness. Shadows flitted about the forest and hid under every bush and beside every boulder. Carter ran blindly, thoughts of slipping into the sinkhole or breaking an ankle on a stone making him pull the flashlight. With stealth no longer an issue, he turned the torch on, and a gaudy cloud spilled over the forest before him.

A wide oak, many dead leaves still clinging to its thick branches, rose from the frozen hardpan like a monolith. Sounds of exertion carried through the forest: huffing, clicking, growling. Carter scrambled behind the oak, using it as a shield as he wrapped his arms around the tree's trunk. He trained the flashlight on the path he'd left in the snow and aimed the H&K.

White light spilled over the frozen waterfall, the elongated shadows of trees like boney fingers reaching out from the forest.

The beast was gone.

Carter panned the light around, the guttural sounds of the Howler still rising above the wind. He looked over his shoulder, though he didn't think the beast could've gotten behind him.

Tree branches snapped, and the pop and crack of footfalls breaking through the verglas was like an approaching elephant in the stillness.

He backed off the tree and spun on his toes, swinging the VP9 around, snow crunching beneath his feet. Carter didn't see the beast under the unforgiving glare of the Maglite, but he squeezed off three shots in random directions just to give the beast pause, and the tactic appeared to work.

An eerie stillness settled over the scene, the gentle sound of water trickling over stones and the tinkle of snow brushing over snow filling the forest.

A huge shadow glided through the woods, and Carter aimed the VP9. Mist lifted from the snowpack, eddying around trees, and settling under bushes as the shadow dissipated like the fading of a ghost. Heart thumping in his chest, muscles shrieking in protest, face stinging from the cold, Carter slowly backed away from the oak, panning the flashlight and H&K around the way he'd seen Bosch do it on T.V., flashlight atop the gun like a sight.

With a cry that sent a shiver of pain clamoring down Carter's spine, the Howler burst from the tree cover, a blinding amorphous dark shape with glowing yellow eyes and four-inch fangs. It moved like smoke and with the speed of a bullet.

Carter tried to aim the VP9, but the beast knocked him from his feet, the Howler's massive paw raking over Carter's backpack—his second lucky break in the last five minutes. The snowpack cushioned his fall, and Carter twisted onto his back as he brought up the H&K.

Moonglow lit the clouds, darkness, and white tree branches spinning before him. He fired twice, the scent of cordite filling the air. Carter crab-walked back, his ass dragging in the snow, the H&K held out before him, the glow of the flashlight dancing around.

The beast slipped from the flashlight's eye, ducking behind a thick evergreen covered in snow.

Carter's heart sank. Hunting was allowed in the Ozarks depending on the season, and what were the odds that the beast hadn't been shot at? Hadn't Jed mentioned something? Though how would he know?

Panic urging him on, Carter pushed to his feet and bolted into the forest, angling away from the beast and threading along the edge of the shallow river valley that met the sinkhole. Tree branches whipped his face as he threw himself forward, the land angling downward as the gurgle of running water and the sounds of pursuit filled the woods.

He stepped in a hole, slipped, and then he was falling, the dark line of the stream rushing up to meet him.

A tree branch snapped, the sound like a gunshot in the deep of night. Carter slid down the embankment toward the stream, grabbing at saplings and dead underbrush as he tried to stop his slide. Thoughts of his family flashed through his mind, memories, goals, and things he'd wanted to see and do. He saw himself on the city street and felt the itch of the rage, the sweet heat of release as he pulled the trigger. Sorrow and regret engulfed him, every bad decision he'd ever made settling on him as he tore at the vegetation, a sense of hopelessness gnawing at his resolve and cramping his muscles.

At the top of the incline the dark outline of the Howler stood watching, its elongated snout in the air as it shrieked. Far off in the distance, an answering wail carried on the wind like lost ambition.

Carter tumbled through the frozen underbrush, the flashlight beam jerking around as he fell, revealing the black tree line, the silvery water, and stone. Thorny vines tore at his jacket and pants, his knit cap getting caught and pulled from his head. His face hit snow and he rolled, the river only feet away, cold moisture rolling off the stream in waves.

Pain stitched up his side as Carter crashed into a boulder and came to a bone-rattling stop. Icy fingers ran down his back, and he sat up, the flashlight beam angling toward the sky, its harsh light painting the Ozark Howler's inhuman shadow on the frozen waterfall.

12

Carter killed the flashlight and got on his hands and knees, his head ringing, lungs on fire. Blood ran down his forearm from his elbow, the joint tightening and swelling. He flexed the arm and it grudgingly moved, pain spiking to his fingertips. The stream gurgled, the blue and white stones beneath him like a checkerboard drawn by Tim Burton.

He pressed to his feet as his gaze strayed to the frozen waterfall. The shadow of the Howler was gone, but the crunch of massive paws charging through snow echoed through the night. Carter searched his pockets for the H&K, panic rising in him when he didn't find it. The gun wasn't in his jacket, and he felt behind his back and checked his pockets, but his search was disturbed by a ferocious roar.

Two yellow eyes glowed in the darkness, levitating six feet above the ground as they slid along the river's edge. Carter's mind spun until he recalled the beast dropping on all fours. Bears could move at terrific speeds when galloping along on all four appendages, and he had no doubts the Ozark Howler could outrun him, whether it was on an open plain or weaving through the forest.

The gleam of metal caught Carter's eye. The VP9 was in the snow halfway up the embankment Carter had tumbled down. He raced for it, clawing at the undergrowth, his gloves tearing on pricker vines, his boots slipping in fresh snow.

He scooped up the H&K and continued his climb, picking up his hat along the way, stones tumbling behind him, his heart hammering in his chest. He spared a glance back, but he saw nothing except the silvery glow of the stream, the encroaching blackness, and snow-covered stones.

When he reached the top, he examined his footprints, which trailed into darkness in the direction of the waterfall. He cinched up his backpack straps and turned on the flashlight. Having almost been caught by the Howler twice, Carter figured being able to see where he was going was more important than stealth, which based on his exploits so far, proved impossible. Not only had the creature tracked him, but it also knew the territory, and if it was anything like a bear it had excellent sensory perception and would hear him trudging through the forest a mile away. Plus, the beast had already circled back on him twice, and as Carter peered into the shadowy woods he despaired.

Fresh snow coated the forest, clean and pristine. The cloud cover glowed, backlit by moonlight and starlight, and a corpse light leaked through the woods. A chill wind muttered and exhaled, the trees talking back and forth in rhyme, their branches rasping and popping.

A deer trail led into the trees and Carter followed it, the flashlight blazing through the darkness like a locomotive. Carter looked back every few seconds as he walked as if on a balance beam, one foot directly in front of the other as he utilized the thin path the deer had trailblazed. Piles of dog food-sized brown scat dotted the whiteness, and hoof and claw prints wove between the trees.

The gurgle of the stream faded, and Carter's heart rate eased, his breathing became less ragged, and his joints settled down to a dull throb. What he would give for an aspirin or a stiff drink. The saliva in his mouth soured at the thought of alcohol. After the incident, he drowned himself in whiskey and wine, but when COVID struck and he could move about again, see his children, he'd begged off, though he missed the numbing bliss and reinvigorating heat.

With a chorus line of frosty martinis dancing in his head like candy canes in a Christmas musical, Carter plowed forward, the harsh light of his Maglite painting the forest in lurid black and white. A shadow slipped from the trees onto the path, and Carter froze midstride, tiny imaginary spiders scurrying over every inch of his flesh.

The Ozark Howler stepped into the cone of light, the massive bear-cat on all fours, its elongated snout sniffing the ground, the sound of sucking air like a vacuum cleaner on full power. The adolescent elephant-sized beast rose onto its hind legs, its piercing eyes locked on Carter, who still stood rooted to the frozen path, the light out before him, VP9 at his side.

The Howler's black, shaggy coat was dusted white with snow, and as the creature stepped forward it separated from the shadows like the night itself was birthing the beast. It trundled toward him, muscular arms hanging by its sides, the glint of curved claws at the end of each digit. Two twisted horns protruded from its head, its eyes never leaving him.

The creature looked different in some way, but he couldn't put a finger on it. Carter brought up the VP9, aimed, but…

Transfixed by seeing something that shouldn't exist, the wonder of experiencing something never thought possible, the surge of adrenaline, curiosity, a need to know, to see, to understand, all kept Carter from pulling the trigger. Then there was convincing himself he wasn't going mad. More than once he'd thought about the car accident on the interstate and he had to pinch himself to ensure that he was, in fact, alive and not wandering around purgatory awaiting his final trial.

The beast howled, its odd bellow wolf-elk call and the chortle of its odd bark carrying through the forest. Nasty mange covered the beast's neck and shoulders, but the blood that had darkened its elongated snout was gone. Its fist-sized nose blew streams of foggy condensation, the Howler's huge jaws hanging half open as it snarled, dark saliva leaking through broken teeth, two thick fangs hanging over pulled-back lips. Cords of muscle knotted the creature's appendages, and its pointed ears stood on end, the beast tuning its sensors to high.

A branch snapped, and the Howler's huge head swiveled in the direction of the sound.

Carter aimed the flashlight into the woods, also searching for the source of the noise. He took his eyes off the creature for two heartbeats. Nothing moved in the forest, the white coating of snow reflecting the flashlight beam, tree trunks casting long spider-like shadows over the trail. When he shifted the light back to the Howler it was gone.

The icy fingers of terror massaged his back as Carter panned the light over the path ahead. Thick trees filled the woods, but nothing large enough to hide the beast. It had faded into the darkness like a wraith, its black fur perfect camouflage.

With the beast ahead, Carter had no choice but to turn back, but once again the Ozark Howler outmaneuvered him. He'd only backtracked twenty feet before the beast appeared in the forest to his right.

Carter brought up the VP9 and fired. The bullet smacked into a tree trunk, splinters flying, but the shot didn't deter the Howler and it disappeared behind an evergreen. He steadied the flashlight, but its beam only caught shadows, the glow of snow, and a dark pyramid of thickly packed needle-like green leaves.

He felt like the north star in the woods with the light blazing, so he clicked off the flashlight. Darkness pressed in on the path as Carter blinked, his eyes adjusting. Suddenly the H&K felt heavy in his hand. He counted the shots he'd taken and calculated how many bullets were left in the fifteen round clip and determined he had at least eight shots left and there was another clip in the backpack.

Snapping branches, heavy footfalls, crackling snow, snorting, huffing, and growling. Carter felt, rather than saw, the beast silently moving through the forest, its shadow appearing and disappearing in the darkness as Carter rotated, VP9 out before him in a double-handed grip. With his eyesight adjusted to the gloom, Carter saw behind shadows, the white shine of the snowpack like a mirror.

A loud gurgle-bark-howl.

He fired twice at a huge shadow as it moved through a tight stand of evergreens. A bullet thwacked into a tree trunk, another hitting the ground, a geyser of snow spouting into the air. But... there was nothing there. What he'd seen was an evergreen branch swaying in the wind.

Time slowed, as if the creature had hit pause on the game that was its life and was relieving itself behind a stone. Carter slowly spun three hundred and sixty degrees, his vision sharp, the H&K at the ready. The wind pushed around snow, tiny tornados twirling through the woods, the crackle of dead leaves like static. A thin layer of mist hung just above the ground, its tentacles eddying around tree trunks, rocks, and evergreens laden with snow. A line of gray feathered chickadees that sat on a nearby branch chortled and cooed, and far off an owl hooted.

An angry yelp blared from the darkness, very close. The chickadees sprayed from the evergreen and knifed into the blackness.

For a heart-wrenching moment, Carter didn't know which direction the beast was coming from, and he spun, weapon up and ready.

The cacophony of the Howler's passage gave away its position, but it didn't matter much.

Carter struggled to sight the H&K. There were so many trees, the beast was moving fast, and it was dark. He fired twice and hit two tree trunks, but the creature kept coming, dodging through the vegetation, its yellow-rimmed eyes alight in the blackness.

The Howler was thirty yards away.

With no time left, and with so many obstructions between himself and the Howler, Carter searched for another way to fight off the creature. He looked around for a stick he could use as a club, but everything was hidden by snow. Then an idea worked its way forward through the dread.

Carter put the flashlight on top of the gun like a sight, holding it in place as he turned it on. He sighted the weapon and light directly into the beast's eyes as it burst through the underbrush, all muscle, fury, and teeth.

He fired until the gun clicked empty, and though he thought he'd hit the beast, the creature didn't slow as it slipped through the final stretch of trees that separated the Howler from its prey.

Carter surged down the deer path, but a gunshot rang out, the pop and crack bringing him to a halt.

"Hey now!" someone yelled. It was a deep male voice. Another gunshot. The scrape of metal-on-metal shrieking through the stillness. Another shot. Both bullets pelted nearby trees and the Howler slowed, a splinter impaled in its left cheek, a puzzle of red dots forming in the snow at the creature's feet.

The Howler changed direction, the massive shadow of its head falling over the path, its twisted horns like elongated knives. Dazzling light reflecting off the snowpack illuminated the scene as the beast disappeared into a thicket of evergreens with the ease of a brick falling through water; fluid, quick, and without hesitation.

Another shot rang out, but no trees splintered.

A tall shadowy figure stepped onto the path.

Carter slipped off his backpack and dropped to a knee as he undid the clasps holding the bag closed.

Branches snapped, snow crunched, and muffled growling floated on the wind.

With a flick of his thumb, Carter let the VP9's empty magazine fall into the open backpack as he pulled a fresh clip free. He jammed the magazine home, chambered a round, and sealed up the bag. He slipped the pack on and stood, the gun at his side.

The figure on the path was coming toward Carter, and his nerves jangled, his palms itching, the H&K cold in his hand. Elongated shadows crisscrossed the deer trail.

Like the Howler, the stranger materialized from the darkness like a ghost, and relief flooded through Carter. "Jed?" He couldn't believe it. How could it be?

"In the flesh, baby," the big man said. He held his rifle, and still wore the new camouflage jacket. His eyes gleamed above his mask, his evil clown toothy grin glowing in the flashlight beam.

For the first time in hours, Carter remembered his mask. He'd worn it for so long he didn't think about it much, but not having it on had been so comfortable Carter had forgotten about it. The gaiter was still around his neck, but it was covered in snow and stiff from frozen sweat. He considered not pulling it up, but he remembered hiding his identity wasn't the only reason for covering his face, and if he got COVID it would be game over.

Carter pulled up his mask and said, "What the hell are you doing out here?"

"Saving your ass," Jed said. "The Howler almost got you. Again. Where the hell did you learn to shoot?"

Something stirred in Carter, some piece of the puzzle not fitting, but he didn't care. He had help, and though he was loathed to admit it, he needed it. Bad.

"Do you have anything to eat?" Carter asked. His stomach hurt. As an American—even as a fugitive—he'd never had hunger pains.

"No," Jed said. "There's plenty of supplies up on the interstate. Let's go."

Carter nodded, calming heat flowing through him like wine as he followed.

13

Borderland Pass, I-49, Ozark Mountains, 6:18 PM CST, March 12th, 2021

"Mask up, sweetie," Aniyah said.

Stacey complied, and Aniyah boosted the child to a rescue worker.

The scent of human waste filled the trailer, and though she hadn't gotten used to it, Aniyah no longer coughed every other breath. She broke the heels off her shoes and put on the galoshes the emergency people had given her and cinched up her jacket.

She joined Stacey outside, and wind and ice bit at her face. Everything was covered in a light sheen of snow, hiding the horror.

Stacey was being checked out by a medic on the hood of the car next to the camper.

"Where're your parents, sweetie?" asked the young female EMT who wore a hunting cap with fur side flaps, her eyes bright above a white N95 mask.

Stacey pointed at Aniyah as she climbed down onto the hood of the green sports car packed against the camper's side, the warmth of love growing in her.

The car's hood flexed and popped.

"This your daughter?" the medic asked, her voice muffled.

Aniyah's heart raced, her hands shaking. What would happen to Stacey if she said no? Would the girl be whisked off and placed in foster care? Aniyah shuddered at the thought. She'd been orphaned when her mom died of heart disease, and there was no close family. She'd struggled through the system, crawled through the sewer pipe, and come out clean on the other end. She was stronger for it, but there were easier ways to gain maturity and wisdom. She said, "Sort of."

The EMT's brow knitted.

"Her parents…"

"My real mom and dad are dead. This is my new mom. Her name is Aniyah," Stacey said with an innocence and ignorance only a child can possess.

Aniyah smiled in support, then realized the medic couldn't see her mouth because of her mask, so she said, "That might be overstating things a little, but I can look after her until the authorities have time to sort things out for her. Find her family."

The EMT nodded. "Let me give you a look then."

"I'm fine."

"Let me take your vitals."

Aniyah sighed and unzipped her jacket.

The EMT jerked back, her face twisting.

"No. No," Aniyah said. "That's... my husband's blood." The front of her shirt was brown with dried blood, and as the medic inched forward and placed the head of the stethoscope inside her shirt the memory of her dead husband came rushing back like a bad dream.

Harry lay dead in the wreckage. Gone. He would never talk to her again. Lecture her about things she didn't care about. All those little things that had annoyed her were lost forever, and she already missed them.

"OK," the EMT said. "You're good to go. Head to the shoulder of the road. There'll be a transport coming to take you to a processing site, and from there you'll be put up in a hotel. See your MD for a full checkup as soon as possible and find a police officer and update them on Stacey here." She tousled the kid's hair, but Stacey pulled away. There was a line forming on the side of the camper as the remainder of the survivors were rescued, so Aniyah and Stacey moved along.

Darkness suffocated the road, snow swirling against blackness. Stacey turned on a small flashlight she'd retrieved from inside the upturned camper. Wind pushed around the dusting of snow that covered the wreckage, and the distant thump of helicopter rotors carried over the interstate as Aniyah and Stacey climbed over destroyed vehicles.

"Where's Ray?" Stacey asked.

Aniyah had been so focused on her sorrows, on taking care of Stacey, that Ray had slipped her mind. "I'm not sure. Hold up." She climbed atop the roof of an SUV and turned three hundred and sixty degrees, straining to see through the gloom, looking for Ray. When she didn't find him, she said, "I don't know, honey, but I know where we can look. Come on."

"The lady with the medicine said not to go far," the child said.

Aniyah chuckled. "I know. We're not."

The pair climbed through the devastation, people sitting around with bandages on their heads, EMTs tending them. The fires had been put out, and a steady stream of support personnel filtered through the tangle of vehicles. Aniyah wanted to help, to ask if anyone needed anything, but she was in no position to help anyone. She could barely help herself... and Stacey.

When the duo arrived at Ray's white Ford Taurus he wasn't there, and she stayed clear of her crushed blue Nissan and the corpse therein. Police officers were going through the box truck with the dead bodies of people who had been smuggling themselves into the United States, and by the sheer twisted finger of fate had ended up dead on the interstate because they'd been in the back of the truck with no restraints.

Ray was nowhere to be seen, so Aniyah led Stacey east toward the shoulder as instructed. The crimson trail was mostly covered in snow, but an occasional dark patch revealed dried puddles of blood. The duo traversed the destruction in silence, Stacey quietly humming the theme song of a cartoon Aniyah couldn't name.

Several crash victims stood on the eastern shoulder waiting for the transport. Aniyah didn't see Ray.

"Let's ask her," Stacey said.

Before Aniyah could protest, the child was walking south toward an old woman sitting in a camping chair wrapped in an emergency blanket and drinking coffee.

"Stacey. Stacey, hold up," Aniyah said as she trailed after.

"Hi, I'm Stacey. My parents are dead, and this is my new mom Aniyah," Stacey told the woman.

"Your new mommy?" the old woman said. "How wonderful." A light coating of snow dusted the woman like she hadn't moved in some time.

Aniyah scooped Stacey into her arms and said, "I'm not her mom. Just looking out for her."

The lady nodded but said nothing. She wore a black knit cap and a smiley-face surgical mask.

"Did you see my new dad?" Stacey said.

The old woman smiled sympathetically.

Aniyah's stomach sank. The trauma of the accident, losing her parents, and Ray, had unhinged the child from reality. "We're looking for a friend," she explained.

"What did he look like?"

Aniyah described Ray.

"Oh, dear," the lady said. "I did see a man with a dirty-blonde crew cut wearing a black ski jacket and face gaiter."

The way the old woman said "Oh, dear" made Aniyah's heart drop.

"Where did he go?" Stacey asked.

Aniyah put her hands on the child's shoulders.

"He ran when... it came," said the old lady. She pulled down her mask and sipped her tea as she gazed at the frozen ground, her face contorting.

"It?" Aniyah said.

"I wouldn't know what to call it. I didn't *actually* see it. But I heard its screaming and fussing. You must have..." She trailed off as her gaze shifted to Stacey. "I saw him run that way." The old woman pointed at the tree line.

"Thank you," Aniyah said.

"Let's go find him," Stacey said as she surged toward the forest.

Aniyah held the child fast.

The old woman frowned, realized her mask was still down and pulled it up. People certainly had gotten used to their facial expressions not being seen, and therefore not analyzed and interpreted.

Aniyah said, "I don't see what you could poss—"

"I can help," Stacey argued. "I've got this light I found." She held the flashlight up as evidence.

"That's not enough, sweetie," Aniyah said.

"I'm not losing another father," Stacey yelled, her tearing eyes staring south toward where the woman had pointed.

"Just watch her for a minute. O.K.?" Aniyah said. "I'll go take a fast look." She rolled her eyes to let the woman know she was humoring the child.

The old lady nodded.

Stacey didn't.

"Can I borrow your light?" Aniyah asked.

The kid reluctantly handed it over as she shifted back and forth on her feet, nervous energy eating away at the kid.

Aniyah hurried along the shoulder of the road, panning the light over the snowdrift that separated the road from the forest. The layer of new snow was a pristine white carpet marred occasionally by a twig, car part, or splotch of blood, but when she came upon what looked like bear tracks and a double set of footprints trailing to the tree line she paused, staring into the forest, the evergreens and white oaks swaying, dead leaves clamoring in the wind.

"Those are his footprints. I know it," Stacey said.

Aniyah started and looked down to find the child standing next to her. "I told you to stay with…" She hadn't gotten the woman's name. She couldn't follow Ray into the forest. That made no sense at all. Especially with some beast lurking in the shadows.

"Let me see that," Stacey said, her little fingers gripping her flashlight. "I just want to see something."

Lost in thought, Aniyah let the child pry the light from her hand. Her primary purpose was to protect Stacey and get her to safety. It was dark, snowing, she wasn't dressed correctly, and she had no supplies. Snow had already worked its way into her rubber boots, chilling her feet. She wore pants, but her legs were freezing, the icy fingers of cold working their way up through her groin to her chest.

But Ray could be just inside the tree break, lying face down in the snow, dying. Didn't she owe him something? He helped her when she'd needed it most, and she felt a responsibility for the man. Not enough to say he was Stacey's new father, and she her mother, but… No. It was too dangerous and risky. She was weak, tired, and she was in no way an outdoors person.

"Let's go back to our new friend and wait for the police," Aniyah said, her fugue broken. She reached out to put a hand on Stacey's shoulder, but the girl was gone.

A flashlight beam bounced through the darkness as Stacey ran across the snow-covered grass strip that separated the wilderness from the shoulder of the interstate. The snowbanks at the edge of the highway were slick with new-fallen snow and below that, a thin coating of ice crackled and snapped as the kid ran.

"Stacey! Stacey, you stop right now!" Aniyah yelled, but the kid didn't even look back.

Aniyah looked around in desperation, then gave chase. Steel drainage grating marked the end of the snowdrift-covered grass and a pile of scree tumbled from the woods toward the road. Gray stones ranging in size from a boulder to a pebble plunged down the embankment like frozen water, every rock slick with ice and a potential ankle twister.

Wind pushed snow into Aniyah's eyes as it swirled and eddied, the dark wall beyond the tree line leaking fog, stray flashlight and headlight beams making everything look one dimensional in the pale light.

The flashlight's glow disappeared into the forest, and the air rushed from Aniyah's lungs, the sense of loss so great she couldn't explain it. She hardly knew this child, yet... Stressful situations create strong bonds, and as she ran after the bobbing flashlight, she thought maybe she could be Stacey's new mother. But that was crazy. In what world would the court give custody of a white child to a widowed black woman who wasn't her kin?

Aniyah plunged into the forest at a full run, calling out Stacey's name, but the child ran on. The trail of footprints was barely visible in the soupy darkness, but she focused on the cloud of light surging through the trees before her.

She came to a sliding halt when a guttural roar followed by a series of stuttering barks echoed through the forest.

Stacey froze, her hands stinging with cold, her nose running, snot leaking into her mouth. She heard Aniyah calling her name, telling her to stop. But her flashlight revealed a trail of footsteps leading into the forest, and she wanted nothing more than to find Ray. She had to find him. She ducked under branches, skipped over holes, and veered around rocks, her small size allowing her to move fast through the snow-covered underbrush.

The sounds of the accident scene died away and the darkness thickened, the blackness eating her flashlight's beam beyond thirty feet. She took her hat off because she was sweating, heard her dead mother's voice scolding her, and pulled it back on. She didn't know how far she'd gone, but as she went on, the unnerving sense that she was being watched filled her with fear.

She was alone. In the woods. Panic gripped her, shook her, reality taking hold and telling her how stupid she was to think she, a little kid, could find anyone or anything in any forest. The trees were so tall she couldn't see their tops, and she cowered under their size and majesty.

Then she remembered the yellow eye. The camper getting flipped over like it was a toy, and her concern for Ray fell away.

Stacey turned off her flashlight. She might only be a kid, but if something was out there, she knew better than to give away her position. She'd played hide and seek and tag in the dark with her friends—one of her favorite things to do—so she knew how to use the shadows to hide, and how to tread so lightly her footfalls weren't heard.

Snow filtered through the tree canopy, bare branches shifted and swayed, a patchwork of shadows writhing over the snowpack. A man appeared ahead. The large shadowy figure dropped to a knee and examined the trail of footprints. He had a long gun hanging from his shoulder and some instinct yet to be fully developed sent a shiver of worry and fear running through Stacey. She stopped running and hid behind a thick evergreen shrouded in snow.

Stacey hunkered down under a branch heavy with ice and stepped on a branch that cracked like a gunshot.

The shadow man spun and brought up the gun; Stacey saw his silhouette clearly in the gloom. The figure slipped into the shadows like an apparition, and Stacey let go of a breath she'd been holding and cowered in the shadows.

14

Ozark Mountains, 3:29 AM CST, March 13th, 2021

Carter and Jed threaded down the deer trail, the wind tearing at their clothes, dead leaves rattling on their branches. Sucking on snow was getting old, and Carter felt grit and sand on his tongue, his stomach aching for something solid. The memory of the beer and the smell of the potato chips as Stacey munched made him think of Aniyah and the girl. They were most likely on their way to a warm hotel, where they would be given food and shelter for the night. His family was snug in their beds, his son getting his rest for his game the following day, his daughter dreaming of things he didn't want to think about like partying, sex, and such. Same things Tommy would be obsessed with in a couple of years if he wasn't already. And Debra? Well, Debra had always been good at taking care of Debra.

"Are you O.K., Ray?" Jed asked.

Carter stared at the ground, lost in thought.

"Ray? Are you alright?"

"Yeah… yeah. Sorry," Carter said. He'd forgotten he was Ray. "Just hungry, and it's been a long night."

"Yes, it has. An extraordinary night."

Carter usually reserved his use of the word extraordinary for good things, and his silence revealed his puzzlement because Jed added, "Seeing the Howler and all."

"I'd rather have missed the thing. Kind of like roller coasters. Thrilling, but given the choice I'd pass."

Jed chuckled, but it sounded much different than his usual laugh. "People force you onto many coasters? Last I checked, that shit was voluntary."

"Not when you have kids."

The other laugh. The fake laugh. "I suppose."

"You don't have children?"

"Not that I know of." The real laugh. Jed stopped walking and turned to Carter. "I didn't see any kids with you up on the interstate? You were alone? Where are your kids?"

This one was easy. Carter had been asked that question many times over the last couple of years. "Home. With their mom. I sell auto parts, so I travel a lot."

"Really? For what company?"

"Glenco. We supply Napa, Advance, all the mom and pops."

"Never heard of it."

Of course you haven't, because it doesn't exist. "Not surprising. Are you a big player in the aftermarket fuel injector business?"

Jed said nothing.

"There you go."

The duo started walking again, snow sifting over the path, the cloud cover growing brighter as it thinned.

"What about you?" Carter asked. "You from around these parts?"

A long pause, then, "I've spent most of my life in the Ozarks."

"Around here?"

"Naw, down south a ways. I was running an errand."

"You figure the Howler was hanging around looking for roadkill?"

Jed didn't say anything for a long while, the wind chirping through the trees, snow shifting over ice, dead leaves crackling. Finally, his voice two octaves below its normal tenor, he said, "Oh, I've seen it before. Or one that looks like it."

Carter's head swiveled, the possibility of the beasts coming at them from multiple angles a new concern. But of course, it made sense. The creatures had to reproduce, and unless Ozark Howlers, which were most likely mutants, were asexual, how would that work if there was only one?

Jed hiked his shoulders and said, "Few know the mysteries of these hills."

In the back of Carter's mind, he heard banjo music. He pulled on his pack straps and checked the VP9 which was stowed in an exterior jacket pocket for easy access. His flashlight beam bounced around, and the snowpack gleamed, tree trunks casting long shadows that disappeared in the blackness that seemed to stretch on forever before them. Bruises pulsed, his head ached, and his lower back spasmed every few seconds like he was running a marathon. He couldn't see or hear the road, but Carter had no idea how far he'd run to escape the beast, or in what direction.

"There are legends about the Howler all over the Ozarks," Jed said. "The town I grew up in is one of them."

Carter said nothing. He didn't really give a shit about a bear-mutant with stilettos for fangs. He wanted out of the forest, now, but he also didn't want to reveal anything to Jed. He checked his mask. Let the guy tell his fairy tales. What did it matter?

"I grew up in Jasper, a sparrow fart of a town to the east of here. I was ten, maybe eleven, and school was out. Boy was it hot." Jed lifted his hand like he was going to wipe his brow, but let it fall back onto the forestock of his rifle as the chill wind funneled down the deer path.

"My friend's cat disappeared. Kenny. The ratty coon was old, but that thing was smart. It would've fought a red wolf if it got the chance, but there ain't none of them this way no more. All gone." He sounded wistful. "Anyway, that cat. My boy Lester loved that damn thing, and I helped him look all over town when it went missing, which isn't much, mind you, but the woods." Jed shook his head, though Carter couldn't see the man's face. "Me and Lester searched and searched, and you know what?"

"You didn't find it," Carter said.

"No, we found it all right. We was checking a section of evergreen forest behind Lester's house and we came across this stink. You know that smell? Flesh baking in the sun."

To Carter, it sounded like the guy was talking about bacon.

"Kenny had been gutted, his legs gnawed on, entrails rotting on the ground beside what was left. Something got that cat. No question in heaven."

Carter wasn't sure what that last part meant, and he said, "Stuff like that can't be that uncommon in this area, what with the wilderness and mountains and all."

"Well let me get to it," Jed said. "Like I said, that old coon was a tough beast, and nothing in the Ozarks is fast enough to catch her. I'd bet everything I got on it."

Carter said nothing.

"When dogs started going missing people took notice. Cats are loners, so when something happens to them people shrug, just like when birds smash into plate glass windows and fish get chomped by bears. Occupational hazard, the call of the wild, the circle of life, and all that shit.

"But with dogs. Oh boy, people treat them like people, so when the canines started disappearing things were taken to a whole new level."

Carter sensed where this was going, yet he was still enthralled as he put his feet in Jed's footprints.

"It took all summer—even with animals going missing the folks that live in Jasper put their heads in the proverbial sand more than most, if you understand me. None of the adults wanted to believe something weird was going on, because then they'd have to deal with it.

"When Kimberly Fonder disappeared, and the staties got involved, everybody finally believed what me and my bud had been saying all summer. That something... not normal was stalking the woods around Jasper."

An owl hooted and cooed.

"So what happened?"

Jed hiked his shoulders, the gloom wrapping him in shadow as he cut through a large stand of white oaks, their dead leaves singing, the crunch

73

of their footsteps carrying through the forest. "They hunted for the thing. Half the town. The state brought in professional woodsmen. The whole deal. They didn't find shit, but the Howler sure found them. Two men were killed and found gutted. One was missing a head." The real laugh. "Even the DEC showed their faces, though they were as useless as flies on a space station, like the rest of our government."

Carter said nothing. Politics in the United States had been the fuel of America's fire for the last two decades, and the orange man had only exacerbated the situation. If you wanted a fight, mention politics. He didn't bite.

"It was late September, 'cause I was back in school," Jed said with disdain. "One of the searchers found a cave up Glory Hole Fall's way." Jed paused for effect, but Carter didn't bite. He knew what a glory hole was, and he didn't want Jed to go there.

"Anyway, the guy didn't go in the cave because of the smell, but he called it in. Me and Lester caught wind of things, and we knew where the cave was—we'd graffitied the walls in there a bunch of times when we were real young, so we went up there." He shook his head. "I could smell the corpse from a mile off, but when we got there the police and everyone were already there. We watched them haul a black body bag from the cave. It was Kimberly. We knew because the bag wasn't no way full.

"As the story went, a bear as big as an elephant with slick black fur, yellow glowing eyes, and knife-like horns was seen leaving the cave, its mange covered in blood. Well, that just about told the story. They buried Kimberly and kept a watch for a while, but the Howler didn't show again. Winter came on, and well…" He fell still.

The sky grew brighter as the night waned, and as Jed finished his story Carter saw a glow of orange light in the forest ahead. He stopped walking, fixating on the light as it shone through the darkness.

Jed kept walking and said nothing.

"Do you see that?" Carter asked.

"Come on."

Carter and Jed pushed on, the glow of flames like an oasis in the distance. Renewed with the hope of making it back to the road, Carter's thoughts drifted to what awaited him back in civilization. He examined the dirty cotton candy sky. The cloud cover glowed strongest behind him. Taking the arc of the moon's passage across the sky into account, the bright spot would be to the southwest, which meant he and Jed were heading east, not west toward the direction of the interstate. He may have gotten spun around as he'd fled, but he knew he'd gone east when he'd left the road, and there was no way he'd crossed under the highway without knowing. He said, "Those are pretty strong flames. What the hell is going on up there?"

"One of the semis was carrying tires, and they're on fire," Jed said. He cackled like that was the funniest thing he'd ever heard—the fake laugh.

"What's so funny?"

"When tires burn, they're difficult to cool down because of their low thermal conductivity. I've seen tires burn inside even if they're extinguished on the outside, and they easily reignite when hot. It's going to take ages to get the hot rubber sludge off the interstate."

"At least the Howler will stay away." Animals were always afraid of fire, right?

Jed said nothing as he continued his trek toward the fiery glow that was growing closer and larger with each step.

Carter shuffled his memories and tried to reorder things so his jumping nerves would stand down, but that wasn't to be. He was to believe he and Jed were being tracked by a mythical creature part of a genus that included Yeti, Bigfoot, the Loch Ness Monster and its associated kin, Chupacabra, and the Jersey Devil? The idea of it was crazy, yet... He'd seen the beast, and it was like nothing he knew to exist, so until another explanation presented itself, he was forced to accept what Jed had told him.

The wind gusted, and tiny shards of ice pelted Carter's face, burrowing into his collar and the gaps between his jacket and gloves. His mouth was dry again, so he sucked some snow, his bladder protesting with each step. The duo took a break, and Carter squeezed out a few drops.

Jed stood watching, the wicked grin of his gaiter mask glowing in the darkness.

When Carter was done shaking the dew off his lily, he zipped up and gathered his strength for the final push. If nothing else, he could stand upwind of the fire and warm himself. The tips of his fingers and toes stung, and a gentle tremor ran through him like a fading electrical shock.

Jed grunted and spat as he walked, but said nothing.

Carter retreated into himself, the movie of his lost life again playing in the theatre of his memory. He had so many things he didn't deserve, and yet he'd paid a price few understood, and it was difficult being the bad guy, especially when only one side of the story had been told. That was his fault, of course. The blast of gunshots filled his mental screen, the click and pop of the H&K as he pulled the trigger, the scent of cordite.

He buried his hands in the pockets of his jacket and nestled into himself, taking away the shiver, and as the night wrapped him in its soothing shroud, he heard the distant muffled call of his name on the wind. Or was it his imagination?

15

"Did you hear that?" Carter asked as he jerked to a halt. He lost his balance on the compacted snow and overcompensated, throwing his weight left. Then he was going down, palms out to break his fall, whiteness rushing up to greet him.

Two muscular arms grabbed him and stopped his tumble inches from the path. As Jed helped Carter get his legs under him, he said, "Hear what?"

Carter tuned his hearing as he steadied himself, filtering out the wind, the push of the snow, the thrum and grumble of the earth and its beasts. There was nothing there. Nobody called his name. Nobody called anything.

"You O.K.?" Jed's mask was hanging below his red bulbous nose, the wicked grin scrunched into a white line.

Carter nodded, but it was becoming clearer with each step that he wasn't fine. His knees ached and throbbed in rhythm with his many bumps and bruises and the gash on his head, and his elbow screamed. Then there was the underlying angst that hung just below his rationality, pecking away at every decision and planting irrational thoughts.

"Come on," Jed said. "We're almost there."

Ahead, light filtered through the trees, a pale orange glow that promised warmth and sustenance. It struck Carter then that he didn't hear the pounding of helicopter airfoils, and there were no sirens, bullhorns blaring instructions, or the chatter and wail of human suffering. The forest was silent save for the arguing wind and sifting snow.

When the pair was trudging down the deer path again, Jed asked, "Do you know why they call this area Borderland Pass?"

Carter searched his frozen brain, came up empty, and said, "No clue."

Jed shifted his rifle, looping his right forefinger through the trigger guard as he gripped the forestock. "First off, we're technically in the Boston Mountains right now, which is part of one of the three sections, or plateaus, of the Ozarks, which are generally referred to as the Ozark Mountains."

"You ever consider doing documentary voiceover work?"

"Oh, I'm just getting going," Jed said. "This area is a deeply dissected plateau, not really mountains."

He paused as if awaiting input, so Carter asked, "I'll bite. What's a dissected plateau?"

"The mountains in this region were created by severe erosion, not like traditional mountain ranges at all. The Rockies and the like were created by the folding and pressing of tectonic plates and volcanic activity— among other things— while the Ozarks show none of these traits. The pass, geologically as the bigheads say, is a basic river valley carved by time and flowing water, though the river that created the valley dried up eons ago. So, what you're left with is a deep demarcation line cutting across a section of terrain where the Caddo and Quapaw Indians traveled regularly. Local historians speculate that the Mayans traveled up this way, and all these myths thrown together is where the name Borderland Pass came from. To pass over the valley meant you'd entered another tribe's territory, and that was punishable by death."

Jed let that sink in as Carter wondered why the man was telling him all this. When he got to the interstate he was heading north and never coming to the godforsaken Ozarks again.

"There were many battles fought here, and there are arrow and spear heads, club and axe heads, and other primitive artifacts like carvings and pottery shards all over the region. One of the more famous legends is about Chief Redcorn, a Quapaw tribal chief who picked fights at certain times of the year because of the potential cloak of bad weather in the pass. Like catching flies on a glue trap the creatures don't see. Then it all seemed to have stopped about two hundred years ago."

"The bigheads know why?"

"Not for certain," Jed said. "It's very common to find Native American structures and cities that show evidence of rapid departures. Personally, me, and I don't hold no degree, and I don't have any special education on the subject, but I think the people that came up this way from South America were running from something about their old way of life that they really didn't like. There are scout posts all over the place, and when a scout came running in yelling, "They've found us" they all picked-up and split. Problem is, in this case, there's little evidence of that. What there is evidence of is the Ozark Howler."

Hearing the beast's name brought Carter back from the enthralling land of Jed's story and he said, "How's that?"

"I ain't never seen any, but there are those who say there are drawings—what do the call them? Picmogrifs… Petrogriphs…"

Carter knew there were two types of cave drawings, one where the images where etched into the stone and another where they were painted. He didn't know the name of either of them, so he said nothing.

"Anyway, there are painted drawings in some of the caves up in these parts, and some say there are depictions of a large shadowy beast taking babies and destroying crops. The Quapaw called the creature a Wendigo. Though the Howler doesn't resemble traditional descriptions of the Wendigo."

An owl hooted, and the faint pop and crack of the fire echoed through the woods. They were getting close.

"As the tales go the local Caddo and Quapaw stopped coming to the pass to fight, and they found alternate paths. There are those who believe the beast owns the pass now," Jed said, and with his tale finished, he fell silent.

"That what you believe?"

Jed said nothing.

Thick white smoke rolled through the forest, but Carter didn't catch the scents of gasoline or burning rubber. It smelled like wood burning. Had the forest along the interstate caught on fire? Smoke stung his eyes, the forest thinning as the glow of flames lit the night. Carter heard no voices, no sirens, and the tickle of suspicion and worry seeped through him, but then his weary muscles and fatigued brain reminded him it had been hours since he'd been at the crash scene. Things were probably under control, the injured having been airlifted to hospitals, and those who got the O.K. from the EMTs were probably already snug in their hotel beds, the crash a memory… or a nightmare.

Nightmares would be on tap for Stacey and Aniyah, and again guilt tore at his stomach and sent shards of pain spiking to the tips of his fingers and toes. In a way, he'd done the same thing to his own family, but this was old territory. Everyone he cared about was better off without him around. He knew on some level that was a cop-out, but he'd been on the self-loathing trail so long he didn't know any other path.

The wind gusted and tore away the smoke, the glow of flames illuminating the forest. The deer path dipped down into a shallow bowl and imaginary spiders crawled up Carter's spine. Something was wrong. Very wrong.

Carter wasn't a particularly smart man, but he was no dope, and he noticed things, though sometimes what he noticed didn't register until later when new information came to light. He recalled his first gut reaction when he'd met Jed. The vibe hadn't been good, and it wasn't until he'd spoken with the man that his fears were alleviated. An image of the pickup Jed called his—Jed with red—crawled from his mind, the picture coming into focus. If Jed lived in the Ozarks as he claimed, why did the red pickup have Oklahoma plates?

All this was too late in coming, and as the flames licked the darkness, Jed paused at the lip of the shallow bowl. A massive fire filled the depression, a giant pyramid of burning wood stacked like a teepee at its center. White smoke trailed into the sky, the tangy bitter scent of burning white oak filling the air.

Carter reached in his pocket for the H&K, found it missing, and frantically padded his jacket and pants pockets. Nothing. He slipped his hand behind his back, knowing the weapon wasn't there because he didn't feel its cold metal against his skin. When he came up empty, Carter recalled his stumble, how his new friend Jed had stopped his fall and helped him to his feet. The gun had been in an outside pocket so he could get to it, and Jed had snatched it.

Firelight danced off the snowpack, specks of multicolor sparks dotting the whiteness, smoke pouring from the depression and biting at Carter's eyes as it filled the woods.

Jed faced Carter, the rifle ready to fire, but pointed at the ground. He'd pulled down his mask, revealing a wicked smile that creased his face, not unlike the wicked grin on the mask. His eyes danced in his head, his cheeks puffy and red. Streaks of busted blood vessels, a map of alcohol abuse that looked to have been laid down over many decades, creased his windburned face, the pulled-down gaiter making it look like there was a mouth in Jed's neck.

The two men stood there, silent, and still. Carter couldn't believe he'd been so clueless. His judgment of Jed aside, he'd known on some level that they'd been going in the wrong direction, and a piece of him, the part tired of running, didn't care.

With no weapon, Carter was no match for Jed, and thoughts of what the man wanted from him conjured a spiral of horrible images that filled Carter with anger, worry, and fear. "What do you want?" Carter asked. Motivation. What did Jed hope to get from him? The answers Carter came up with made his stomach sink and grumble, and if he'd had anything to eat in the last twelve hours it would have made a curtain call.

Jed said nothing. He simply stared at Carter, his unhinged smile hanging low on one side. His eyes, which had seemed full of life just moments before, were now vacant and resigned. A line had been crossed, a border, and suddenly Carter understood that the Howler wasn't the only animal that called Borderland Pass home.

Heated smoke pushed up from the bowl, the fire still raging. It must have taken a long time to prepare, to collect all the necessary materials. The amount of wood, the size of the flames, and the fact that it had been burning for a couple of hours without being tended.

Carter's head jerked to the right, then left. Was Jed alone?

"Don't worry, Mr. Renfrow. The Howler isn't around." His voice was half a whisper, as if the words themselves knew they were a lie.

He reeled at the use of his name, Carter's reality coming apart at the seams. How had Jed—

The memory of his mask slipping down as he and Jed talked amidst the wreckage of the crash site smacked him like a hammer blow to the temple. Jed had known who he was... knew who he was. Don't worry? That was laughable, and even as his hope fled, the call of the Howler rose above the crackling bonfire and the shrieking wind.

Carter backed away from the hollow, eyes darting about as he searched for anything he could use as a weapon, even though he knew there was nothing around that could best a bullet.

Jed said, "Take it easy, man. I'm a fan."

The world spun as Carter tried to keep hold of his sanity. He felt lightheaded, all his pains and worries throbbing and popping and pounding, his hands shaking with fury and fear. "What do you mean?" Carter knew exactly what the man meant, but he needed to hear it. Know for certain that Jed understood who he was and what he'd done.

"The way you took care of that punk. Put him down like a dog." Jed's eyes gleamed as he smiled wider. "They should've given you a medal."

"That's why you're doing this?"

"This country is a mess and taking the law into your own hands is necessary sometimes. You can't let mutts take what's yours and do whatever they want, now can we? Question is, are you qualified to have such power?"

"Are you going to turn me in?" Carter asked.

Jed laughed his real laugh, long and hard. "No, what I've got planned is much more fun. You'll see."

"What makes you think I'll cooperate?"

Jed raised the rifle and said, "That's not going to be a problem."

16

"Put this over your head." Jed tossed a black bag at Carter.

"On?"

Jed sighed. "Look, I'd like an even match, but I'll blow out a kneecap if you keep acting the fool."

Carter said nothing.

Jed put the stock of the rifle to his shoulder and aimed it at Carter. Again.

The bag was black fabric, some thin synthetic stuff, and it felt like silk as Carter pulled it over his head and the world went dark.

"That's better."

"I'm going to trip within ten steps. There are vines running beneath the snow, and I can't see where th—"

Jed lashed out with the butt of the rifle and struck Carter in the stomach.

The blow knocked Carter back a step, pain burrowing into every corner of his body, his breath betraying him.

"Put out your hands."

Carter considered noncompliance, but his throbbing head and shrieking elbow made him thrust out his hands.

Jed tied a loop of rope around his wrists and pulled it tight. "I'll lead you like a dog. We'll go slow, and it'll only be for a church second. Can't have you knowing where the farm is."

The wind gusted, and Carter thought he heard his name woven in the shrieks, bellows, and gentle static-like roar.

"Not that it needs to be said, but you weren't in the accident, were you?" Carter said.

"Aren't you a bright little bulb."

"You were up by the interstate looking for roadkill just like the Howler." As soon as the words left his mouth, Carter wished he could have them back.

Carter's leash went taut, and he was jerked forward, the rope tightening around his wrists. He felt like the fellowship trekking blindfolded through Lothlorien, Gimli and Legolas bitching the entire way. When he looked down, he saw his feet shuffling in the darkness, so he stepped in Jed's tracks and took stock of his situation.

Jed took his pack, his gun, and the bumpkin was leading him to his private farm in the middle of the Ozarks. Perfect. His head hurt, he'd lost his phone, he had no food, his body ached, and he stank like he'd been rolled in shit and tossed in a hog pen.

Then there was the Ozark Howler to consider.

The Howler hadn't shown itself since Jed arrived, and Carter thought of running, but all that would accomplish was pissing off Jed and he'd most likely break a leg in the process. It came down to the question of did he want to take his chances with Jed alone, or did he want to try and draw in the beast? With the creature in the fray, Jed would have trouble fighting two foes, and maybe Carter would get an opportunity to escape.

His hands stung from the cold despite his gloves, and because the rope was restricting blood circulation. Whatever decision he made, taking down Jed would be difficult. He had the rifle, the H&K, Carter's hands were bound, and he had no idea exactly where Jed was. Carter stared at the ground and put one foot in front of the other as self-pity wormed its way through him, his muscles aching under the strain.

Carter judged they'd walked for twenty minutes when Jed tugged him to a halt. He said, "We're going to get to know each other a little before the contest, and I'm going to let you take your hood off now, so the local terrain isn't a complete surprise. I don't want things to be easy."

"What things?" Carter knew Jed was egging him on and wouldn't tell him shit until he was good and ready, but Carter always asked questions. It was how he talked to people, and if he could talk to Jed, distract him, maybe he'd slip up.

Jed said nothing, his wicked smile wider than the one on his gaiter, which was pulled down around his neck. Carter still had his mask up under his hood, though the odds were greater that he'd give Jed COVID then vice versa. Jed pulled the hood off Carter's head.

Dark backlit cotton candy clouds packed the sky, the snowpack shimmering, the shadows frolicking and fighting. Jed stepped away, rifle at the ready. The duo stood in a small clearing at the center of a dense thicket of evergreens. Carter saw their trail in the snow and based on the glow in the sky he was sure they'd gone east.

"My place is up ahead. Go on now." Jed pointed through the trees and waved his hand in a 'come forth' gesture.

With his hood off Carter was conjuring all types of Jack Reacher-type escapes, but he wasn't Reacher, and he was in no condition to fight anyway. Whatever Jed had in mind, he wanted him alive, and food and warmth most likely awaited him at the end of the road. He took a hesitant step forward, Jed smiling and rolling the tip of the rifle in the direction Jed wanted Carter to go.

Icy green needles pricked his face and tore at his clothes as he fought through the evergreens, snow cascading onto him, the muffled chuckle of Jed carrying through the trees.

When he broke free of the thicket, rolling hills covered in snow filled the dark horizon, short leaf pines, and white oaks with dead leaves clinging to their branches packed the mountain in patches like a rash. The scent of smoke carried on the breeze, and atop a hillock sat a cabin, its windows glowing orange with the light of a dying flame.

A barbwire fence trailed across the path, and Jed said, "Take a left. There is a trail that winds up the hill."

Wind dusted Carter with snow as he headed down the dirt path, the fence running to his right. He tried to take note of his surroundings and follow the line of the fence, but in the shadowy darkness it was difficult. Two smaller buildings dotted the compound, but they were nothing more than dark square smudges in the snowpack. He heard the nicker of a horse, or donkey, and the swish and pop of a windmill churning. Carter's heart sank. Just how far off the grid was this asshole? If he wasn't connected to municipal services, the cops may not even know he was living out here.

Rolling mountains wreathed in darkness and glimmering snow filled the horizon in every direction. He saw no other lit windows, and no headlight beams cut through the blackness.

A branch snapped and Carter's head jerked toward the sound as he stuttered to a halt, slipping on the snowpack.

"Stay still," Jed said.

A shapeless dark shadow glided through the trees, but there were no glowing eyes or the glint of fangs.

Gurgling, sniffing, the creak and pop of tree branches, the whistle of the wind.

Jed urged Carter on with the tip of his rifle. "Hurry up now."

Carter considered making some serious noise so the beast could track them, but he could barely walk.

A patch of moonlight broke through the thinning cloud cover as the remnants of the storm pushed east to Tennessee and the Smoky Mountains.

One of the dark outbuildings materialized out of the gloom, and Jed stopped at its entrance, keys jangling. The door swung open with a creak, and the click of a light switch echoed from the shack. Yellow light spilled from the open door, casting long shadows over the glowing snow.

Both men stepped into the shelter and Jed closed the door.

The building was a firewood shed, and half its fifteen-foot by fifteen-foot space was filled with cut logs. The air was thick with must and dampness, and the hay on the floor crackled beneath his feet. A cot bare of any amenities was pushed against the far wall, and there was a bucket and an upturned brazier in a corner.

Jed pointed at the old brazier, and said, "You can start a fire, but don't let it get too big. This place will go up like tinder and that wouldn't be fun."

"What? No food? Water?"

"Later, if you behave."

"What now?" Carter asked, but he wasn't sure he wanted the answer.

Jed chuckled—the real laugh—and said, "I've got to go carrot shopping. Try and get some rest, you're going to need it." His wicked grin was back, and as he slipped out the door the wind pushed snow into the woodshed. The door slammed closed and the clang of the lock bolt driving home sucked the hope from him like radiation.

He was freezing, so he set about starting a fire. The brazier was rusted, the old metal thin. It had strange designs on its side that looked like hieroglyphics, and colored tile was embedded therein. Jed had left matches and fine kindling, and it only took Carter five minutes to get a nice flame going. He cleared away the straw around the fire—last thing he needed was a spark igniting it—and for a second layer of protection, he picked logs of hardwood from the pile and placed them around the cleared area. With the brazier blazing at the center of brown frozen hardpan ringed in hardwood, Carter flicked off the overhead light and dropped onto the cot.

The wind hollered and sang, pushing through every crack in the shed's façade. The flames flickered and danced with each inrush and pull of air, heat building in the shed. He unzipped his jacket and lay back, staring up at the mismatched wooden ceiling. Boards of every thickness and color made up the roof, and planks with their bark still attached made up the walls.

Carter gazed into the woodpile, his mind conjuring spiders. Would they venture out? He doubted it, but he'd have to sleep with one eye open.

Anger and frustration fought for control of his emotions, the heat of helplessness leaking through him. His eyelids fluttered, and he imagined his daughter standing next to the cot, looking down at him. He was dreaming, and he smiled, but as his daughter's face contorted with pain and horror, he knew it was no dream.

Carter sat in his warm easy chair in the den at the back of the two-story cape he and his family called home. The T.V. grumbled, and he was nestled within a three-beer cocoon, the warmth filling him with peace, his muscles relaxing, the stress seeping from his pores. Darkness crept in around the edges of his vision as his eyes drooped. The fuzziness of sleep took his hand, but before he was ushered off to dreamland he was pulled from his rest by the wailing of his phone.

The Imperial March echoed through the house, and as Carter fought from sleep, he reached for the device and knocked it off the end table.

"Shit," Carter said as he gripped the chair's adjustment lever, yanked it forward, and the footrest slammed back into the chair's frame with a thud.

He picked up the phone. It was 12:21 AM and the caller ID showed the Leister County Police Department's name and number.

The police.

Cold fingers prodded his back, the icy dancing of fear and angst filling him as he tapped Answer Call. Thoughts flitted in and out of his mind, which was still fighting off sleep. Was Katie home yet?

"Hello?"

"Is this the Renfrow residence?" asked a calm female voice.

"It is."

"I'm Officer Gladly. Who am I speaking to?"

"Carter Renfrow. What's this all about?"

"Mr. Renfrow, I'm going to need you to stay calm, but there's been an incident involving your daughter. She's at t—"

"Oh, my god." Carter vaulted from his chair. "Debra! Debra!"

"Please calm down, Mr. Renfrow. Your daughter is in the hospital and doing fine."

"Car accident? What?"

"There are officers and counselors at the hospital, and they'll fill you in when you get there. Are you O.K. to drive? I can send a car if that will be a help."

"Yes, please do."

They exchanged information and as he hung-up Debra shuffled into the room rubbing sleep from her eyes. "What are you yelling at?"

Carter filled in his wife, and she was weeping in his arms when the squad car arrived to transport them to the hospital. Carter and Debra sat silently in the back of the cruiser, the squawk of the radio fraying Carter's nerves.

The officer said nothing, and when he pulled into the carport at the front of the hospital he asked, "You need help getting inside?" The cop wouldn't meet his eye, and Carter thought he noted pity in the man's reddening cheeks.

Carter and Debra ran the gauntlet of security, and nobody told them anything as they hurried to their daughter's side. Katie sat propped up in her bed sucking on juice. A dark bruise marred her left cheek, and fear lines creased her smooth face, but otherwise, she looked fine.

"What happened?" Debra asked.

Katie's eyes welled with tears, her face going red. She looked at the floor and said, "Danny... He attacked me."

Carter's stomach went cold, and harsh pain stabbed his lower back. Danny was Katie's boyfriend, and they'd been dating for a few months. Attacked…

Before Carter's astonishment and fear wore off and he could start asking questions, a doctor entered the room and introduced herself as Dr. Gretta Harger. "I'm sorry to meet under such circumstances, but the police insisted we follow rape protocol, and they're right. It's just…" The doctor's eyes strayed to Katie who studied a wrinkle in her sheets.

The word rape sat there like a grenade taking its time exploding. White-hot anger tinged Carter's vision and a steady ringing filled his head. This couldn't be happening. His baby, her life forever changed.

"The police took a complete statement and we've done all the necessary tests here at the hospital. I insist she sees a counselor every day for the next couple of weeks, but physically she's fine and she can go home," the doctor said.

"Has… will Danny be arrested?" Debra asked.

The doctor looked at the floor and said nothing.

"Did he… Was he successful, with his… attempt?" Carter needed to know. He knew it was a sexist thing to ask, and he was concerning himself with his own feelings when he should be concentrating on his daughter's, but the rage that churned his stomach was unlike anything he'd felt. The world shrank away, and a fever rose in him.

Katie began to cry in earnest and Debra sat on the bed and cradled her daughter.

He didn't know what to do, to say. He wanted to hit something. Find that little shit Danny and break his neck, but not before he cut his little pecker off.

A nurse brought the clothes Katie had been wearing when she was brought in, and Carter couldn't bring himself to look at them. Where had this occurred? Why? When exactly? Were you making out and it went too far?

None of that mattered, and as his daughter cried, he felt the life drain from him. In the months after, he would remember that moment. Use it as fuel and justification. But that supply was running thin, and Carter felt his time slipping away.

17

Carter came awake with a start.

The fire had gone out, but orange embers still lit and heated the woodshed. Someone was unlocking the shack's door. The bolt fell back with a clang, and the door swung open. A huge dark shape stood silhouetted in the doorway, faint rays of moonglow leaking into the shed. With a *snap*, the lights came on. Carter was momentarily blinded, and he brought up his arm to cover his eyes.

"Brought you some grub," Jed said.

The door slammed shut and the serenading winds dulled. Jed held out a bottle of water and what looked like a sandwich wrapped in wax paper.

Carter accepted the food. Brief questions of poison raised red flags, but what sense would it make to go through all the trouble of bringing Carter to the farm just to poison him? The food and water could be drugged, but what choice did he have? He could go without food, but he needed the H20.

"I know what you're thinking," Jed said. "But why would I poison it?" He unzipped his new hunting jacket and slipped it off. "Hot in here."

Some of the things Carter had noticed about Jed now made more sense. He said, "Did you steal that jacket off a dead person?"

"Steal? The guy was deader than disco, what's he gonna do with it?"

"It's not yours, so it's stealing."

Jed took two fast steps toward Carter as he pulled back his massive paw to take a swing, but he held himself back. A wicked smile spread over Jed's face that reminded Carter of the man's mask. Jed chuckled, the real thing, and said, "The jacket would probably have ended up in Goodwill, so I just saved everyone time."

Carter was somewhere in the middle of the Ozark Mountains, a prisoner, and all his possessions had been taken, so surely it made sense to argue with a madman about the theft of a dead man's jacket.

When Carter stayed silent, Jed said, "Eat." He tossed the jacket on the woodpile, and chose a log to serve as his stool. Jed's tattoos danced and slithered in the firelight, shadows reaching out from the wood pile.

The wind picked up, and it played the woodshed like an ancient flute, the whistles, howls, and chirps oddly relaxing.

Carter unwrapped the wax paper mystery and found a sandwich— ham and cheese—and as he ate, Jed studied him. He needed to get the big man talking. The more information he had the better off he would be, so he started with a common enemy. Between bites, he said, "Do you see the Howler often?"

Jed leaned forward and put his elbows on his knees, his eyes aglow, his perpetual smirk fading. "The Ozark Howler is a sly creature. It can go unseen and silent when it chooses. As you've seen. It is an apex killing machine not of this time… this world. It's magnificent."

"What world is it from?"

"Another time when the world was wild, and it was a king among beasts."

"It told you this?"

"The legends are there for those who look hard enough," Jed said.

Carter sensed the man working up to something, so he stayed silent.

"It is said that the first settlers to come here fought the Howler. I already mentioned the Mayans, but Spanish conquistadors also came through this land. Not to mention Native Americans, which I've also already told you about. They all fought the Howler and tried to capture the beast.

"One of the tales told to all youngins in these parts to make them behave is the tale of the Ozark Howler and the great hunt. This one originated back in the mid-1800s when the country was wild and raw, and a massive bear-cat with tall pointed ears, three-inch claws, fangs, and yellow-rimmed eyes stalked the land. The creature was said to come for young children who got out of bed—that was all bullshit, of course— but what wasn't was the beast stealing cows, goats, and occasionally people, such as I've already mentioned.

"The Howler wiped out the livestock of a rich landowner up Searcy way. Cows, sheep, pigs—everything dead, throats ripped out, entrails littering the ground. What angered people most was the random waste. Almost like the creature killed for fun and sport. Folks back then understood that wild animals sometimes defended their property, and stole chickens, eggs, and such, but the stuff was always eaten. American Indians knew this better than most. They use every part of an animal they kill, and some of the folks up this way took to those traditions.

"Anyway, the town was rightly pissed, and the farm owner whose livestock had been murdered organized a hunt. Paid local folks to scour the Ozarks for the beast. Three dead hunters later, they gave up."

Carter recalled firing at the beast, how it used the forest for cover, its stealth as a weapon.

"The hunt itself was a thing of real-life legend. I found copies of journal pages online. A first-person account of the expedition as seen by Freddie Weston, a local farmhand who was paid to join the hunt. The pages read like a King novel. All blood, chaos, and sorrow." Jed paused and rolled his shoulders, looking at Carter with wide eyes as if searching for a reaction to his words.

So far Carter hadn't heard anything that couldn't be applied to every alleged cryptid creature ever imagined, right down to the Boogeyman.

"The main hunting party found the first guy strung up in the trees by his ankles, caught in his own trap," Jed said. "The hunter's face had been clawed off, and his gut opened up, intestines spilling out. Weston called the scene 'grizzly beyond his imagination's ability to create.' Deep shit.

"They tracked the Howler across the Ozarks, which by all accounts is where the name Ozark Howler originated. Weston talks about the beast baiting them, creating false trails, almost like it was leading them on. When the party found the second body, the head man decided to go back and call off the hunt."

Wind argued and bitched, pushing into the woodshed through every gap and hole. Jed grabbed a log from the pile and threw it into the brazier atop the glowing cinders and it caught immediately. He threw two more pieces onto the fire, and within moments flames were once again pushing away the creeping darkness. Smoke filled the enclosure and Jed stood and cracked open a window covered in wooden planks.

"The second hunter's head had been crushed, and it's said there was a bloody rock nearby, but Weston didn't see it because he didn't mention it in his journal, at least not on the pages I read. The guy was missing fingers that looked to have been gnawed off, and there were stab wounds all over the man's body. They figure the punctures were from the tips of the Howler's claws or horns," Jed said.

Cold fingers poked his back, a block of superheated ice forming in Carter's stomach. Why was Jed telling him this story? He had the feeling he was supposed to be reading between the lines, seeing something just below the surface. He finished his sandwich, opened the water, and took a shallow pull. He'd have to conserve because he had no idea when he'd get more.

"So, they headed back, the forest thick and untamed," said Jed. "The main party had traveled for four days and were deep in the Ozarks. Like I said, the beast led them out there. At least that's what I believe.

"The Howler attacked their camp at night, sneaking past the night watch and pulling a man right from his tent. Weston described the night in great detail. The chaos, the men fleeing, some wanting to go after the Howler to save the taken man, others wanting to run for their lives, including the man paying the bills. Despite the big man saying no to going after the creature, Weston joined a small party that went after the Howler. The man who was taken was Weston's friend, and he didn't feel right going back to town without at least trying to find him.

"They followed the trail for two days, and then they started finding body parts. First a thumb, then an ear, a hand, a leg. By the time they found the corpse there was nothing left but the torso, muscle, gristle, and shattered bone leaking from where the head and appendages should've been.

"Crazy shit, right? When I first read it, I was certain the beast was playing with them, but then I figured probably not. We give animals too much credit. They're just following their instincts and sometimes that makes them look smarter than they are. Anyway, Weston and the rest ran then. They didn't stop for sleep, nothing, and when they staggered back into town, they learned the Howler had struck again. The townsfolk blamed the hunters, and they were shunned. For helping. Can you believe it?"

Carter could. People did and thought some stupid shit when they were scared for themselves and their families. He asked the question that was on the tip of his tongue. He couldn't help himself. "Why are you telling me all this?"

"I'm a hunter, as you might have figured out," Jed said. "I've hunted everything in these woods, and some stuff not of these woods. Could I kill the Howler? Maybe. Do I want to? No. Hunting animals for sport is like playing hide and seek with a young child. It's fun being out in the woods, breathing the clean air, but there's no competition. No real challenge. I hunt deer with a bow, but still. I'm in a stand, with a laser sight, and I spray fake urine on the ground. That all sound fair to you?"

"Not everything is fair."

"Ah, now you've got it. Most of the time it ain't, and I wanted to make sure you knew that because the next few days are going to be hard, and you might even think it's easier to just give up and die, but I want you to understand all hope isn't lost."

Now Carter was confused, so he waited.

"What I'm saying is, your own life might not be enough to motivate you. I think you're going to make excellent prey, but to motivate you I've got a little surprise," Jed said. He pushed up from his stool and threw his log seat onto the brazier, a cloud of sparks and smoke puffing into the air. Jed glanced over at the bucket in the corner, saw it was still overturned and unused, then headed for the door. On his way, he shut the wooden window. "This'll be locked on the outside, so don't think of escaping." Jed left, the clang of the door lock falling into place ringing through the shed.

The fire cracked and popped. Carter's mind raced, and with a sinking dread he thought he understood what Jed meant to do. He would make excellent prey, and the comment Jed had made about how he'd like an even match. It all led to one thing.

Carter's frustration boiled over, and he surged up from the cot and paced about the woodshed. He had to escape, get back to civilization, to his... life? Did he have a life? Would he ever have one again? What had Jed meant by motivation? Carter didn't want to find out.

He checked the door first, knowing it was locked, and when it didn't budge, he moved on to the shuddered window. The wood gave way a little, and a sliver of darkness worked its way into the shed. The thump of a metal lock twisting in its hasp told Carter that unless he had a saw or a huge crowbar, there was no way he would be able to work the window open.

The fire lit most of the shed, but Carter couldn't see the rear of the woodpile because it was stacked to the rafters. There might be a vent or window behind the logs. He looked under the cot, and went over the walls, searching for any crack or hole that could be exploited. When he found nothing, he began digging through the woodpile. He didn't expect to find a way out, but he couldn't just sit still and wait for Jed to come back.

Or could he? He'd need his rest—Jed had said so, and Carter had to agree with the man. Would his time be better spent sleeping? Could he sleep?

Carter took a small pull of water and capped the bottle. He threw logs on the fire until the flames were as large as he'd risk, and continued digging through the woodpile, searching for what he didn't know.

Splinters bit his hands, his mind straying back to the story of the Howler and the great hunt. It was all so clear now, and though Carter hadn't shipwrecked on a rocky jetty off a deserted island, he was about to play a very dangerous game.

He peeled away logs, stacking them to the side as he cleared a row along one of the walls. There were no windows, no vents, and as he worked his way around the outside of the room, filling the path behind him with wood, the futility of his situation settled on him.

When he reached the far end of the shed, and he was walled in by cut wood, he sat down and let his head fall into his hands. It occurred to Carter that he could stay right where he was, hidden and protected by logs of wood. But that would only buy him a few minutes and would most likely piss off Jed, so Carter continued digging and stacking until he'd worked his way all around the exterior walls of the shed. There was no other way out.

Helplessness washed through him, and Carter felt like the day in the hospital when he'd learned his daughter's innocence had been stolen, her sense of safety and trust. Would Katie ever be able to trust someone of the opposite sex again? Probably, but it would take time and patience, as well as an understanding partner. His daughter would know what to do, she always did.

He lay on the cot, the warmth of the fire seeping beneath his skin as he drifted into a troubled sleep.

18

Borderland Pass, Ozark Mountains, 7:09 PM CST, March 12th, 2021

The snow picked up and Stacey paused beneath an evergreen bough laden with snow and ice. She heard voices on the wind. Sometimes Aniyah yelling for her, and other times… Stacey felt the heat of fear, like when she knew there was something hiding under her bed even though her mom and dad had told her there was nothing there.

Mom and dad. When she thought of them tears welled in her eyes. She'd been to her grandad's funeral, seen his dead body, so she knew what death was. They put you in the ground and bugs ate you. But the idea that she'd never talk to her mother again. That her dad would never yell at her to put away her toys. It all hurt in places she didn't know she had, in ways she didn't understand.

Stacey pulled her hat lower and checked her mask. She knew she didn't need it out here, but at the same time, it helped her stay warm. The snow was coming down hard, the wind creating cyclones of ice and snow as tree branches squeaked and crackled.

The dark figure with the gun she'd been following had paused and dropped to a knee. It looked to Stacey like the man was studying the same set of footprints she was tracking. Why was he looking for Ray? Did the man know him? Stacey wanted to call out for help. Judging by the person's size it was an adult, with a gun, and though her mother had taught her never to talk to strangers, Stacey figured her current situation might be an exception.

Despite her fear, hunger, and the cold biting at the edges of her fingers and toes, she held back. Something about the way the man moved told her to keep her distance.

When the shadow person moved on so did Stacey. She skipped along like she was playing a game, jumping forward and putting her little feet into the footprints that in places created knee-deep holes. Snow was working its way into her boots, and her stomach grumbled.

Stacey was humming silently in her head, eyes down as she focused on placing her feet in the tracks when the dark shape of a man materialized before her out of the gloom. She knew it was a man because his rancid stink carried on the breeze. He brought a rifle to his shoulder and Stacey held her breath, though she couldn't see what the man was aiming at.

The dark silhouette shifted as the man looked over his shoulder.

She held her breath and stayed completely still. The guy was twenty feet away, and if he turned a flashlight on her he'd... what? See her? This man didn't know her. Why would he want to hurt her? The tingle in her stomach told her it wasn't the 'why' that mattered. There are strange people in the world. She knew that. Had seen it with her own young eyes. Sometimes she didn't understand, but when she did, she felt sad and lost. Stacey didn't think she was going to be a very good adult because she didn't like hurting people and wasn't good at it. Since that was what most adults did, hurt themselves and others, usually over money, she didn't feel like she would ever fit in.

If the man saw her, he didn't let on because he turned his attention back to his gun, the stock of which was still pressed to his shoulder.

Moonglow filtered through the clouds and snow, colorful bursts like tiny stars falling through the forest. The snowpack glowed white under the weight of the darkness, and a tall shadow fell over the snow-covered underbrush. Taller and larger than the man. Much bigger.

Stacey's skin crawled and every part of her wanted to run, but she was too afraid. Her teeth chattered and she pressed them together to stop the noise as she hugged herself, willing the larger shadow to go away.

Crunching footsteps, huffing, sniffing, and pig-like grunts carried through the forest.

The urge to run became so strong Stacey stood, but her feet were cemented to the snowpack, her eyes locked on the massive shadow as it writhed and eddied through the woods.

With a whine and a roar, the Howler appeared from the darkness, its yellow eyes ablaze.

A flashlight beam arced through the forest.

Stacey's breath caught in her young throat, her mind not believing what she was seeing.

The Ozark Howler drew itself up onto its hind legs, its muscled body rippling, its dark fur covered in a thin blanket of snow that shone under the glare of the flashlight. Its front claws glinted as it pulled back its cat-like head, its pointed ears out straight, twisted horns beside them.

Stacey cowered. It was so big, but... She'd never seen anything like it, and she didn't know what to believe.

A clamoring and yelling came from the forest behind Stacey, and she jerked her head in that direction along with the Howler and shadow man.

"Stacey! Where are you? Stacey please. If you hear me, call out. Please, honey."

Aniyah saw light ahead and she stopped calling out for Stacey. Her throat was dry and raw, her feet and hands frozen. She came to a halt, her breaths forming clouds in the cold night. Snow still fell, but it was nothing more than ash-like flakes that cycled around trees, the wind pushing them around. The snowpack glowed in the darkness, and she focused on the bright light, which had to be a flashlight. There were so many trees and the undergrowth so thick that all she could make out were dark shadows flitting about within the white nebulous cloud.

She surged forward, following the beaten trail, her heart hammering, the cold stinging her face. Aniyah's knees ached and her chest hurt. She wasn't in shape—but dang, she hadn't realized she was out of shape. More time walking and less reading and sipping chardonnay would do her some good, but those dreams were for another day.

A primordial screech echoed through the forest, not of a person, but of an angry, or hungry, animal. Shadows danced in the cloud of light ahead, the surreal scene reminding Aniyah of giants fighting within the dust clouds of their destruction.

Stacey bolted from the darkness, saw Aniyah, and pulled up short, her eyes going wide. The kid ran forward and hugged Aniyah, who wrapped her arms around the child like she was bobbing on a storm-swept sea without a life preserver.

"I thought I'd lost you," Aniyah said as she studied the child's face in the darkness. "Why didn't you listen? Are you O.K.? Did you see Ray? Who's out there with you?" The questions spilled from her so fast she forgot she was talking to a child. She took the kid's face in her hands and kissed her cold cheek. "I'm sorry. Are you alright?"

Stacey stared up at her, looked back over her shoulder, and said, "We need to go. Now."

Aniyah and Harry were never able to have children, and it had never bothered her much. She'd always had Harry, and they had built a comfortable life. Did she regret not having a piece of him now that he was gone? Maybe, but a child without a father canceled out any justifications she might build. She knew many kids and loved being around them, but it was always cool when she got to go home to her house where everything had its place and was in its place, and she didn't have to take orders from a child who needed help going to the bathroom.

Her instinct fought the urge to question the child and attempt to understand why she was panicked. The person with the light could help them. Despite all these thoughts racing through her brain like they were all late for a coffee break, she took the girl's hand and darted back along the beaten path through the snow the way she'd come.

The Howler appeared on the path before her, crouched on all fours like a cat coiling itself to strike. Its eyes ranged around, its massive snout dipping as it sniffed the snowpack. Then the beast laughed. There was no other word Aniyah could think of to describe the sound. The cackle-bark went on for a few seconds as the creature inched forward on all fours, its huge paws crunching the beaten path. The beast's thick black fur shimmered in the faint light as it moved, a cloud of light growing around the beast like it was caught in the headlights of an oncoming truck.

Aniyah cycled Stacey behind her as she backed away, her eyes locked on the creature as it came forward, the cone of the approaching light pushing away the blackness.

With a squeal and a surge of rippling fur-covered flesh, the Howler came at Aniyah, who screamed.

A gunshot rang out, and a bullet smacked the trunk of a white oak next to the Howler. The guy with the gun was either a really bad shot, or he was just trying to scare the beast. Aniyah wanted to yell, "Shoot it! Now! What are you waiting for?" But she said nothing, the wind yelling and whispering for her to stay still.

The Ozark Howler changed direction midstride, splinters spraying the beast as it slipped into the cover of an evergreen, the crunch of footsteps carrying through the woods as the creature fled. A howl of pain pierced the night, and Aniyah saw black dots in the pristine white snowpack.

The glow of the flashlight approached, and Aniyah saw the man holding it. The guy was huge, and he wore a neck gaiter with a mouth full of teeth painted on it and a camouflage jacket that looked new. He held a rifle at the ready, a flashlight pinned to its forestock.

The beast screeched again, but it didn't sound close.

"What are you ladies doing out here? Were you in the accident?" the guy said.

Aniyah pasted Stacey to her legs with both hands as she stared at the man. He stank, and the vibe rolling off him told Aniyah to stay away.

"Just looking for my girl here," Aniyah said. "She ran off. Do you know which way the highway is?"

The man chuckled, but it didn't sound genuine. "I can take you there. I was tracking those footprints. Thought maybe an injured person wandered off in their delirium."

That all sounded like it made sense, yet...

"Let me take you, this way," the guy said, and he turned and started back down the path.

Aniyah was no hiker, and though she'd taken some walks in the woods, she'd never ventured off the marked trails, but that didn't mean she had no sense of direction. She and Stacey had followed Ray east off the interstate, and though her direction might have shifted slightly as she traversed ditches, stands of vegetation, and thickets of evergreens, she knew she hadn't been completely turned around. The man was taking them east, away from the highway. She said, "Excuse me, but why are we going this way?"

The man stopped walking and turned. The teeth of his gaiter glowed as he turned the flashlight on Aniyah and Stacey. He lifted the rifle and said, "You want help, or not?"

Though buried deep under years of non-use and callus, Aniyah's motherly instinct took control, driving out rationality as she sprang forward, reaching for the barrel of the gun.

The man stepped back and swung the rifle, but he was too slow, and the snow too deep. Aniyah barreled into him and knocked the gun barrel aside as a shot rang out.

A deafening ringing filled Aniyah's head as she screamed, "Run, Stacey!"

Aniyah took a breath, and a hand the size of a bear paw raked across her face, and she went down like a wet sack of potatoes and faceplanted in the snow. She rolled on her side, eyes fluttering. A smile crept over her face as she watched Stacey bolt into the trees and disappear into the shadows and darkness.

The man grunted, loaded another shell into the rifle, and hauled Aniyah to her feet by her hair. The pain was excruciating, and she squealed.

"That was really stupid," the man said.

Aniyah backed away but didn't dare run. The longer the nut was with her, the more time Stacey had to get away.

"You know you just signed the kid's death warrant, don't you?"

Confusion, fear, and disbelief fought for control of Aniyah's senses, but she settled on indignation, though she was in no position to stake claim to that ground. "From where I'm standing, I just saved her life."

"Really? She can survive out here by herself? In the dark? The cold? No food? No understanding of the wilderness and its... creatures."

Aniyah's heart sank. The psycho had a point.

"No matter. You'll do. Hold out your wrists."

Aniyah set her chin, but when the man put the tip of the rifle barrel to her forehead, she complied.

"You can call me Jed," the guy said as he tied Aniyah's wrists and held the end of the rope like a leash. "You go first. Follow the path."

With no other choice, Aniyah started walking down the beaten trail.

Jed gave her directions like a GPS, and Aniyah didn't see their destination until she bumped into it. An old hunting shack, holes in the roof, windows long broken, sat nestled within a copse of evergreens protected from the wind.

The door was closed, but a chain with a lock at its end hung from an unsecured hasp. Jed ushered her inside and positioned her next to an old, rusted potbelly stove. He tied her ankles, resecured her wrists, and then used rope and chain to tie her to the cold stove. When he was done, he pulled a water from a pocket and placed it on the floor beside her.

He said, "You can scream if you want. Nobody will hear you. Might as well save your strength. I'll be back to collect you."

With that he pushed out the door, slamming it behind him.

The rattlesnake tinkle of a chain being drawn through the shack's handle, then the click of a lock. Even if Stacey was able to find her in the dark, she wouldn't be able to set her free. Aniyah leaned against the cold stove, fear stoking her inner rage, her spinning mind asking questions she couldn't answer. Like what if he was lying and never came back? What if he was killed while he was gone? Hurt? She'd starve here chained to an old potbelly stove.

Aniyah was exhausted, and if she didn't get some sleep, she'd have no strength to run if an escape opportunity presented itself. She butt-inched forward, lifted the water bottle, and struggled to unscrew its cap with her wrists secured, but managed. She took a mouthful, only swallowing it a little at a time. She didn't want to piss her pants, and she had no idea how long she'd be tied up. She capped the water and pulled her knees against her chest so she could rest her head. The wind hollered and sang, and beneath it, the steady beat of her terrified heart thumped in her head like a bass drum.

19

Ozark Mountains, 7:18 AM CST, March 13th, 2021

Carter was spared reliving the end of the incident by the clang of the door lock disengaging. He came awake, rubbing crud from his eyes, shards of gray light leaking into the woodshed, the fire nothing but a mound of ash. He shivered. It was cold in the shack and as the door swung open, and the wind ushered in snow, he had the crazy idea of rushing Jed and trying to take his gun, but even the primal side of his brain which was usually up for anything nixed that idea. He was starving, dehydrated, weak, and bruised, and his elbow throbbed with constant dull pain. Yeah, that was why he couldn't take Jed.

The shed door fell back against the woodpile and Carter instinctively covered his eyes, though the gray corpse light that filled the shed was anything but bright.

Jed tossed Aniyah into the woodshed, and she hit the wooden floor hard, her head bouncing off the straw-covered planks.

Carter jerked up his mask and went to her.

Aniyah sat up and he helped her to the cot, anger burning through him like jet fuel. Carter turned on Jed and screamed, "What the fuck is wrong with your twisted hick mind? A woman? Are you one of those pussies who need to carry a gun into the supermarket?"

The blow caught Carter on the chin and his head rocked, his mask slipping. Pain raced down his back, creeping through him like darkness. As he rubbed his chin and conjured up a tough reply, the pain faded, and Carter realized Jed hadn't hit him with his full strength. Not even close. The big man didn't want to hurt his prey. That would spoil the hunt.

"Not as dumb as you look," Jed said as he tossed a paper bag to Aniyah. "Make sure you convince each other how fucked you are. Because you are fucked."

Carter and Aniyah's eyes met as he willed her the question that tormented him. Where is Stacey?

Aniyah looked at the floor.

Reading the situation, Jed asked, "The girl? No worries. I'll find her. Now you two miscreants eat up. I'll be back for you later, amigo." Jed slapped Carter on the shoulder so hard his teeth rattled in his head. "That first one be a love tap."

Carter licked the inside of his lips, the taste of fresh blood from a gash caused by Jed's blow reminding him of his current situation. He said nothing.

Jed nodded and left the shed.

Aniyah threw her arms around him and said, "Ray, I never thought I'd see you again."

Guilt washed over Carter as he gently returned the hug. "Are you O.K.? Did he hurt you?"

"Not physically. You?"

"I've been better. What are you doing out here, Aniyah? You should have stayed up on the road."

"I did," she said. "Then Stacey ran off, and well, there was no way I was leaving her out here alone." She quickly recounted her run through the forest, finding Stacey, Jed, and the attack of the bear-cat beast with horns.

"Where is Stacey now?" Carter asked.

Aniyah shook her head, smiling, tears welling in her eyes. "She ran."

Carter hoped the kid didn't decide to try and help. If she ended up Jed's prisoner things would become much more difficult for Aniyah and himself. He said, "What of the Howler?"

"The what?"

He told Aniyah everything Jed had said about the Ozark Howler, his mask tickling his nose the entire time. Carter had just gotten used to not having the damnable thing on.

"Shit," she said. "That all makes sense. The thing I saw was huge, Ray. I've never seen or heard of anything like it, but it matches the description of what you saw. Huge cat-bear, a long snout with a mouth full of teeth and two large incisors, and two twisted horns. Its fur seemed to shimmer and change color under the beam of the flashlight, but it was definitely black. And the eyes." She shook her head. "They were the worst. They made me feel like the thing was seeing through me, judging me for every wrong I'd ever committed. You know what I mean?"

"A little," he said. "So, you think you saw blood? Did Jed hit it?"

Aniyah shook her head. "He hit a tree next to it, and I think the beast caught a splinter or two."

"That would explain the blood."

She nodded.

He had many questions, but the grumble of his stomach called a recess. Carter opened the bag and found two waters and two peanut butter and jelly sandwiches wrapped in foil.

As Aniyah took a bite of her sandwich, she asked, "Is this home-baked bread?"

"It's home-baked, alright. Like our boy Jed." He tore off pieces of his sandwich and cycled them beneath his mask.

She chuckled and took a long pull of water.

"Go easy with the water. I don't know how long we'll be in here, and Jed doesn't appear to be a very attentive host."

Aniyah frowned. "How did he get you?"

"I met him up on the interstate."

Her eyes went wide as she took a bite.

"Yup. Had several conversations with him. I had no clue. I mean, I'm not a cop, but I'm usually pretty good at identifying shits. I totally missed this one, though there were clues. When I was chased from the road I tangled with the Howler, and Jed helped me out. Pretty much how he did you. I had a feeling we were going the wrong way, like you, but the snow was thick, I'd been twisted around, and I had no reason to believe Jed was a few gallons short of a full tank."

"That sounds horrible."

"Not as bad as what I think he has planned," Carter said.

"Which is?"

"I think he plans to hunt me."

Wind pushed through every crack in the woodshed and the old shack sang like a busted bassoon. Carter's neck ached from sleeping on the cot, and his eyes were bloodshot and red from the brazier's smoke. He flexed his legs, rolled his shoulders, and cracked the joints of his fingers, the faint sound of them popping echoing through the shed.

"You... we, can't let that happen, Ray."

Every time she said his alias the heat of guilt, shame, and frustration filtered through him. There wasn't another person on Earth that knew his entire story, what he'd been through. Jed knew what he'd done, and why, but lives are comprised of many puzzle pieces, and he was the only one who knew where all his pieces fit.

"Is something wrong?" Aniyah asked, her brow wrinkling.

He took her hand. Carter cared for this woman. He knew stressful situations created unusual bonds and stronger than normal feelings, but he didn't think that was it. He thought that, maybe, in another life, he and Aniyah would've been good together. But he was on the run, and she had just lost her husband, yet that still didn't stop the persistent feeling that he needed to unload on someone. Relieve the burden he'd been carrying for over two years, and for reasons he wasn't certain of, he trusted this woman.

"My name isn't Ray. It's Carter, Carter Renfrow." He pulled down his mask, searching her face for clues, any sign of recognition. Fear and angst that he'd get COVID filled his mind, and all the worries about doctors and hospitals came rushing back. He took a bite of his sandwich as she studied his face.

"Why did you lie?" she said with an air of nonchalance. She didn't look angry, but disappointed.

"You don't know who I am?" A strange sense of disappointment leaked through him, and he damped it down. People not knowing his past was a good thing, but dang. Didn't the woman watch T.V.? She read his mind.

"Don't watch the news much. All bad shit. What did you do? Kill a bunch of people?" She chuckled, but then her face went taut with embarrassment. "Not an appropriate joke. I was just trying to lighten the tension."

"Didn't kill a bunch of people. Just one." He studied her face as he took another bite of his peanut butter and jelly sandwich.

Aniyah's eyes narrowed in thought as she sucked on her lower lip, but she said nothing.

"A kid named Danny Tesco. A few years back in Memphis. I shot him on the street." He was surprised at the bluntness with which he stated his crime. It felt good.

Her eyes went wide with recognition. "You're that guy who killed the kid that raped his daughter. I remember now." She went on eating her sandwich like he'd told her he was Batman, and he was leaving to go to his cave.

"You... don't care?"

"Honey, if I had a baby—shoot—if anyone tried to force Stacey to do anything she didn't want to do I think a shot to the noggin would be the easy way out, 'cause what I'd want to do to the pervert would be a bit more sadistic."

Carter sucked on his lips but said nothing.

"Listen, Ray... Carter... we're in the shit together right now, so character references will have to wait. For all you know, I'm a serial killer."

He chuckled.

"OK, maybe I work at a nondescript call center doing useless work for shitty pay."

"Why?"

"Great question," she said. "Especially now with Harry gone."

They sat in silence for a time, gray light filling the room, the wind brushing snow against the shed.

"What did it feel like? I mean... oh, shit, sorry." Aniyah took a pull of water, her brown cheeks going a shade of pink.

"How did it feel to kill someone?" he said.

Aniyah said nothing.

"I guess I'm a cliché." He sucked in a long breath. "I never thought of killing anyone in my life until I read Katie—my daughter's—account of what happened. That anger, the feeling of utter helplessness was what did the most damage. I was so ashamed of myself. My daughter was hurting, and all I cared about was revenge. I told myself it was for her, but it was for me."

"Because you couldn't protect her?"

Carter nodded. "That took me a long time and many bottles of whiskey and wine to realize. Then a bunch more to realize it was bullshit, but still…"

Aniyah nodded and crumpled up the foil that had wrapped her sandwich.

"They were drinking," Carter started, and suddenly he was a kid again, in the little booth at the church telling a priest things nobody had any business knowing. Aniyah's expression deepened and soured as he spoke, but the confession felt good as the burden was lifted. "Katie says she had two beers, but Danny was drinking the hard stuff. They were making out, some light petting, but when Danny rounded third base Katie gave the holdup sign."

"I love the baseball analogies."

"Makes it easier to tell," he said. "The police report was harsher than a King novel. Anyway, she says no, he doesn't stop, a struggle ensues, and Danny rips her panties and forces himself on her. Thank someone that she didn't get pregnant.

"It was the aftermath that really got to her, and if I'm being fully honest, me as well. Physically she was fine, but the story went all around the school when Danny was questioned. The little fucker gave the standard asshole excuse provided by every abuser since the beginning of time. She wanted it. Led him on. It was consensual until they were in the middle of the act." Carter felt the heat rising in him, the rage.

He continued, "Kids can be way crueler than adults, and I watched Katie get tormented, called a slut, and other names not worthy of repeating. It all blew over. She started at a different school, and life went on."

"But not for you." It was a statement, not a question.

He shook his head no. "I just wanted to talk to Danny. Give the little turd a piece of my mind. Threaten and scare him." Carter shook his head.

"Why'd you bring the gun then?"

"I told myself it was a safety precaution, but that was high-grade bullshit. In the months after I realized I'd always intended to kill him. Maybe not on that day, on that street, with witnesses, but killing Danny had become an obsession I wasn't even aware of."

"You were married, right?" she asked.

He nodded. "Still am. When the cops came looking for me, she basically disowned me. Wouldn't help me run, nothing. She said I made the situation worse, and of course, she was right."

Aniyah frowned. "That's harsh."

"But true," he said. "Now my children have lost their father."

"You just ran?"

Carter shrugged. "It was that or jail. People understood—shoot, I saw newscasters say what you said. To some, I was a hero, but the law is the law, and nobody has the right to go around shooting people. Did the punishment fit the crime in my opinion? Yes, it did. But I'm not a judge and jury and I didn't make the laws."

"I'm sorry, Carter." She put a hand on his leg. "But know that I understand. I guess your wife was right, but still... who wouldn't understand?"

"You'd be surprised."

"If you got a do-over would you do it again? Could you?"

Carter said nothing. He knew what she was asking, but he was unsure of the answer.

"Kill again, I mean."

"You mean Jed?"

She said nothing, her wide glowing eyes all the answer he needed.

"I'm worried for Stacey, so maybe... I definitely felt the rage, and he is holding us like gerbils, so... Yeah, I can do it. But something tells me it's not going to be a fair fight."

"What are you going to do? Run?"

"I can't."

"Because of me." Aniyah looked at the floor.

"I will die before I leave you here."

She looked up, her face softening.

"And that's not your fault," he said.

"Or yours."

Detente achieved, they settled in to wait.

20

The wait felt like days, but when Jed came to collect Carter, it was like no time had passed. Their captor wore the same camouflage jacket and held the same rifle, a basic one-shot slide long gun that looked old but newly polished. The gaiter mask was gone, and when Jed saw Carter's mask was down, he said, "She recognize you?"

Carter said nothing.

"Did you get to know each other?" said Jed.

So the big man didn't know he and Aniyah knew each other from up on the road? Carter didn't see how it could matter, but the less information the guy had the better. He stayed silent.

Aniyah also said nothing.

"Whatever," Jed said. "I don't really give a flying fart. If you two mor—"

A non-human shriek followed by growling laughter carried on the wind that pushed its way into the shed.

"Is that the Howler?" Aniyah blurted. She jumped back, as if struck by her own words.

"That's the wild card," Jed said. "The random element to even things out."

The pair said nothing.

Jed jerked Carter to his feet and pushed him toward the door. "For practice, we'll use a tranquilizer dart. Shit I use on bears. It probably won't kill you, but it'll hurt, and you'll feel like shit for a few hours."

Anger built in Carter, the urge to strike out so great his neck pulsed with pain.

"If you don't do your best, well, then." Jed stepped forward and ran his fingers through Aniyah's dark hair. "Then she'll die, Carter. And it will be on you, and this time you won't have any grand cause to justify it. She'll be dead because you were a coward."

"Run, Carter," Aniyah said. "Leave me. You don't owe me a—"

Jed's massive mitt duffed her on the back of the head, and she fell still.

Carter took a step forward, fists balled.

Jed swung the rifle until it was aimed at Carter's chest.

Go at him, now! Carter screamed in his mind, but Aniyah was rubbing the back of her head.

Carter went cold. "What makes you think I give a shit about her? I don't know her from a hole in the ground." Then to drive the depravity home, he said, "And she's not... my type."

"Yeah, I don't go in for the dark meat much myself," Jed said. "Yer full of shit, though." A lecherous smile crept over his face as he looked at Aniyah, who was focused on a splinter of wood on the floor. The man's gaze shifted like a glacier as his eyes ranged to Carter.

Carter's stomach crawled with anger and shame. Hopefully, Aniyah understood what he was trying to do, but words were deeds, and he'd just dropped a nuke.

Jed ushered Carter out of the woodshed and jerked him to a stop. The chain rattled with a finality that made imaginary mice scramble up Carter's spine as Jed locked up.

A gunmetal sky thick with cotton candy clouds blotted out the sun, a dense layer of gray gloom hanging over the farm and surrounding forest and mountains. Rolling hills gave way to dark skies in every direction, and Carter couldn't hear the highway, or helicopters—nothing but the singing of the wind and the tinkle of snow being pushed over snow.

It struck Carter then how difficult beating Jed was going to be. They were on his turf, and anywhere he went he'd leave a trail in the snow. Desperation took hold of his stomach and squeezed, and he said, "I don't give a shit about her."

"Right."

"What do I get out of this?" Carter said, stalling for time.

"You live to breathe another day."

Carter lifted his chin toward the rifle. "I thought you said you wanted a fair fight. Do I get a weapon? Make things fair?"

Jed chuckled. "Any man of average intelligence can manufacture weapons with what can be found in the forest as well as here on the farm."

"So I have nothing to fear."

"Get free and tell the cops where I am," Jed said.

I don't know where I am, shitbag! "That's my plan. Thing is, I won't be going to the police," Carter said.

"Oh, right. I forgot you're a criminal and nobody will miss you, and from what I overheard of your conversation with Aniyah there ain't nobody looking for her either. When it comes to you I'm helping the police. Am I right?"

Carter said nothing. He was looking around while trying to not look like he was looking around. When he'd been marched onto the farm it had been dark, but in the half-light of the overcast day, he saw there were more than three buildings. He looked back over his shoulder at the path that trailed away into the trees. Down that path there was a gate in the barbwire fence that ran around the property—he assumed in its entirety. No matter, wire can be cut.

Jed nudged Carter in the direction of an old dirty house that sat at the center of the compound. When they'd gone about twenty feet, Jed said, "Get on your knees, hands behind your head."

If Carter hadn't known better, he would have thought Jed was going to execute him. He dropped to his knees and knitted his fingers behind his neck.

Jed moved around behind him and leaned in, putting his mouth just above Carter's right shoulder, his stinking hot breath puffing in the chill air. "I'm going to go finish my coffee," Jed said. "When I'm done, I'll be coming. Should take me a few minutes. Use the time well. Close your eyes and count to ten. If you open them, I'll shoot you." He said it with such nonchalance Carter had no doubts he would do exactly what he'd said.

Carter pressed his eyes shut and started counting. In the blackness of his mind's eye, two yellow eyes stared at him, the gurgle of the Howler's laughter transforming into the crunch of footsteps. When he reached ten, he inched open his eyes like a child who didn't want to see what the light of day would reveal.

Jed was gone, and there was a fresh set of footprints in the snow leading to the house.

His neck ached as Carter shook his head. Yeah, you go finish your coffee. Carter spun around and headed for the path he knew led to a gate. When he was halfway there, the locked shed on his right, he slowed and came to a stop.

"Aniyah, can you hear me?" he said.

"Yes, oh God, Carter. I hear you."

"You know I won't leave you, right? I just said what—"

"You're wasting time!" she roared.

"Right," he said. "I'll be back."

Instead of continuing toward the path, Carter pressed his back to the woodshed and surveyed the farm. The property was carved from the forest, and he estimated it was roughly twenty acres. Barren snow-covered fields surrounded the house on three sides, the front yard filled with buildings including the woodshed, a large barn, and several smaller outbuildings the purpose of which Carter could only guess at.

Lights shone from several of the house's windows—Jed and his damn coffee. There should be tools in the barn, pitchforks for the hay and such. Jed would never expect Carter to bring the fight to him, so he decided to ambush the psycho in his house when he'd least expect it.

With a plan he felt good about, Carter worked his way to the barn, hiding behind large oaks devoid of leaves that dotted the land between buildings. A snow-covered pickup sat nestled between the house and the barn, and a driveway disappeared into the evergreen forest.

The barn was an old-school affair, open on both ends, stalls running down both sides of a center aisle. There were bales of hay strewn about and an old gray horse with glassy eyes stared at him in silence as Carter searched the place. He heard the clock ticking in his head and he figured he'd used at least half of his allotted time. He considered commandeering the horse, then remembered he was an O.K. rider at best, the ground was covered in snow, he didn't know the terrain well enough, and the beast would give away his position. Carter saw no pitchforks or shovels, but an old wheat scythe with a broken wooden handle and a rusted curved blade hung from a support post.

Carter hefted the weapon and swung it, the air hissing. A smile he had no business wearing slid over his face as he crept out of the barn, hiding behind the pickup as he watched the house.

Yellow light spilled into the gloom from several of the downstairs windows, and a shadow flitted about therein.

He saw no faces peering through the windows, so he bolted across the corner of the field, pounding over a crisscross of trampled footprints in the snow. Carter got low when he reached the house, and as he crept onto the front porch the floorboards popped under his weight.

A laugh-howl filtered from the forest as if the Howler was warning Jed.

Carter looked over a shoulder and started, but it wasn't the Ozark Howler that made his stomach drop out his butt.

Stacey stared at him through the snow-laden branches of a thick evergreen, her eyes aglow.

Hope and the heat of love blossomed in his chest. Carter wanted to go to the girl. Take her in his arms and run. Everyone would understand. Stacey, a young child would live, and Aniyah would be the cost. It made sense, but as the wind threw snow in Carter's face, he knew every part of that rationalization was complete dog turd. There was no way he could leave Aniyah and judging by what he saw the kid was doing just fine.

Carter raised a finger to his lips in the universal 'stay silent' gesture.

Stacey shook her head back and forth fast and hard, the clear sign of 'no'.

He didn't know what she was trying to tell him. Lights were going out in the house, the windows going dark. He had run out of time. Carter moved across the porch, the old wooden planks beneath his feet popping and shrieking. He put his back to the front of the house and peered in a dark window. Nothing moved. The place certainly had a back door, and there were several windows on the first floor Jed could climb out.

Carter tested the window he peered through. Locked.

Still nothing moved within what he assumed was the living room, so Carter eased along the porch, back pressed to the wall for cover as well as to stop the screaming floorboards. When he reached the next window he ducked down, peering into the darkened room beyond. Nothing moved, so he continued until he got to the corner of the house, where he paused, his heart hammering, sweat dripping down his back, the tips of his fingers and toes stinging with cold and fear.

The screws in the wooden handle of the scythe were drilling pinpricks of stabbing cold into his palm, so he shifted the blade to his other hand. He cracked his neck, building his courage to look around the corner, but froze when he heard a door slam. It sounded like metal on metal, and as he spun around only shadows greeted him. He'd failed to consider a cellar door.

Carter darted forward, hopped over the railing that ran around the porch, and crouched within a tangle of dead weeds and creeping juniper bushes dusted with snow. He fine-tuned his hearing, dropping out the wind, the push of snow and ice, and... nothing but his knocking heart.

Time dripped away, his nerves dancing as the element of surprise slipped away. The longer he waited, the better chance Jed would track him. He needed to move.

He coiled himself to spring and run for the pickup.

Jed strolled across his field of vision as he headed for the barn.

Carter eased back into the shadow of the house, but he was exposed, the low vegetation around him not providing enough cover. If Jed looked back...

But he didn't. The big man made his way across the corner of the barren field next to the house and went into the barn. The whinny of the horse soon followed.

A chill wind massaged its way into Carter's collar as he ran, curved blade in hand, legs pumping as he sprinted for the barn.

He was about halfway when Jed stepped from the barn, the rifle pointed at the ground in low carry position. The big man planted his feet but didn't raise the weapon.

Carter didn't slow, but changed course, heading for the cover of an oak tree on the corner of the empty field.

Jed put the stock of the rifle to his shoulder and fired, the pop and thwap of the dart leaving the gun barrel echoing over the farm.

There was a hiss, and Carter felt a stabbing pain as the dart plunked into him. He went down in slow motion, his strength draining from him, the gray world going hazy, his vision turning blurry. He dropped to his knees, everything spinning as he fell face down in the snow. He rolled onto his side, but his arms and legs weren't obeying commands.

Carter watched, unable to move, as Jed strolled toward him, rifle over his shoulder. The snow bit Carter's face as anger, fear, and humiliation fought for control of his emotions. He wanted to get up and fight, yell, and scream, make demands, but instead, he lay there paralyzed.

Jed's feet appeared in front of his face. The big man dropped to a knee and said, "You alive?"

Carter was unable to speak or move, and it was taking all the energy he had left, all his focus, just to keep his eyes open.

"Sure you are." Jed hauled Carter through the snow to the woodshed.

He heard the click of the lock disengage, the creak of the door opening, but everything was fading, blackness pushing away the gloom.

Aniyah shrieked, but he barely heard her.

Jed guided Carter to the cot and laid him on it as Aniyah scurried out of the way. She considered running. The door was open, and Jed was preoccupied.

Carter struggled to speak, to yell, to move, but as his eyes slipped closed a sobering thought flitted through his failing mind: Stacey was fine, and now he only needed to worry about Aniyah.

Jed tossed something to Aniyah, and she caught it. "There's first aid stuff in there. Fix him up and have him ready for the real thing tomorrow. I'll bring by food in a bit."

Aniyah said something, but all Carter heard was mumbling as the blackness took him.

21

Flames writhed in the darkness, white smoke swirled, and shadows danced on the walls as Carter came awake. He was on his back, lying on the cot, arms at his sides. Aniyah sat beside him, wiping his forehead with a wet towel. She looked angelic, her face backlit by the fire, her brown eyes glowing in the semi-darkness.

"Welcome back," she said. "How do you feel?"

Carter was afraid to answer for fear of having no voice, but when he tried to speak his vocal cords vibrated and scratchy broken words came out. "How long was I out?" He flexed his hands and legs; they felt like they were filled with cement, but he could move again. Carter tried to sit up, but only got an inch off the cot before Aniyah pressed him back down.

"About three hours. Rest. There's nothing to be done. Are you—"

Outside, the call of the Ozark Howler cut through the driving wind.

"Nothing to be done and we're probably safest right where we are," she said.

"At least for tonight."

She shifted gears. "Are you hungry?"

He nodded.

The meat stew was cold, but not half bad, and Carter ate it all and drank half his bottle of water. When he was done, he felt much better, and Aniyah let him stand up and stretch. Pale light still leaked into the shed, but Carter figured the trials were done for the day.

"What happened out there?" Her voice was frail, beaten, and it set Carter's stomach aflame.

"I walked right into his little trap. I underestimated him. Jed might look like a dumbass, and on many levels, he probably is, but he's a hunter." Carter told Aniyah about his failed ambush attempt.

"I don't think what you did was stupid at all. I think it was smart, and took guts, you just didn't have any time to make a plan, let alone execute it."

She had a point. He needed to use what he'd learned. Carter rummaged around the shed until he found a wood splinter the size of a pencil. He cleared away a section of straw before the cot and gathered dirt and sand with his feet.

"Sit," he said, as he sat on the cot, the empty sand and dirt canvas on the floor before him.

Aniyah sat next to him, the heat between them hotter than the warmth of the woodshed warranted.

Carter drew a box in the dirt with a square at its center. "The box is the house," he said as he drew in the other buildings: the barn, the pickup, and the fields. He made a mark along the fence line where he thought the gate he'd come through should be, then drew in the driveway. Lastly, he added a compass rose in the upper right corner but didn't mark the direction.

"Judging by the way the fields are laid out, the glow above the clouds I saw yesterday, and what I believed the direction to be when I was brought in, I think this is north." Carter marked an N at the top of the compass rose.

"I agree," Aniyah said. "When he brought me in, I thought the moonglow was in the southwest."

"Yup. So..." Carter used the stick to draw a thick line along the western side of his map. "So that should be the highway."

"Is that what you're thinking? Go that way?"

He shook his head. "Too obvious. I'm thinking I start at the barn, take the horse, and head up the driveway."

"Seems too simple."

"I'm open to suggestions."

"Set the place on fire."

Carter nodded. "A possibility, but even if I could manage it, what about you? Let's not forget you're going to be locked in here."

Silence fell. The fire crackled, the arguing wind bitching and complaining as snow and ice pelted the woodshed.

Carter's muscles were loosening, his head clearing, but despite the food and water, he was still starving.

As if reading his mind, which she appeared to have a talent for, Aniyah said, "Are you still hungry? I saved half my stew for you."

"Don't be crazy," he said. "No way—"

"Will you stop with the macho bullshit? You don't need to be polite to me, Carter. You're the one who needs strength. I want to live, and right now the best chance I have is you. So why wouldn't I help my champion in any way I can? I'm no Cersei for shit's sake."

"Who the hell is Cersei?"

She stared at him like he was from another planet. "Cersei Lannister? Game of Thrones?"

Carter shrugged. He hadn't seen much T.V. over the last few years.

"Annnnyyy wayyy. When we get out of this, we'll watch it together, O.K.?"

Carter frowned. "Are you just giving me something to fight for?"

"What do you mean?"

"Did you forget who I am?"

"We'll worry about that hurdle when we get to it. For now," she said as she pointed at the map on the floor, "...you need to worry about getting us out of here."

With that settled the pair sat in silence, the fire popping, the wind and tinkling snow serenading them. The gray light pressing into the shed faded to black, and as Carter prepared to sleep on the floor next to the brazier, Aniyah said, "You should take the bed."

"Not happening."

Jed had brought a few blankets when he'd dropped off the food, and Carter wrapped himself in one and laid down on the hard floor next to the fire.

"Thank you," Aniyah said.

"For what?"

"Not leaving me."

The rattle of the chain, the pop of the lock.

Carter and Aniyah sat up as one as if they'd spent their dreams practicing. As Aniyah rubbed the sleep from her eyes Carter pressed to his feet, stretching sore muscles. His head pounded like he'd tied one on, and his chest burned with worry and fear. He rolled his shoulders, cracked his neck. As Jed entered the woodshed Carter again felt the urge to attack the man, but the shed was small and the last thing he wanted was for him or Aniyah to take a stray bullet.

Jed stood in the open doorway looking exactly as he had the day before. "Rise and shine, my little pretties." The man reeked of body odor, smoke, and alcohol, and his eyes were a red spider work.

Carter and Aniyah said nothing.

"You." Jed pointed at Aniyah.

"Wait, I thought—"

Jed stepped into the shed and pushed Carter aside. "I'm gonna take her to the bathroom so she doesn't get skanky."

Aniyah got up and let Jed lead her to the door. She looked back over her shoulder and shot Carter a wane smile, but fear creased her face, and perspiration dripped down her forehead.

"It will be O.K.," Carter said as he reached out for Aniyah as Jed hauled her out of the shed.

"Good. Good. If you do good, she'll live to see tomorrow," said Jed as he dragged Aniyah from the woodshed. The door fell back on its hinges, but there was no rattle of the chain, no click of the lock engaging.

Seconds dripped away. No sounds of the door being secured. Had the contest started?

Carter looked around the shed, searching for a weapon, though he'd been through the place numerous times and knew there was nothing of use. The fire sizzled as his gaze shifted to the closed door, indecision eating at him like acid.

He pulled on his jacket, hat, and gloves, and put his ear to the door.

It cracked open, wind whistling through a one-inch gap.

Carter pressed harder, and the door opened all the way.

The gray of early morning covered the farm like a death shroud. Jed led Aniyah toward the house, their footprints crushing the frozen snow. Carter stepped from the woodshed and gently eased the door closed.

Dead leaves clinging to branches hissed and preached in the wind, the tinkle of snow like breaking glass.

Jed still had a hundred feet or so before he and Aniyah reached the house, but this time around Carter intended to use every precious moment he'd been given. Being careful to stay on the beaten path through the snowpack so he didn't make noise, Carter ran-jogged-hopped toward the barn, the open maw of its southern end like a dark portal to another world.

Carter glanced at the house as he ran, and the scythe he'd stolen from the barn caught his eye. It hung from a nail on the corner of the house's porch like a fishing lure floating in the crystal-clear water of an immaculate pond.

He was no moron, and Carter had seen The Hunger Games and knew a trap when he saw one. He wanted the weapon, but Jed was just getting to the house with his prisoner and Carter didn't see how he could get the scythe without taking a huge risk.

The dark mouth of the barn loomed before him, and Carter pushed the scythe from his mind as he passed inside. It was warmer out of the wind, and he wasted no time going to the stall that housed the horse. Just as it had prior, the beast stared at Carter with glazed, vacant eyes, and didn't make a sound. He recalled the beast whinnying with pleasure when Jed had entered the barn, and a stitch of worry worked down his spine and settled in his lower back.

Carter had ridden several times in his life, but he was an amateur with just enough experience to get into trouble. He'd never ridden bareback, but he didn't have time to put a saddle on the horse, even if he could find one and he knew how to put it on the beast, which he didn't.

A set of worn reins hung from a peg next to the horse's stall, and Carter grabbed them as he opened the swinging gate to set the beast free.

"Come on," Carter coaxed as he tried to get the beast to leave the comfort of his 8' by 10' home.

The horse stared, unmoving.

"O.K.," Carter said as he played out the leather reins through his fingers. "Let's put this on." He tried to loop the reins over the horse's head and the beast tried to bite him.

Carter jumped back and squealed like a child. "Hey, you be nice." The clock in Carter's head was ticking loudly, and he heard a door slam. He tried to put the reins on again, and the beast snapped at him again, stomping its right front leg in anger.

"This isn't going to work out." Carter judged it was time to cut his losses. The beast didn't want to cooperate, and every horse he'd ever ridden had been a willing participant, and he had no experience dealing with unruly beasts, and without a saddle and reins—

Another door slammed, much louder. It sounded like the slap of a screen door.

Carter dropped the reins and searched. The peg where he'd found the scythe was empty, and he found no other tools or anything he could use as a weapon. There was a hayloft, but the ladder looked rickety, and he didn't have enough time to explore up there. He ran past the hay pile and empty horse stalls, and as he passed through the open door at the opposite end of the barn the gleam of metal caught his eye.

He skidded to a halt and backed up into the shadow of the barn door. In the empty horse stall at the end of the aisle, there was a hammer resting on a ledge just inside the doorway. Carter hefted it, the old metal head polished clean, the wooden handle tarnished with grease and chipped from usage.

A length of rope was on the ground, and he scooped it up as he looked back at the area where the reins lay in darkness. Carter retrieved the reins and bolted with his bounty into the gray gloom of morning.

The pickup sat at the end of a dirt driveway that trailed away east into the trees. Snow blew and eddied over the empty fields, the wind biting his face as he crossed the open area between the barn and the truck. He put the hammer in his belt like a sword, threw the rope over a shoulder along with the reins, and hid behind a thick oak as he peered at the house.

Nothing moved on the porch, but several of the windows shone with light, though he saw no shadows gliding about therein.

Carter surged from cover and bounded over open space until he was behind the pickup, his skin prickling with tension and unease. Still, nothing moved in or around the house. He scanned what he could see of the rest of the farm, but saw only stark buildings, dancing snow, and lurking shadows.

He backed away from the pickup, his back to the forest as he stared at the house. The driveway was nothing more than two snow-covered dirt ruts in the hardpan. Carter used it as a guide and he turned and strode purposefully into the forest.

The driveway was barely a path. It meandered around oak trees and thickets of short leaf pine, the weeds at the center of the two ruts brown and dead. Potholes and stones appeared in the snow like broken teeth, the forest growing thicker as he jogged.

Carter broke into a run, legs pumping, an urgency driving through him that he hadn't felt since the incident. Trees packed the sides of the driveway now, and ahead Carter could make out an opening that appeared to lead into a clearing. He doubled his pace, his heart screaming, his knees moaning.

He broke free of the trees and sputtered to a halt, his stomach dropping, pain cycling through his chest.

The driveway ended in a clearing dotted with stones and dead vegetation. Perhaps in the summer, it was a field of wildflowers… or poison ivy. A chaotic mix of crisscrossed snow-covered ruts went in every direction, the dirt driveway splitting into several tributaries like a river breaking on a giant stone.

Carter gazed at the confused tracks, the heat of fear and disappointment leeching through him.

In the distance, the crack of a rifle shot pierced the gray day.

An inhuman howl followed by barking laughter answered.

22

Ozark Mountains, 7:21 AM CST, March 14th, 2021

A ray of sunshine, like manna from heaven, knifed through the thinning cloud cover and broke over the clearing, a spotlight shining on a road rut that appeared to bend north like a giant snow-covered viper. After the storm, the endless night, and being locked up, Carter would take whatever sunlight he could get. A gray haze hung over the clearing, dead leaves tinkling in the bickering wind. His feet were planted in cement, the echo of the gunshot and the Howler's return call hanging in the air, his mind still processing that the driveway led nowhere.

Carter looked over his shoulder, but as he stood at the edge of the clearing, shadowy fingers of darkness reaching out from the forest, he was unsure which way to go. The sun was in the east, which meant he'd been traveling east. Something itched at him, an unease, the sense that he was being watched.

Rolling mountains filled the horizon in every direction. He looked back into the forest, and nothing moved. Moss normally grows on the northern side of tree trunks, and many of the bare white oaks had brown ribbons of dead moss running up their lengths on their northern sides. This cemented Carter's mental compass, and some of his stress fell away as he pictured his map of the area: the green patch labeled the Ozarks and the stretch of I-49 running north to south. The interstate was in the west, so he had to circle around or head in another direction and hope for the best.

Growling, sniffing, huffing, and the scrape of claws on wood.

Shadows writhed and darted about in the forest, flitting from tree to tree like nymphs. Carter scanned the snowpack inside the woods, but he saw only the tiny prints of birds, deer, squirrels, and chipmunks.

His skin crawled with terror as he peered down the path the way he'd come, searching for the beast's fog light yellow eyes.

A branch snapped and he spun around.

The Howler exploded from the trees on the opposite side of the clearing, a dark shape slick with snow, two yellow eyes hanging above a snarling tooth-filled maw. Muscles rippled beneath the beast's fur, its twisted horns pumping up and down with its head as the creature loped across the clearing on all fours, moving at a fantastic speed, its footfalls like a coming storm, the crackling snow its lightning, the beast's gurgling growl its thunder.

Carter started to run back the way he'd come, remembered Jed, and veered north as soon as he entered the forest. The underbrush along the tree line wasn't thick, but bare vines with thorns all along their length tore at his pants as he crunched through pristine snowpack. He knew he was leaving tracks, but if he didn't get away from the Howler it wouldn't matter.

A deer trail appeared to his right, and Carter shifted course and followed it.

Breaking branches, tittering chickadees, and crunching footfalls rose above the wind as Carter pushed onward. He glanced back and saw nothing but swirls of snow, pole-like tree trunks, and an endless blanket of white with dead vegetation reaching from it like emaciated arms.

When he turned his attention back to the path, he saw the glint of something at his feet. A wire ran across the path, suspended two inches from the ground.

Carter jumped, throwing himself forward in an awkward attempt to avoid the tripwire. Arms out for balance, the hammer dangling in his belt, his right leg took all the weight, and Carter danced for a heartbeat on one leg before getting his feet under him and hopping over the wire.

"Fair my ass!" Carter screamed.

The Howler roared, a guttural squeal of hatred that tore away the windblown silence.

Carter skidded to a halt, pulled the hammer, and turned to face the Howler. Getting taken down from behind was no way to go. He'd engage the beast head-on, and if he died, he'd do so fighting for his life.

The Ozark Howler burst from the trees onto the path. It rose on its hind legs, eyes gleaming, front paws up in attack position, its three-inch claws gleaming in the pale light. Its insidious growl rose in volume and pitch as it came forward, mouth open, railroad spike-like fangs hanging over dark gums.

A gunshot pierced the day. It wasn't far off, but it wasn't close.

The beast slowed, the pointy ears next to its twisted horns going straight, then shifting around frantically.

Carter's hands began to sweat as he gripped the hammer handle so tightly pain stitched across his knuckles as he ran.

The Howler was moving at half the speed it had been, but Carter still felt it gaining on him as he sprinted down the deer path, eyes focused on the snowpack before him. He needed to get off the path into the cover of the trees where he might have a chance. That meant he had to take his eyes off the ground before him, and he had no desire to end up with a swinging rock pounding his head or a spike impaling him.

Ahead, the main deer path widened, but a secondary trail curved west into a stand of evergreens. If the local deer didn't think going straight was smart, he'd follow their lead. He veered into the thicket of trees, the sound of pursuit close as he wove around short leaf pines stacked with snow, the snowpack littered with brown pinecone scales.

Cold branches whipped Carter's face, his knees aching, lungs on fire, as he worked his way through the thick undergrowth the deer had slipped through. Tall white oaks appeared ahead, dim rays of gray light leaking into the forest.

Carter broke free of the pines and a gunshot rang out.

A bullet whizzed by his head and plunked into the tree next to him, and splinters sprayed the right side of his face, thousands of tiny needles digging into Carter's cheek. Specks of crimson marred the white snowpack, and he felt the heat of blood dripping down his face into his collar.

He dropped and rolled, his jacket getting caught in the underbrush, his face hitting icy snow. Another shot, but this one hit the ground several feet away from him, a tiny geyser of snow rising from the ground. The shots appeared to be coming from the west, and Carter crawled to the nearest oak and planted himself on its eastern side, putting his back to the trunk and using it as leverage to push to his feet.

The Howler had disappeared like smoke, and an eerie silence settled over the woods. The wind died away, the tinkle of snow on ice falling to a low static. No birds cooed or chirped, and no squirrels tittered. His breathing echoed in his head as he bent carefully, staying behind the tree, and scooped up some snow and forced it into his mouth. He wiped his face with the back of his gloved hand, and pinpricks of pain cascaded over his face. A bloody splinter was stuck in his glove, and Carter pulled on the tips of his fingers as he began pulling the glove off. His hands were sweating, and if he wasn't careful, he wouldn't be able to get the glove back on.

The distant trudge of footsteps carried faintly on the breeze. Carter had no idea how far away Jed was, or what the range of his rifle was. He'd come close to taking off Carter's head, so he assumed the nutter was nearby because a precise shot through the trees required skill, and the longer the range, the more difficult the shot.

He reconsidered pulling off his glove, and instead of taking it off, he pulled it on tighter, securing the glove's drawstring around his wrist. Slowly he inched his head around the tree trunk and peered west.

The cloud cover was breaking up. There were white patches mixed within the dark, and stray beams of sunlight arced into the forest and cast indiscriminate spotlights on the forest floor. The undergrowth was thick all around him, and white oak intermixed with evergreens filled his field of vision. There was no sign of Jed, and there was no gunshot.

Carter's skin itched. He'd been in one place for too long. He needed to make some time and put as much distance between himself and Jed as he could.

To his left, a thick knot of pines filled the southern approach, and the northern and eastern paths were no different than the western; an open forest of oak packed with underbrush and slick with new-fallen snow. The rolling mountains of the Ozarks were everywhere, yet they seemed distant and forlorn.

He went tree to tree, expecting the snap of a gunshot each time he moved. As his confidence grew, and no gunshot came, he broke into a run, weaving in and out of trees, staying away from thick patches of vegetation and lifting his feet clear of the snow with each thrust forward.

Carter came across footprints in the snow, colossal four-toed paws that formed double tracks like those of a bipedal creature, three-inch slices at the tip of each digit outlining claws. The tracks trailed away north into the trees.

Pain settled in his lower back as the adrenaline ebbed. He put the hammer back in his belt and made a mental note to look for a large straight stick he could use as an extended handle for his weapon. The rope and reins were tangled, but still hanging from his shoulder and Carter paused a moment to re-orientate the stuff and pull it across his chest.

He looked back. Nothing moved, and no birds sang, but the wind had resumed its debate, and the murmur and holler echoed over the snowpack, the chill wind biting his face but easing his wounds.

The deer path he'd abandoned for the evergreen thicket appeared before him, the snowpack pristine and white. It ran north to south, but if he used the path he'd leave a trail in the snow that even a child could follow. Perhaps he could use that to his advantage. If he could find a place to ambush Jed, he could use his footprints as bait for his trap.

Carter headed north along the path, trudging right up its center in the foot-deep snow, his pants getting caught on pricker vines that pushed through the snowpack.

A cry carried on the wind, but it didn't sound like the Howler. The bears were asleep for the season, and foxes and wolves no longer lived in the Ozarks, having long been run out, or in the case of the red fox, were teetering on the brink of extinction, so he puzzled over the source of the sound. His head pounded in rhythm with his heart and Carter looked over his shoulder every few seconds. He felt Jed coming on, back there somewhere in the forest, watching, tracking, waiting for the right opportunity to take down his prey.

Not today, pal. Not today.

The ground gave out beneath Carter's feet.

His arms shot out, fingers searching for anything to grab as he plummeted in a maelstrom of snow and dirt. The scent of wet earth filled his nostrils, snow pouring onto him, working its way into his collar and up his shirtsleeves and pantlegs. His mind had just enough time to conjure a series of sharpened wooden spikes planted at the bottom of the pit before he crashed into a pile of leaves and debris covered in snow and came to a stop, his face planted in dirt and snow, dead leaves pushing into his mouth.

Carter lay still as he took inventory of his body and spat out leaves. Pain lanced his back and side from the hard landing, but he felt no spikes skewering his torso, and there was no blood running down his legs. Using his elbows for leverage, he pushed onto his side, cold pain gripping him. His breaths puffed in the air, mist filling the hole.

A few of the splinters in his face had been pushed in deeper, and thin rivulets of blood ran down onto his jacket collar. Heart racing, rasping for air, he rolled onto his back and stared up at the gray cloud-filled sky. He was in a dirt pit, at least fifteen feet deep. There was no way he was climbing out.

He sat up, rubbed his eyes, and inadvertently pushed a splinter deeper into his cheek. As he carefully pulled off his right glove, he tuned out the wind, his racing heart, and the thump and wheeze of his breathing.

Footsteps crunched in the snow above, but the hairy face of the Howler didn't appear over the rim of the pit.

With the glove off, Carter set about plucking splinters from his face. A large one had impaled the side of his nose, and when he pulled it free its ragged end tore a bigger hole. He cursed and stifled whimpers of pain as he pulled out the rest, each splinter coated in his blood. When he was done a pile of eight bloody shards of wood sat next to him. He knew he hadn't gotten them all, and there were sure to be small needles beneath his skin, but he'd done all he could, so he slipped his glove back on. It took a little work to get his fingertips in, but he managed, his nerves dancing as the sound of crackling footsteps got louder.

Carter searched the darkness of the pit. Roots stuck from the walls, and white stones stared out like eyes. Carter grabbed a baseball-sized rock and hefted the hammer.

"Ray?" The voice was like the coo of a dove, simple, kind, and infinitely concerned.

Carter got to his feet, heart racing. "Who is it?"

More shuffling feet in the snow, then a flashlight beam arced down into the pit and Carter covered his eyes.

"Ray?"

"Stacey?" said Carter, hope blooming in him.

23

Stacey's young face appeared in the grayness above, her eyes glowing in the gloom. "Ray?" she repeated. "Is that you?"

Carter closed his eyes and took a deep breath. "Yup. It's me, sweetie." Worry and concern leaked through him. Jed was up there. The beast. "Are you alright?" he asked. "The How… a strange creature was after me. Do you see it? Hear it?"

"It's gone off," the child said. "It doesn't like the big man with the gun."

"Where is he?"

"I'm not sure, but he's coming."

The searing pain in Carter's lower back eased as what he needed to do became clear.

"Stacey, turn off the flashlight," he said.

She complied.

"The most important thing you can do to help me is paying attention to everything around you. Jed… the man with the gun… he wants to shoot me, but I'm sure he would hurt you if he caught you. And the beast, the Ozark Howler, it moves around like smoke, so I need you to constantly be looking around, and if you see the monster or Jed, I want you to promise me that you'll run."

"And leave you?"

"Yes. I know you don't understand, but I'll have a much better chance of making it through this if I don't have to worr… If I only have to look out for myself."

"You mean like now?"

Carter laughed. He couldn't help it. "Point taken. Will you promise to keep an eye out at all times? Even when you're helping me?"

"Why does Jed want to kill you?"

"Because he's crazy," Carter said. He didn't have time to teach the girl about the garbage that lived among them. "Do you promise?"

"Yes."

"Good. Now, look around for the tree closest to the hole. Something big enough to hold my weight. A tree as thick as a telephone pole."

Stacey's pale face disappeared, and Carter cracked his neck, tension massaging every muscle in his back. He felt time slipping away like the clouds overhead and heard Jed's footsteps in his mind.

"O.K. Got one," the kid said. Jed barely heard her over the wind, but he was happy the child was smart enough not to yell and draw attention to their location.

"Come back," he whisper-yelled.

Stacey's face appeared above.

Carter holstered his hammer, pulled the looped rope from his shoulder, and played the length of it out through his hands. He had about thirty feet. "How far is the tree from the hole?"

The kid looked back the way she'd come but said nothing.

"Bigger than your living room from end to end?" He had no idea what the size of her living room was, but it would give him perspective.

"Not that big," Stacey said.

"Your bedroom?"

"Sort of."

Ten feet-ish plus the roughly fifteen-foot depth of the pit. "Should be enough," he whispered.

"What?"

The distant call of the Howler echoed over the Ozarks like a siren's song.

"Nothing," he said. "Wait one minute."

Carter made a hitch knot loop at one end of the rope and coiled it. "Step back from the edge," he said.

Stacey disappeared from the lip of the pit and Carter hurled the rope. It hit the ledge, bounced back, and got tangled in a root halfway back down to Carter.

Three tosses later he managed to get the rope out of the hole and explain to the child how to wrap the rope around the tree and put the straight end through the looped end. The line was barely long enough, and when Stacey had completed her task the end of the rope hung above Carter's head.

"Hurry, Ray! Someone... thing, is coming."

"Go hide." Carter secured the hammer in his belt, made sure the horse reins were tightly hitched over his shoulder and climbed. It was arduous work and would have been impossible had it not been for the frozen ground. Despite the extra support the frozen ground provided, patches of earth broke away as he dug the tips of his boots into the earth for footholds.

He slipped back to the bottom of the pit four times, but on his fifth try he made it out and rolled exhausted onto the trampled snowpack, the gunmetal sky fleeting by overhead, the sound of crunching footsteps carrying through the forest.

Stacey burst from the trees and pounced on him. "Ray. I'm so happy you're here."

Carter patted the kid's head and draped an arm over her shoulder. Guilt worked his way through him like bad news through a crowd, and though he didn't have the time, one of his errors needed to be corrected as soon as possible.

As he coiled the rope, he said, "My name isn't Ray."

The child stared up at him with eyes so innocent he would have melted had he not been made of cynical granite.

"It's Carter. Carter Renfrow." Though their masks were down, their true identities revealed, the kid was too young to know who he was, what he was.

"Why... why did you say your name was Ray?"

The truth only went so far, and Stacey was just a child after all. "I'm sorry. I... We were in a bad accident. I was confused, and..."

Stacey's face twisted, even her undeveloped bullshit meter registering an anomaly.

"And my brother's name is Ray, and people get us confused all the time. Scrambled eggs is all."

That final lie appeared to have satisfied the burgeoning detective, and she asked, "Do you hear that? The footsteps?"

He nodded. "We need to get out of sight."

"Can I help? Please."

"You sure can. You've been wandering around these woods longer than me and you seem to have a knack for getting around."

"Mom and Dad used to take me hiking all the time."

The memory of the child's dead parents came rushing back like a nightmare, their bloody corpses folded into their vehicle in a way human bodies weren't supposed to bend.

"There's a cave not far from here," Stacey said.

Caves were dangerous business at any time of year, but in the winter, they posed the added danger of the possibility of bears calling the place home for their long sleep. He didn't like it, but he didn't have anything else. He needed to find a good location to confront Jed. That was priority one, and the sooner the better, before hunger weakened him to the point where he would be unable to beat Jed in hand-to-hand combat—not that he could on his best day. He looked down at the hammer in his hand.

A roar echoed over the woods, and Carter thought he heard a faint scream in return.

"How far is the cave?" he asked.

"Not far."

"Which direction?"

The kid pointed north toward a sheer cliff face where a slice of the mountain had broken off and slid into the valley below. Its peak looked like a broken tooth, and the mountain stood out within the rolling hills of the Ozarks. It didn't look far off, and heading that way meant going in a direction that led away from Jed and the Howler.

Wind gusted, clouds of snow twisting between the trees and through the underbrush. Carter sensed the sun had moved toward noon, the sky still packed with dirty clouds, though they were thinning, and there were faint blue patches above the western horizon.

The pair joined a trampled deer path, Stacey's tiny feet fitting easily atop the thin well-trodden trail. Carter did the balance beam walk, one foot directly in front of the other, the horse reins dragging behind him and scuffing the marks left by the treads of their shoes.

The forest grew sparse as the cliff face grew, and tumbled boulders and patches of frozen devil grass and evergreens replaced the white oaks as the path split in several directions like the duo had reached a major intersection on the deer highway.

A hill packed with a tumbled field of scree climbed toward the cliff face to the north, but the most well-used path bent west and looked to run back on itself. "Watch your step. Time to lose Jed," Carter said.

The kid zipped her coat and pulled down her hat.

Carter gathered in the horse reins and slung them over his shoulder along with the rope. He picked the largest stone within jumping distance and leaped to it. It had a thin coating of snow, and he slipped upon landing but managed to stay perched atop the rock. He shifted his feet like he was cleaning the bottom of his shoes on a doormat, then jumped to the next stone. So he went, stone to stone like a child crossing a stream. When he'd gone ten stones or so he paused atop a big boulder and looked back.

Stacey stood on the path watching him, her eyes aglow in the gloom. There was no sign of his passage in the snow leading up to his position.

"You can do it," he whisper-yelled.

And she did. Hesitantly at first, Carter had prepared each stone for her, stripping away the ice and snow with his boots. When she was a couple of rocks behind him, the wind hollering, he continued up the slope, jumping from stone to stone.

When Carter reached the top of the incline he paused, staring down at Stacey as she worked her way toward him. He felt exposed and hid behind a boulder, peering around its edge as he gazed back at the forest in the direction he'd come.

It was difficult to be sure with the glare of the snowpack, the thickets of evergreens covered in snow, and with so many dead leaves still clinging to the white oaks, but Carter thought he saw a solitary figure working through the forest to the southwest.

Stacey made her final jump and planted herself at Carter's side.

He patted the child's head, and said, "We need to stay out of sight. I don't think Jed can see us from down there, but…"

"The Howler."

He nodded. "Lead on as fast as you can."

With a new sense of urgency, the partners abandoned the stone hopping and plunged into the forest, heading directly for the cliff face.

It was slow going. The underbrush was thick and packed with pricker vines, and there were slick stones hidden beneath the snowpack. Carter fell twice as the duo struggled up the mountainside, and he was dusted like a powdered donut when they arrived at the cliff face.

Stacey, being much lighter of foot and youthful dexterity, had to wait for Carter several times as he untangled himself from thorns and ate snow, his stomach a jumble of pain, angst, and disgust.

Randomly Carter wondered if his son won his game? He chuckled, the thought of watching his son through binoculars as normal as the coming of day. But it wasn't normal. Nothing about this life was, and if he lived through this ordeal things would change. He didn't know exactly what that meant, but it still brought him some comfort knowing that if he died out here, he could go to his maker knowing he intended to own up to his actions. Who knew? Maybe the powers that be would cut him a break.

With that impossible thought gestating in his mental incubator, Carter followed Stacey up a narrow path that had giant cracked slabs of stone on both sides. Carter was no geologist, but it was pretty clear what had created the cliff face and the cave. He'd visited a few caves, and he knew the entire Ozark region was created by erosion. Water had split the mountain, the crack widening until a huge chunk of the southern mountainside broke off and slipped into the valley. As Carter traversed the path, his tiny partner leading the way, the crack widened, the dark maw of a cave mouth appearing against the gray and black stone.

There were four-toed footprints in the snow, thin lines at the end of each. They were all around the cave entrance, but they were filled with a dusting of new snow. Dead vines and weeds covered in snow surrounded the cave entrance, and several white oaks leaned over the opening like teased eyebrows, their roots exposed as they clung to the side of the mountain.

The tinkle of water carried on the wind, snow pushing over snow, and Carter figured a stream ran below the snowpack. A faint clicking, like a lead line tapping its aluminum flagpole, emanated from the cave. The stench that wafted from the opening was anything but sweet; a toxic mix of rot, feces, animal body odor, and the scent of earthen moisture. Red warning lights flashed all over Carter's mental dashboard.

He stopped and looked back.

Stacey said, "What's wrong?"

Carter wasn't sure. An undefinable dread had crept over him, the rational side of his brain telling him going into the cave was a bad idea.

Would Jed follow? If so, it could be the perfect place to lay the trap. He examined the paw prints in the snow once more, and said, "I don't think the Howler is in there. Look at the tracks, and it would have to be really fast to have beaten us up here." Or it knew a better way. Or there was another entrance, and there could be bears, he added to himself but didn't say aloud for fear of scaring the child.

Stacey glanced back the way they'd come but said nothing. What needed to be said? Jed or the beast would eventually find them if he didn't take the fight to them.

Carter shrugged and pointed at the cave mouth. "You've been in there?"

She shook her head no. "Yesterday I saw the cave opening. It's easy to see from Jed's farm."

A chill crawled up his back, and thoughts of traps and other horrors within the cave gave him pause yet again. Jed surely knew of the cave and had been in it. It was on, or very close to, his property, and it was unreasonable to believe he'd never explored the cave. Carter rolled his shoulders. He could apply that logic to the entire Ozarks.

"First, let me make something that at least resembles a weapon," he said.

As if on cue the wailing laugh-growl of the Howler echoed up the mountainside. This time it was much closer.

Stacey's eyebrow rose, and her woolen hat inched up on her forehead.

"Look around for a stick. Straight as possible."

As the pair searched, Carter beat himself up for not obtaining a stick when they were trudging through the woods where there would've been many options. He'd thought about it, but he'd been preoccupied.

There weren't many oaks around the cave mouth. The trees were mostly evergreens, but the dead leaves and branches of the white oaks that angled off the cliff face above had created a small deadfall between a series of tumbled rocks at the base of the cliff. There Carter found an oak branch with a relatively straight section that measured five feet long. He broke the section free and used one of the leather straps from the horse reins to secure the hammer to its end.

Carter swung his new weapon in a wide arc. It felt good in the hand as it sang through the cold air.

The crack of a gunshot carried up the cliff face, and a bullet smacked into stone two feet from Carter. Rock fragments sprayed him, but this time no shards impaled his face.

"Get down!" he yelled, but Stacey was already running for the dark crack in the side of the mountain.

"Come on," the kid shrieked.

Holding the hammer-club with one hand like a spear, Carter crawled over the beaten snowpack into the dark maw of the cave opening.

24

Carter scrambled through the cave mouth, the palms of his hands chilled through his gloves, his pants wet with snow, knees aching from crawling over the frozen stone. The echo of shattering rock still hung in the air as darkness consumed him, and the rancid scent filling the cave assailed him. He gagged as he got to his feet, looking back at the triangle of gray light that marked the crack in the mountainside.

Stacey flicked on the flashlight, and the cave filled with harsh LED light. The clicking sound was a dead branch hanging from a root just inside the cave entrance. It swung back and forth in the breeze, tapping the stone wall as it angled upward. Shadows danced, frozen rivulets spidered down the cave walls like snot, and the sound of dripping water accompanied the wind, which whistled, shrieked, and piped through stone. Ribbons of solid rock hung from the walls like hair. Most caves in the Ozarks weren't much more than cracks in the limestone created by erosion, but some of them had what was called flowstone, stalagmite-like formations made of calcite or other carbonate minerals, formed from flowing water.

The formations were stunning, and as Stacey panned the flashlight across them, the rank scent of death filling Carter's nostrils, he waded deeper into the cave.

There were drawings on the walls, primitive stick figures wearing Native American garb, and praying to the moon, which was represented by a huge, pocked circle. The figures danced, and several symbols that looked like Mayan writing ran below the drawings like a narrative. Carter recalled what Jed had said about the ancients in the area, the warring tribes that he believed originated in South America. He'd even mentioned the cave drawings, which further proved Jed had been in the cave.

"Why do they pray to the moon? I learned the Egyptians, who lived way before, prayed to the sun," the child asked.

"The moon represented night, which was cooler. The sun was an enemy, as it can get very hot in most of the southwest United States." Carter chuckled. "At least that's what I remember. Who knows?"

Stacey stopped arcing the flashlight around, and its beam illuminated a particularly disturbing image.

The scene depicted four stick figures in elaborate dress. Feathers of blue and red festooned their heads, and they wore black loincloths that had squiggly white lines running across them. The figures held spears, and the hunters were arrayed around a beast that could only be the Ozark Howler. The bear-like form was three times the size of the stick figures. It stood on its hind legs, front paws up in attacked position, dark smudges of paint depicting drool or blood seeping from a tooth-filled mouth. But it was the yellow speck-like eyes. They seemed to follow Carter's every move.

A rank wind wafted from within the mountain, and the hairs on the back of Carter's neck stood on end.

Stacey said, "You know… maybe we shouldn't go any farther."

Their situation was dire, and he couldn't shake the feeling that he and Stacey were doing exactly what Jed wanted. There was no way the man could've known what direction he'd head, but now that Jed knew where they were Carter felt he'd given the nutter the upper hand.

The sound of trickling water reminded Carter that the cave might have another outlet. Limestone caves created by water often had many side passages, and the cave they were in most likely had tributaries, but what were the odds one could lead them out? Slim.

A musical wind pushed into the cave. Carter said, "I think you're right, kiddo. My guess is there isn't another way out, so going deeper would trap us."

The child nodded, and again Carter was impressed with her maturity.

"But he's out there," Stacey said.

Carter nodded and coughed, the smell of rot unbearable. He hadn't mentioned the other reason he didn't want to venture farther into the cave. He figured words weren't necessary. Stacey had a nose, had seen the beast, and it wasn't a stretch to assume the beast had hung out in the cave, perhaps more than one of them.

The pair went back and paused just inside the cave mouth, peering out into the gloom of the overcast day. The path they'd followed through the large boulders and slabs of stone was clear, their footprints running down its center until they met the jumble of Howler prints. The view beyond was blocked by the fallen rocks, and Carter deemed that Jed wouldn't be able to see them from his position lower on the mountainside.

"Hold this and get on my back," Carter said as he thrust his hammer-spear at her.

Stacey stared at him like she didn't speak English.

"Trust me."

The child looked at the ground, but nodded.

Spear in hand, Stacey mounted Carter's back, one arm around his neck, the other holding the weapon as Carter held onto the kid's legs. She was light, and as Carter carefully backtracked, putting the tips of his toes in his footsteps, he barely felt the child's weight on his back. He went slow, even though the alarm in his head was ringing, his muscles bitching, and hunger pains pierced his stomach every few seconds. The backtrack trick hadn't worked on Jed prior, but Carter figured that may have been because the man was able to see Stacey and him jumping from stone to stone up the hill. It didn't matter, because Carter was running on empty, and the low oil light was on, and soon his engine would seize.

As the path opened, byways shot off in every direction. "It won't work beyond this spot because I don't know which way he'll be coming," Carter said aloud to himself.

Stacey looked back up the path toward the cave mouth, which was now up the incline about a hundred feet. Boulders and scrub pine dotted the area. "What won't work?" she said, the innocence in her voice making Carter's chest ache.

Carter turned and faced the cave as he hitched up Stacey, who still clung to his back. He placed his feet in his own footsteps for a second time as he headed back the way he'd come, the patch of darkness marking the cave looming over them.

When Carter reached a tall stone that leaned out over the trail, he dropped Stacey to the ground and said, "See that rock over there surrounded by pricker bushes?"

"Uh-huh."

Carter leaned in and took the hammer-spear from the kid, and said, "You don't need to worry about what I'm going to do. Go hide beyond that rock and don't come out no matter what you hear. Do you understand me?"

The kid's lips twisted, but she stayed silent, defiance creasing her face.

Carter hadn't yelled at a child in… he didn't remember the last time he'd ripped into Katie or Tommy. Anger welled in him, but he tamped it down. Stacey cared about him. She was concerned. He dropped to a knee and took her by the shoulders. "Listen, kiddo, you've been a real trooper so far, but I need you to be tough a little longer. Can you do that?"

Still the child made no sign.

He sighed. The kid had been in a massive multi-car pileup, lost her parents, been separated from Aniyah, her surrogate mother, and now she was being chased by a madman and a creature that should only exist in fairy tales. Carter said, "You've been through more in the last forty hours than most people in a decade, but if you want to help me… no. You need to help me or we're not going to survive. Do you know what that means?"

"I'll be with Mom and Dad?"

Sorrow, shame, and then cold hatred seeped over him. No, kid, when you're dead worms eat you. God is bullshit and Heaven is a construct to keep you in line. What he said was, "That's not what your mom and dad would want."

"How do you know?" the kid yelled, tears welling in her eyes. "You didn't even know them!"

He didn't have time for this, and he felt Jed's hot breath on his neck, but there was nothing for it. "I have children of my own, so I do know. Your mom and dad would want you to have a great life, and then, someday, many many years from now, when you pass from this world, you'll see them then. If you were to go to them now, they would feel responsible for you not having the life you deserved. Do you understand?"

"I guess."

The sound of footsteps crunching snow carried on the harried breeze.

Carter and Stacey both looked downslope in the direction of the sound.

"What are you going to do?" the kid asked.

"End this," Carter said. "Will you do as I've asked? Please? And if things go badly, and we get separated, head back to the farm. I'll meet you there."

Stacey didn't answer but instead hurried to her hiding place.

As Stacey nestled into her spot, Carter smudged her footprints and positioned himself behind the slab of rock that leaned out over the path. Without the sun shining there would be no shadows, so he'd have to rely purely on instinct, reflexes, and sharp eyesight. If he was wrong, or off by just a second...

The footsteps slowed as his pursuer became wary, but came on. Carter gripped the hammer's stick handle and raised it over his head. One swing was all he'd get, and it had to count.

He stood frozen, the hammer-spear cocked and ready, eyes locked on the corner of the stone. The footsteps were getting closer, and he heard the echo of ragged breathing. Sweat dripped down his back, a chill seeping through him like raw sewage. He was doing it all over again, losing himself in his hatred. He'd just resolved to turn himself in, and here he was preparing to kill. He reminded himself that the two situations were markedly different—he was fighting for survival now, not revenge—but still doubt gnawed at him. When it came time to swing, would he be able to kill again?

That thought barely had time to register as Jed's camouflage jacket inched past Carter's hiding spot.

He swung with everything he had, the hammer scything through the air with a *swish*, the branch flexing like a golfclub shaft, building momentum and force. Carter let loose with a battle cry that echoed over the mountain and bounced off stone.

Mid-swing the hammer flew from the end of the stick like a bullet and shot across the trail, smacked into a rock with a clang, and fell to the ground.

Carter's eyes widened as he completed his swing, the stick without its hammer head striking Jed on the shoulder as the man struggled to aim his rifle. The stick snapped, and Carter threw what was left at Jed's face as he lunged forward like a cat, grabbing the rifle barrel with one hand, and planting a massive roundhouse punch on Jed's right cheek with the other.

The big man staggered back and jerked the rifle barrel from Carter's grasp.

"Now you've gone and got me angry," Jed said. The punch hadn't even fazed the man, and as he drew himself up to his full height, he tossed Carter aside like a bug. Jed put the rifle stock to his shoulder and aimed at Carter where he lay prone on the snow-packed path.

A stone came from the direction of Stacey's hiding spot and struck Jed on the side of his head, and the nutter turned in the direction the rock had come from. Blood exploded from the wound, and Jed screamed, not in pain, but in fury.

Carter vaulted to his feet, wrapped up Jed's legs, and attempted to take him to the ground.

Jed shuffled back, one leg easing back further than the other as he braced himself. He brought the butt of the rifle down on Carter's back as he drove Jed back, but the man was like a tree trunk, and wouldn't go down.

A roar echoed through the narrow pass, and for a heartbeat, he and Jed froze like an ancient statue posed in battle for eternity.

Carter was outgunned and outmanned, but he had one desperation move left. As he and Jed struggled, he punched at the big man's right hand, the index finger of which was curled around the rifle's trigger.

The rifle discharged, the bullet shooting into the sky. The gun was a one-shot bolt rifle and reloading it would take time. Whether it was to keep things somewhat fair, or for the fun of the sport, Carter's H&K had yet to make an appearance.

Jed sensed this plan, so he broke their embrace and flipped the rifle in his hand, using it as a club as he held the gun's barrel.

"Come on, city boy. You think you can take me?"

Carter squared himself, and planted his feet, fists up. In a blow-by-blow fight, with Jed holding the gun-club, he had no chance.

Another stone sailed from where Stacey hid, but this one missed and smacked a stone behind Jed.

The man's attention shifted for the briefest of instants.

Carter bolted, slipping by Jed as the big man swung the gun, his eyes ranging for the source of the stone.

Sounds of pursuit filled Carter's head as he wove between boulders and around thickets of pricker bushes and creeping juniper. The shriek of metal sliding over metal carried over the scene—Jed reloading as he ran, the crunch of his furious footfalls like breaking bones.

A flash of black, like dark smoke, surged from behind an evergreen with a roar-cackle of anger.

Carter saw slick black fur, heard the beast's horrible growl, and felt the heat of the Howler's passage as it knocked him aside, heading for Jed. Carter hit the snow-covered ground hard, the stone beneath unforgiving. In his peripheral vision, he watched the beast, its muscles rippling as it drove forward on its hind legs, rising like a horrible specter, its twisted horns glinting in the pale light of the overcast day.

Jed slammed the rifle's bolt home and fired, but the beast was too fast and was in too close.

The Ozark Howler's massive paw knocked the gun barrel aside, and the shot went wild.

With a roar that Carter thought shook the ground, the beast raked one of its massive front paws across Jed's face, shoulder, and chest, curved claws leaving bloody ribbons of clothes and flesh.

With clouds of foggy condensation lifting from the crimson snow, Carter pushed to his hands and knees and looked for Stacey. The girl was nowhere to be seen, and his chest loosened as he got to his feet.

Jed went down, the gun falling from his hands. The Howler stood over him and screamed as it dropped onto all fours, its elongated snout surging forward, mouth open, teeth bared as the beast tried to take a bite out of Jed.

To Jed's credit, he was still fighting. He lay on his back, both arms up to protect his face and the wound that covered the upper half of his body.

Carter searched for Stacey again, and when he didn't see the girl, he jumped down the slope, heading for the forest. If the kid stuck to the plan she'd head back to the farm, but plans rarely survived implementation, and as a wail of human pain echoed over the Ozarks, Carter felt pity for Jed.

It passed quickly.

25

Ozark Mountains, 7:14 AM CST, March 14th, 2021

Aniyah struggled through the snow as Jed drove her like cattle. She stumbled as cold bit her face, the wind dusting up the newest layer of snow, the scent of wood smoke thick in the air. There was an old white house ahead, a large barn to her right, a pickup, and empty snow-covered fields. The rolling mountains of the Ozarks walled in the farm on all sides as if the acreage had been carved from the land with a giant ice cream scoop.

Her heart sank. Finding a way out of Jed's valley in the summer when there wasn't a madman chasing her would be difficult; given her current position, it was next to impossible. Aniyah's thoughts went to Ray… Carter… and she told herself Jed hadn't locked the woodshed. Had she imagined that?

The last forty-eight hours were one long slow-motion tragedy, the events so close together each occurrence was slipping away from her, her husband's death-darkened face starting to fade.

When the pair reached the house Aniyah noticed a curved blade hanging from the corner of the old porch.

Jed slowed as he mounted the porch steps as if he was giving her a chance to go for the weapon, or whatever the hell the thing was. A surge of anger and overconfidence ran through her, but the idea was slapped down by the ever-present voice of her dead mother telling her that was the dumbest thing she'd ever heard.

But what did Jed plan to do with her? He clearly thought she was less than human because of her skin color, but there were good old boys that screwed cows, and slave owners had regularly forced their property to perform more services than cooking and working in the fields. She had no mental illusions that Jed wouldn't use the toy he'd found, regardless of its make and model.

The screen door shrieked and as Jed pushed open the main door, he said, "Don't mind the place. I didn't have time to clean."

Jed ushered her into a living room that looked lived in, but the den at her place was more of a mess.

Aniyah paused on an inside doormat that read, "Welcome," then below in smaller type, "ONLY if you've got meat or beer."

Jed grabbed her arm, pulled her down a short hallway, and threw her into a bathroom. The light flicked on, and the door slammed.

Aniyah steadied herself as she listened to a deadbolt slam home and click into place, then the rattle of metal slipping through metal, then a snap as a second lock was secured. She pounded on the door and screamed "Why are you doing this?"

No response.

She stopped hitting the door and rubbed her hands, trying to drive out the pain.

"Clean yerself up. There's a towel, soap. Don't try nothing dumb. You can't get out. I'll be back later with Carter's head, and we'll have a little dinner. How's that sound?"

Aniyah's stomach turned, and if she'd eaten anything other than water and PB&J in the last eight hours she would've hurled.

Silence fell, a finality that eased her nerves, despite her desperate situation. Outside the wind pressed against the old house, whistling and singing, the tinkle of snow pelting wood a faint murmur.

The bathroom was tiled in baby blue, and the toilet, bathtub, and sink were the same color. It was circa mid-60s, she guessed, and she'd seen the same ugly four-by-four tiles in many bathrooms throughout the southwest United States. A cracked mirror hung above the sink, and a single towel rested on a rusted bar, a bottle of Ivory hand soap on a shelf next to the drawn-back shower curtain.

She had to pee, and she unzipped her jacket, pulled down her jeans, and plopped onto the cold plastic seat. Aniyah braced her elbows on her legs and let her head drop into her hands. What the hell was she going to do?

Harry's specter fluttered through her mind, telling her everything would be O.K. She thought of Carter, a man she cared for more than she had any reason to. He was a killer, straight up, and she'd never abided by violence, but there was something... Maybe it was the accident, Harry's death, Stacey, and their fight for survival, but she no longer thought what Carter had done was so bad.

She rolled free some toilet paper, finished her business, and pushed up and flushed. As she pulled up her pants, she scanned the small room. The shower was a standing tub with tiled walls and a curtain hanging from a pole. There were no windows, no art on the walls, no shelves filled with knickknacks. She checked the cabinet beneath the sink and found a toilet brush, a cardboard canister of Ajax cleaner, and a dried-up nasty sponge.

Aniyah threw her weight against the door, and it didn't budge. The air vent in the ceiling was a thin rectangle that a raccoon might fit through, but no way she was crawling out through ductwork like they did in the movies. She closed the lid on the toilet and sat in frustration.

Dripping water drew her attention to the stained tub. She could flood the bathroom. But what good would that do? The water would leak under the door and serve no purpose other than to flood the house. That would surely piss Jed off, and she didn't see how that could help her.

The door was hardwood, and she'd need a hammer or an axe to break it down. The untiled portion of the bathroom wall appeared to be sheetrock, and perhaps she could make a hole, but how?

She got to her feet and searched the room again, hoping to see something that might spark an idea.

The toilet was two pieces. The tank was bolted to the lower bowl, and it didn't look like it would take much to break the tank free. Aniyah took the lid off the tank. It was heavy, and the rectangular shape was awkward. She tried anyway.

Aniyah drove the rectangle of porcelain into the bathroom door, striking the area just to the left and above the doorknob. The door splintered, paint peeled, but the wood was too thick, so she went to work on the doorknob. It broke off after three swings and that accomplished nothing.

In her fury, she hurled the top at the door. It bounced off, barely leaving a mark, and crashed to the floor and broke into several pieces, the broken edges of the shards of porcelain razor sharp.

She turned off the water via two valves below the toilet tank and kicked at the tank until it broke free of its mounting bolts. Water spilled from the tank as she tore out the flush mechanism and hefted the tank. It was considerably heavier than its lid, but she managed to heave it at the door. The tank hit home and shattered on the tile floor just like its lid.

Aniyah chose a shard of broken porcelain from the toilet top. It had a smooth beveled edge on one end, and as it tapered away the broken edge was blade sharp. She picked a spot next to the door above the tiles and began hacking away the sheetrock.

Turned out the walls weren't sheetrock like her and Harry's place... like her place back home, it was old school plaster with rows of wood lath nailed to the 2" by 4" support columns. She kept at it, anyway, thinking if she could clear enough plaster, she might be able to use the towel bar or the shower curtain rod to break through the lath.

It was slow work, and she didn't know how long it took her to make the small hole before she gave up in frustration. It was like escaping from Alcatraz. Given enough time she might make a hole big enough, and be able to work free the wood lath, but Jed would be back soon, and if she was exhausted from her futile escape attempt, there would be no hope left.

She rinsed her face and sat on the closed toilet lid, head in her hands, sobbing. She sat there a long time, wind and snow battering the house, images of sexual torture dominating her thoughts.

"Aniyah?" came a voice from beyond the bathroom door.

26

Ozark Mountains, 11:39 AM CST, March 14th, 2021

Stacey tossed another stone at Jed. Exhilaration and confidence coursed through her until she felt Jed's gaze. She knew he couldn't see her where she'd ducked behind a boulder, but he knew she was there, and it was more than just the stones she'd thrown. The icy fingers of dread massaged her back, and her cheeks stung from the cold and fear.

She peeked around the edge of the rock.

A flash of black, like a ghost, drifted from behind an evergreen, its thunderous roar echoing over the Ozarks.

She saw slick black fur, heard the beast's awful snarl. The Howler went for Jed.

Stacey squealed when she saw Carter hit the ground, a puff of snow rising around him, the beast pushing up onto its hind legs, its twisted horns glinting in the gray light.

Jed slammed the rifle's bolt home and fired, but the beast moved like smoke.

The Howler's gigantic paw knocked the gun barrel aside, and the shot missed. With a roar that hurt Stacey's ears, the beast scraped a front paw across Jed's chest.

With Jed's blood drenching the snowpack, clouds of foggy condensation lifting from the crimson snow, Stacey watched Carter run for the cover of the woods.

Doubt, fear, and the shame of abandonment held her in place, a tear leaking down her face into her mask that was still hanging around her neck. Her parents had been so worried about COVID, and now they were dead, and she an orphan.

Stacey rubbed her eyes as the snow from the dustup settled and the Howler didn't reappear. Hope blossomed in her as she recalled what Carter had told her. "And if things go badly, and we get separated, head back to the farm. I'll meet you there."

She bolted from her hiding spot and headed downslope. Stacey saw Carter in the distance, the black form of the Howler chasing him. She wanted to scream, to call out and tell Carter he was going the hard way, but instead, the wind cried in answer, specks of ice pelting her cheeks.

Carter was beyond her help, and her thoughts strayed to Aniyah and the farm. She'd become familiar with the surrounding woods, and she headed south along the slope, avoiding the large patch of fallen stones Carter and the beast were traversing. There was a trail that headed west toward the farm. She hadn't led Carter up that way because they'd started too far to the north, and though going that way was longer in distance, the path would allow her to move fast.

A thicket of tangled short leaf pines blocked her way and she cut through it, no longer heeding her footprints. To her left, the slope climbed up to the cave mouth, and to her right, the land fell away until it met a line of white oaks that stood on the edge of the forest like sentinels.

Stacey picked her way through underbrush, vines with thorns scratching and tearing at her. She felt much better when she reached the cover of the forest, the creak and moan of the barren trees, and the push of ice over snow comforting.

A guttural inhuman wail rose above the wind, followed by barking laughter.

The call was answered by a louder, angrier howl.

Stacey's nerves danced down her spine and started a party in her stomach as she doubled her pace, following footprints in the snow. She was sweating, and she unzipped her jacket as she ran, but left on her gloves and hat. She knew from playing in the snow that once the palms of her hands started to sweat and got wet, there was no way she'd get the damp gloves back on.

The white oaks were replaced by creeping juniper, scrub pine, and tangled underbrush, and soon she came upon the area where Jed's dirt driveway separated into multiple paths, the mounds of snow-covered dirt ruts trailing away in all directions.

There were no sounds of pursuit, and she no longer heard Carter and the beast barreling through the forest. As she hurried down the driveway to the farm, she saw no living thing and heard no cooing birds or the chittering of squirrels and chipmunks.

The old house appeared in the gloom ahead, and she saw the gleam of metal peeking out from beneath the snow as the pickup came into view.

Stacey hid behind the blue truck. Nothing moved except twisters of snow. She glanced into the barn, saw the doors on both ends were open, and bolted into the dark maw of the barn's southern entrance. The sweet scent of fresh hay assailed her, and she paused to stare at the old horse that watched her with glazed eyes. She ran through the barn, out the opposite end, and using trees for cover, made her way to the woodshed, where she found the shed door swinging in the breeze, nobody inside.

She looked toward the house. An odd blade hung from the porch eaves, and the house was dark. There were other buildings strewn about the farm, but she figured there might be food, water, and weapons in the house, so she ran for it, no longer hiding behind trees or paying heed to her footprints.

The main door was closed and locked, but a brief search revealed an unlocked window, and she climbed through into the darkness.

Dust motes floated in the air and cold wind pushed snow through the open window, but she didn't close it. When she played hide-and-go-seek, she always left herself an escape route. She eased through the darkness, her eyes adjusting to the dim light, but she froze when she heard weeping coming from down a hallway that branched off the foyer.

Stacey followed the sound and stopped before a locked door, the sound of muffled crying leaking from within.

"Aniyah?" Stacey said.

The sounds of misery ceased.

"Aniyah, are you in there?" The kid pressed her face to the wooden door, closing her eyes and wishing harder than she'd ever wished in her life.

"Stacey?" Aniyah's muffled voice filtered through the door.

"Yes, it's me!" Stacey's skin itched with excitement.

At the same moment, they both yelled, "Are you O.K.?"

Aniyah assured Stacey she was fine, and the child gave her a brief update about what had happened with Carter, the cave, the beast, and Jed.

"Was Jed..." Aniyah's voice trailed away.

"Was he dead?" the child stated. "I don't know."

"And Carter?"

"The Howler... it was right behind him, so..." Stacey held back tears.

"You need to get me out of here," Aniyah said. "Can you open the door, sweetie?"

Stacey turned the deadbolt, and the lock disengaged, but there was nothing she could do about the combination lock that secured a secondary latch. The child jerked on the doorknob, and it came off in her hands. She peered through the hole and saw Aniyah's brown eye peering back at her.

"I tried to get out and broke the knob on this side," Aniyah said.

"There's another lock... and I can't..." Stacey was so frustrated she cried.

"Stop that, now," Aniyah said. "I need your help. Look around for something to break the door with."

Stacey glanced back up the hallway into the gloom. She didn't want to leave Aniyah's side, even though there was an inch of hardwood separating them.

"Someone's coming," Stacey said. "I hear footsteps." She knew it could be Carter, but it could also be the Howler or one of Jed's demented kin.

"Hide!" screamed Aniyah through the door.

Stacey ran down the hallway and crawled behind the living room couch.

27

Carter bounced down the slope with reckless abandon, icy rocks sliding around him, the snarl and huff of the Howler close behind. When he reached the tree line he didn't look back as he plunged into the dense forest of white oak and pine. The underbrush was thick, and his progress slowed, tension crawling down his spine as he struggled. Time slowed, his breath coming in ragged bursts, his stomach screaming, muscles shrieking for rest. Tree trunks, evergreens covered in snow, and snowdrifts barred his way as he threw himself forward, sinking into the snow, pricker vines grabbing at his pants and jacket.

The ground fell away, and the trees were spaced further apart, many of them bent at odd angles and slanting downslope. He could move faster in the thin forest, but so could the Howler. A huge boulder that looked out of place on a hillside devoid of large stones rose from the snowpack before him like a giant gray eye with brown spidery moss blood vessels.

His heart hammered in his chest, but he no longer heard the sounds of pursuit. Carter paused behind the boulder and stared back up the hillside.

The Ozark Howler stood perched on the lip of the incline, its yellow eyes peering down at him. The beast sat on its haunches like a dog, arms hanging at its sides, claws dangling in the snow. The creature's mouth was closed, but even in the gray haze, Carter could make out the thick fangs over the Howler's dark gums. Pointed ears gyrated and twisted, the horns protruding from the creature's head behind each ear like daggers stabbing at the heavens.

The beast lurched onto all fours and stalked to the edge of the incline, the low murmur of its growl like approaching thunder.

Then it was gone.

Carter did a doubletake and jerked back, searching the hillside for a dark amorphous blur surging through the trees, but there was nothing. Tree limbs cracked and tapped, dead leaves sizzled, and the wind preached.

If Carter was right in his reckoning he was heading west, and he should come upon the path he and Stacey had used to get to the cave. Once he found that, he could move faster.

Even though he couldn't see the Howler, or hear it, he felt its presence, an unseen menace in the shadows stalking him, waiting for the perfect moment to strike as it had with Jed.

He randomly changed direction, zigzagging northwest, moving around to the northern side of the farm. Maybe he could shake the beast, but he was losing precious time.

The Howler let loose with an earsplitting cry that sounded close, but Carter thought the scream had come from the west. Had the Howler anticipated him going back to the farm? Why not? The creature had been playing cat and mouse with Jed for some time.

Another bark-howl degenerated into hyena-like laughter, and to Carter, it sounded as though that howl had come from the south.

Lost in his thoughts, confusion gnawing at him, he moved through the woods as fast as he could while maintaining some level of caution.

Carter came upon footprints in the snow, two tiny sets of prints partly stomped out by the treads of his boots.

With new energy and hope driving him onward, Carter followed his own beaten path. Tree trunks, snowpack, and evergreens blanketed with snow spun across his field of vision as he ran as hard as his malnourished body would allow.

He slowed when he reached the area where Jed's dirt driveway split in several directions, but he didn't stop. Carter followed the driveway through the woods toward the farm, his steamy breath fogging the air, his knees threatening to come unhinged.

The forest thinned and fell away, and Jed's house materialized out of the gloom, the blue pickup wedged next to the barn.

Carter skidded to a stop.

A Howler wandered casually through the thick oaks that decorated the house's front yard. It was smaller than the beast he'd just seen, and that revelation sent a red-hot knife of pain into his gut. Carter had speculated about the possibility of there being more than one beast—the odds and biology almost dictated it—yet still, he'd hoped.

The beast didn't notice him, and Carter hid behind the pickup, its cold steel like a giant ice cube chilling his bones. As he watched the Howler weave through the oaks, his thoughts drifted to the pickup. If there was a key box, maybe—

With a roar that sounded equal parts fury and surprise, the Howler loped toward the corral, its attention focused on something Carter couldn't see. The beast disappeared from view around the western side of the house.

The scythe still hung from the corner of the porch, and as the curved blade twisted in the wind it looked like a rusted crescent moon. There was no sign of Stacey, and Aniyah could be in any of the outbuildings. The house was the best bet for weapons, tools, and supplies, and wherever Aniyah was, he was going to need something to break whatever lock assured her captivity.

He sprang from cover and bolted across a corner of the snow-covered field to the front of the house. There he paused and concentrated, filtering out the wind, the creak of metal tapping metal, and the crinkle of snow marching over snow. Nothing. No beast. No Stacey.

Did he dare call out? That might alert the Howler... Howlers... to his presence. Carter decided on a half measure, and he called out Stacey and Aniyah's names, the volume of his voice a notch above his normal tone.

Nothing answered but the wind.

The porch steps creaked as he mounted them, his head on a swivel as he looked over his shoulders. The Howlers, Jed... he was most likely dead, but Carter hadn't seen a body. He retrieved the scythe, and the wooden handle felt good in his hand, like an old friend. The blade whistled through the air as he swung it, Carter half expecting the blade to fly off the handle like his hammer-spear.

Carter chuckled to himself as he checked the front door. Locked. He turned to head back down the steps so he could check the backdoor and the cellar doors, but he noticed curtains wafting from an open window at the far end of the porch.

He eased along the front wall of the house. The porch popped and moaned; despite the care he was taking to put his feet as close to where the deck met the wall as possible to limit the stress on the floorboards. A dusting of snow covered the windowsill, and inside tiny muddy footprints trailed across the living room.

Being careful not to snag his new blade on the curtains, Carter climbed through the open window and closed it behind him.

The house was quiet. Somewhere a clock ticked, and a compressor hummed softly. Pale light leaked into the house, and he looked around for a light switch, found one, then thought better of it. He didn't think the Howlers would attack the house—though he had no idea why he believed this. Maybe because Jed had lived here amongst the creatures? Had he routinely frightened them off? Were the beasts coming around now because they'd sensed Jed's demise?

Carter wiped these thoughts from his mental slate. He needed to find Stacey and Aniyah, the keys to the pickup, and get the hell out of the Ozarks.

Dust motes floated in the stale air, a steady stream of heat coming from a vent in the ceiling. With the curved blade out before him, like he was entering a dungeon or some ancient tomb, he crept through the living room toward the kitchen.

"Stacey? Aniyah? It's Carter," he whispered. "Are you here? Stac—"

Wood scraped over wood and Carter spun on his toes, bringing up the scythe.

"Carter!" Stacey emerged from behind a couch and ran to him, throwing her arms around his legs and squealing. The child had done this before, and Carter was starting to like it. He dropped to a knee and hugged the girl.

"Are you alright?" he said.

The kid nodded.

"Do you know where Aniyah is?"

More nods as she took his hand and led him down the hallway to the bathroom.

"Aniyah, it's Carter," he yelled, no longer caring if the Howlers heard him. "Are you in there?"

"Yes," came Aniyah's pleading voice through the wooden door. "Thank God you're here. Is Jed... done?"

"As far as I know, but there's more than one Howler, and one of them is lurking about. We need to get you out of there and hit the road."

"Yes," came her muffled voice in response.

"Sit tight, I need to find something to break off this lock."

"O.K."

Carter took Stacey by the shoulders and said, "Listen, kiddo. I need you to search the house and make sure all the windows and doors are locked. Can you do that for me?"

"I think so."

"Did you see a phone?"

Stacey shook her head no.

"Alright, let's get to it."

The girl scurried off and Carter started his search in the kitchen. There were the normal knives, pots and pans, and silverware. He found a utility closet that most likely held tools, but it was locked. Carter grabbed a glass, filled it from the tap, and gulped it down. There was leftover chicken in the fridge and some snacks in the cabinets. He threw it all on the kitchen table and snagged a bag of chips to eat as he searched.

There was a gun cabinet in what looked to be Jed's bedroom, but it was locked, and there were no other weapons to be found. There were four hundred and thirty-six dollars in cash in Jed's nightstand, and Carter pocketed it. Reparations, he thought, as he searched the living room, and the dining room, which had piles of newspapers and magazines hoarded therein. He hadn't seen a phone anywhere, but that wasn't unusual these days. Many home phones had been replaced by cellular phones.

Carter found Stacey sitting on the couch, the light of a lamp spilling over her face. At that moment the child looked much older than her years, and again Carter wondered how the last few days would mark her. Would the tragedy serve as a rallying point to help her thrive? Or would it become a reason to give up?

His children faced the same challenge, and if he had anything to do with it, Carter would figure out a way to change the odds. He said, "All done?"

"Yup."

"Did you notice anything of use in the basement?" he asked.

"Not much of a basement. More like a dirt hole, but no."

"Probably just an old root cellar."

"A what?" the child asked.

"Another time. I think—"

The living room suddenly became darker. The bulb in the floor lamp next to Stacey twitched, sputtered, and went dark with a tinkle of breaking tungsten.

"That's it!" Carter exclaimed aloud in his excitement.

Stacey took a step back, her eyebrows lifting, her face going rigid.

Carter laid his blade on the couch and grabbed the floor lamp, an old wrought iron thing with a metal base, twisted support pole, and a light with a shade that was so old there were moth holes in its fabric. He jerked the lamp's cord from the wall, tore off the shade, and hefted the lamp, using the support pole as a handle.

Stacey clapped her little hands and laughed. "A hammer."

The pair hurried back down the hallway to the bathroom.

"Aniyah, stand back," Carter said.

"There's no room."

"Lay down in the tub."

There were a few moments of silence, then, "Ready."

"Stand back, kiddo." Carter swung the floor lamp, pounding the metal latch affixed to the door's frame. Metal rang on metal, and the lock twisted in its hasp. He let go of all his fury, the lock becoming the face of his daughter's rapist as he swung, his back aching, his vision going blurry and red from the effort and rage.

Carter wasn't sure how many times he swung the lamp, or how long it took, but when the latch broke from the doorframe, the lock still intact, he screamed in triumph and fell on his ass, exhausted.

Stacey opened the door and set Aniyah free.

The three of them hugged each other, crying, the moment overwhelming Carter. It had been so long since he'd touched another person intimately, felt the heat of their concern and love. He held onto Aniyah and Stacey like they were his family, and in some strange way, they now were.

"Eat and drink. Both of you," Carter said as he gulped down more water and ate a peanut butter sandwich. "I'm going to look for the truck keys."

"You mean these?" Aniyah held up a set of keys. "One says Ford on it. They were on the hook next to the fridge."

"O.K.," Carter said. "All that's left to do is find out where exactly we are and what's the fastest way to a road."

Aniyah headed for a bookshelf and Carter went to search the paper hoard in the dining room. He gave up after several minutes. The newspapers were from all over the region, and the magazines were national.

"Find anything?" Carter asked when he got back to the living room. "I'm going to check upstairs."

"What about the T.V.?" Stacey asked. There was a flat-screen mounted on one wall and the child sat on the couch before it.

Carter gazed out the front window. Nothing moved outside that he could see. "Hand me the remote," he said.

Stacey complied and Carter turned on the T.V. He flipped around until he hit the local twenty-four-hour news channel KATV. A reporter was talking about the weather, and Carter handed Aniyah the remote and said, "Call me if anything useful comes on. There's got to be a map somewhere in this place."

With Stacey and Aniyah monitoring the downstairs and the T.V., he headed back up to Jed's bedroom. Again, he came up empty, but in the spare bedroom, there was an old painting on the wall that showed the northwest corner of Arkansas during the 1800s when native tribes still populated portions of the Ozarks. Carter stood before the map, frustration ebbing through him. The interstate wasn't on the map because it hadn't existed until the 1980s, but there was a compass rose in the upper righthand corner and a jagged line marked the Western Trail where he thought the interstate should be.

The map was useless without knowing his position on it, and he was about to give up and head back downstairs when he saw faint pencil marks on the painting. He pulled it down off the wall and looked at it closer under the light of a lamp that sat on the nightstand beside a double bed.

There were markings, a smiley face, and other drawings that looked to have been made by a child using a pencil, and subsequently erased, most likely by an angry parent. A section in the mountains was marked with a faint star. Whether it had been Jed, one of his children, or some distant relative, Carter was certain the star marked the farm.

Not that it mattered. They already knew the interstate was in the West, and they knew what direction that was, but Carter had hoped for a much closer road. He had the truck keys, and it was—

"Carter! Come quick!" Aniyah's voice carried up the staircase.

He double-timed it downstairs and found Aniyah and Stacey staring at a young male reporter standing on the side of I-49, a spattering of emergency vehicles, fire trucks, and tow trucks in the background.

"…and it has been three days since the tragic events that led to the deaths of twenty-six people. But that's not the worst part of this horrible story."

The scene shifted to a crushed box truck and Carter gasped.

"Twenty-three dead bodies were found in the back of this truck, and law enforcement has determined that human traffickers were transporting inventory on that fatal night. Both drivers were killed upon impact, and there were no survivors in the rear of the truck, so we may never know the ending to this sad story. Officials are saying several crash victims are still unaccounted for, and law enforcement believes the missing persons may have fled the scene for safety early on. The massive fire of burning tires is under control, but the DOT says it will take weeks to fully clear the hot sludge-like material before the northbound lane of the interstate can be reopened. More on this story as more inf—"

Carter shut down the T.V.

"Any luck upstairs?" Aniyah asked.

"Didn't learn anything we don't already know. I think we should get in the truck and go. One of the driveways must lead out of here. There are things here that came from a grocery store, and Jed's supply of beer can't be far away."

Aniyah nodded.

A pop and snap, like a gunshot, pierced the stillness.

Stacey screamed and pointed.

Jed stood staring through a window into the living room, his jacket crimson with congealed blood. He smiled and punched the window, his fist surging through the glass and spraying the living room with tiny knives.

28

Carter dove out of the glass spray and grabbed the scythe where it sat on the couch next to Stacey. The child was protected by her size and the furniture as shards of glass pinged off the floor, snow pushing through the broken window.

Aniyah threw up her arms and ducked, but still caught a few pieces of glass. She was far enough from the window that the tiny knives only scratched and bruised her right arm and the right side of her face.

Jed used his blood-soaked arm to break the pieces of glass that still protruded from the window frame like teeth, his massive body folding itself as he prepared to climb through the window.

"Run!" Aniyah screamed, and she slipped and slid on broken glass as she darted down the hall that led to the rear of the house.

Stacey launched off the couch as if propelled by the ringing of the ice cream truck's bell, and the tightness in Carter's chest eased as he heard the crunch of the kid's little sneakers crushing glass as she chased after Aniyah.

Jed was through the window, rising to his full height, but he held no weapons.

Carter remembered the scythe in his hand, and he gripped the old wooden handle tight as he planted his feet and coiled himself, preparing to put the tip of the blade in Jed's ear.

With a scream of fury Jed surged forward in an awkward gait, the bloody side of his body a tattered mess of slashed skin and torn clothing. His hat was gone, and gashes crossed his face, his cheeks and neck covered in dried blood.

Carter swung the scythe with everything he had, taking out all his frustration, settling all family business.

But Jed wasn't done yet. He stopped coming at Carter, eased his right foot back for support, and turned his body as he plunged his good hand into his jacket pocket and pulled Carter's Heckler & Koch VP9.

The blade missed Jed by inches, and the big man brought up the H&K.

Wind and snow gusted through the open window as the irony of getting plugged with his own pistol almost made Carter laugh in his desperation. The heat of depression and loss seeped through him, his muscles betraying him.

But the spark of survival that had lit the way the last two years ignited his fury and brought forth a horrific hatred he'd only felt one other time in his life.

Jed fired, but he was off balance and Carter too close.

The shot whizzed by Carter's left ear and burned his earlobe, his head ringing, his vision going blurry.

Carter swung the blade again, and this time he hit his target.

The thwap of cutting meat, the crack of metal hitting bone, then Jed's scream of pain filled the living room, blood splattering the couch and floor. Jed's hand hung from cut tendons and broken bones, and the big man staggered back, staring at his hand as it dangled from his dead arm.

Over Jed's shoulder through the broken window Carter saw a Howler the size of a massive grizzly bear stalking between the oaks at the front of the house.

Jed saw Carter staring and looked over his shoulder.

Carter lashed out with the scythe again, aiming for Jed's gut, but the big man blocked the blow.

With a pig-like cry of pain, Jed seemed to remember the H&K in his remaining hand and he raised the weapon.

Carter dropped and rolled as Jed fired, the crack and pop of the VP9 and the plunk and snap of bullets hitting furniture and walls filling the room. Plaster dust clogged the air, providing some cover, but Carter's ears were ringing so loudly he heard nothing else.

With the extra dose of survival adrenaline fueling his aching body, Carter vaulted to his feet like a surfer getting up on a longboard. Head ringing, Carter bolted down the short hallway, passed the broken bathroom door, and through a mudroom filled with boots, dirty clothes, a snow shovel, and more stacks of old magazines.

Aniyah and Stacey stood in the open backdoor, gazing out at an Ozark Howler that was staring at the trio like they were food, and the beast hadn't eaten in a long time.

Carter hadn't seen this Howler before, he was sure of it. The beast was old, was missing its right eye, and thick mange covered its breast and crept down its muscular legs, which had red patches of bare skin where the creature's fur had been stripped away, and one of its twisted horns had been broken off halfway down its length. Yellow eyes bounced up and down as the Howler strode toward the house, the gurgle of the creature's growl rising above the ringing in Carter's head.

"We can't stay here," Carter said as he pushed through the screen door out into the cold and wind.

"Did you... ?" Aniyah's gaze fell on the bloody scythe in Carter's hand.

"The guy won't die!" Carter said. "Come on, now. There's no time."

A demented cackle carried down the hallway, and Jed's dark form appeared in the gloom.

The Howler hadn't slowed, and the beast was making straight for the backdoor of the house.

Carter grabbed Stacey's arm and pulled her with him as he jumped off the stoop and pressed his back to the rear wall of the house. He eased forward and cycled the child between the house and himself, using his body as a shield.

The screen door slapped into its metal frame as Aniyah leaped to the right, putting her back to the house on the opposite side of the stoop.

The Howler came on, all teeth and fury, its claws digging into the snow, angry snarls carrying on the wind.

Carter brought up the bloody scythe, but what it would do against the gargantuan beast he didn't know.

Jed stumbled from the backdoor, blood leaking onto the ice and snow built up on the uncleared stoop. His head jerked right, he saw Aniyah, and the big man rotated his broken body like a zombie trying to work muscles that were no longer attached to bones.

Forced to choose between the barrel of a gun and the oncoming Howler, Aniyah bolted, running along the edge of the house.

Jed fired three times, the pop of the gun echoing over the Ozarks.

The first shot hit Aniyah in her upper left shoulder. The second tore through her neck, and the third took off the top of her head.

Carter watched in stunned silence, his body instinctively shifting in front of Stacey so she couldn't see the horror playing out before him.

Aniyah continued to run, blood spraying the white snowpack that covered the field behind the house. Like a person turning to stone, and then dust, Aniyah's right leg gave out and she stumbled to one knee in slow-motion before collapsing face down in the snow. A halo of red leeched into the whiteness around her, steam rising from the crimson puddle.

Carter screamed, pain grating his throat, his eyeballs popping from his head.

The Howler wailed in return and drove forward into Jed, who hadn't seen the beast in his fury to kill Aniyah. The massive beast pushed onto its hind legs, its claws tearing across what was left of Jed's chest. The sounds of tearing meat and cracking bone reverberated over the farm, the rusty scent of blood filling the air.

Jed and the Howler went down in a tangle, the creature's jaws snapping closed, its teeth tearing into Jed, blood spattering the snowpack.

"Come on," Stacey pleaded, and Carter realized the girl was tugging on his arm.

149

Carter wanted to go to Aniyah, see if she was alive, get her to safety. Stacey needed her, and so did he. The heat of love and loss brought tears to his eyes, but he fought them back. He needed to be strong for Stacey.

"Come on!" The kid gripped Carter's jacket and was pulling as hard as she could, her white freckled face red with the cold and strain.

Carter chuckled to himself in the chaos. He needed to be strong for her?

Jed gurgled, blood pouring from his mouth as the Howler's head jerked forward and back as the beast took bites from the big man.

Jed fired the H&K, six shots at point-blank range.

The Howler was driven back as some of Jed's shots hit their mark. The mighty beast threw its head back and roared, blood spraying from its mouth and dripping down its fangs, stains of dark crimson marring its slick black fur.

"Go to the pickup," Carter screamed.

Stacey hesitated, the deep pools of her innocent eyes peering up at Carter in desperation.

"I'll be right behind you."

The kid bolted.

Realizing it couldn't match the power of a 9MM bullet, the Howler retreated, shuffling over the open field behind the house and leaving bloody footprints in the snowpack.

Carter went to Jed where he lay on the frozen ground, chest heaving, his eyes glassy and staring at the overcast sky. He reached down and retrieved his VP9.

Jed coughed up blood, and sputtered, "Do it."

Carter obliged. He aimed the H&K, then thought better of wasting ammunition, so he let the gun fall to his side as he raised the blade.

Jed stared up at him and smiled.

"Why?" asked Carter, scythe poised to strike.

"Because I could."

Rage worked its way into the cracks of Carter's rationality, the burning fire of hatred summoning its friend revenge. Jed didn't deserve death. That was too easy, and Carter's mind flashed back to the incident. Had death been the easy way out for Katie's rapist? Or would rotting in jail have been more of a punishment? Like then, the system had failed, and Carter had no choice. He was no judge, but he was the jury.

Carter looked to make sure Stacey had passed around the corner of the house—he didn't want her to forever remember him as a killer—and when he didn't see the girl, he brought the blade down with a finality that left no doubts about Jed being alive or dead. He didn't know how many swings he took, blood spraying his jacket and pants, specks of heat dotting his face, but when the job was done, he felt no guilt.

The wind hollered and sang, whispering of revenge, and of first digging two graves. He dropped the scythe onto Jed's dead body. Carter stood there for several moments, his breaths clouding the air, the warmth of having done the right thing, the just thing, telling him he wasn't a killer. He'd been forced to do what he'd done. Again.

He ran to Aniyah's body and turned her onto her side as he took her pulse. Nothing. Her brown eyes already stared into the next world, her hair splayed about her head on the snowpack like a crown. Carter dropped onto his ass, tears leaking from his eyes. He reached out, closed her eyes, and said, "Goodbye, Aniyah."

Carter sensed he was being watched, and he jerked his head up.

Two yellow eyes peered from the gloom along the tree line to the north, the snout of a Howler poking from the forest.

He eased the clip from the H&K and thumbed the 9MM shells into his palm. Seven bullets plus one in the pipe. Carter reloaded the magazine, jammed it home, and re-chambered a round.

The new arrival inched from the forest on all fours, horns swaying as it sniffed the ground.

Carter got to his feet and staggered through the snow, the sound of his footfalls echoing over the farm. Thoughts of what the Howlers would do to Aniyah's body filled him with loathing and disgust, but he needed to worry about the living. There would be time to mourn if he survived. He started for the pickup where he expected to find Stacey waiting, then realized he didn't have the Ford's keys. Holding his breath, nausea threatening to take him down, pain gripping his stomach, he searched Aniyah's dead body for the truck keys. They were in her jacket pocket, and sorrow washed over him as he retrieved them.

The Howler sniffed the blood trail left by its brethren, and was joined by a second, smaller beast. The juvenile's horns were shorter, and there were no fangs visible, but the Howler was twice the size of the biggest bear Carter had ever seen.

He hurried around the house, cut across the corner of the eastern field, and found Stacey standing next to the truck. There was no fob on the keyring, so he used the Ford key to unlock the truck's doors and hoist Stacey inside.

"You alright, kiddo?"

"Aniyah's dead, isn't she?"

Normally Carter would attempt to sugarcoat bad news for children like he used to with his students. "Yes, student X, you've failed, but it's not the end of the world and there's always summer school if you don't want to fall behind." But Stacey had been through too much, and she was too smart, so Carter didn't insult the child and said, "Yes."

Stacey cried, Carter patting her on the back as he watched the house and the empty field, expecting the Howlers to appear at any moment.

"We're almost free. Can you hang in there a little longer?" Carter wasn't sure he could.

Stacey nodded.

Carter put the Ford's key in the ignition and turned it.

Nothing. Not even the clicking of a dead battery.

"No, no, no!" Carter yelled as he pumped the gas pedal and twisted the key.

Nothing.

"Stay here." Carter grasped the hood release, popped the hood, and slipped from the truck, slamming the door behind him as he stuffed the H&K in his waistband.

Carter was no mechanic, but he'd worked on his own car when he was young, doing brakes, tune-ups, and other basic maintenance. Snow slid off the Ford's hood as he lifted it and Carter immediately saw the problem.

There were no sparkplug wires running to the distributor cap.

He slammed the hood in frustration, and within the echo of the resulting boom Carter heard the cry of Howlers and he spun on his toes.

The smaller Howler that had tracked the blood trail of the injured alpha rounded the rear of the house at a full gallop, legs pumping, head bouncing up and down, yellow eyes cutting through the gloom. The beast churned across the corner of the barren field, a hundred yards from the truck.

Carter knew there was no way he and Stacey could outrun the beast, and as he ran around to the passenger side door to get Stacey so they could flee he felt the H&K digging into his back.

"Lock the door and get down in the footwell," Carter yelled.

"No! What are you going to do?" Stacey pleaded. "I want to help!"

"Get in the footwell, now!" Carter screamed with such force his voice cracked and his throat hurt.

A wave of pain broke over Stacey's face, but she complied, and Carter watched with relief as the kid slid from view.

Carter drew the VP9 and faced the Howler. With his children's faces staring at him from the void he planted his feet as he brought the gun up in a two-handed grip and aimed it at the beast.

29

The Ozark Howler came on, muscles knotted, pointed ears pinned back next to twisted horns. The beast churned up the snowpack as it bounded over the field, the wind taking hold of the snow and clouding the air.

Carter took a deep breath and filtered out the shriek of the wind as he ranged his thumb over the H&K, making sure it was ready to fire.

Barks, answering howls, and broken hyena-like braying came from all directions now, and as Carter focused all his energy on keeping his hands steady, perspiration seeped from every pore. There were more than two Howlers, and the realization that he had no idea how many there might be sent the imaginary mice scurrying down his spine.

The young Howler was close, thirty yards off, snow clouds rising from the ground, yellow eyes locked in, steam jetting from flaring nostrils, jaws distended and open in a toothy grin.

Carter rolled his shoulders and cracked his neck, took a deep breath, and squeezed off three shots.

Pop, pop, pop echoed over the Ozarks, the scent of cordite thick in the swirling snow.

The Howler stumbled and went down in a tangle of limbs, blood leaking into the snowpack as the beast disappeared in a cloud of white fog.

Thoughts of more beasts urged Carter on, and with the Howler's death wail still hanging in the air he jerked open the Ford's door and pulled Stacey from the cab.

The child hugged Carter's legs, and the pair stood there, swaying in the wind, clutching each other like they never wanted to let go.

A shrieking moan of pain came from the barn, a braying-bark that ended in a prolonged groan like a giant human dying. The roar of a Howler, then the sounds of tearing meat as the cries of the horse died away.

Carter grabbed Stacey's shoulder and guided her east down the driveway. Third time had to be the charm.

Stacey trudged on in silence, walking beside Carter with her head down.

Pain shot down Carter's spine and his stomach bubbled with anger and disappointment. How would Stacey have a normal life after the trauma she'd been through? To that, the practical and rational side of his brain argued that kids were tough, their memories short, and Stacey seemed smarter and tougher than any youngster Carter had ever met.

The wind played the trees, limbs clicking and tapping, dead leaves rattling. Carter heard no birds, no titters or rustles of small creatures moving about. It was as if the entire forest knew the monsters were on the prowl with nothing holding them back, and it was time to lay low.

The pair reached the end of the main driveway where it forked into many directions. Carter and Stacey's footprints trailed off in two directions, and from what Carter could see that left three more options.

"Pick one," he said.

Stacey considered, then chose the southernmost path.

Carter led, the kid skipping and jumping in his footsteps. The snow was deep in spots, drifts having built up in the dips in the road and around turns. Stacey was humming a tune he recognized from some children's show, sniffing the crisp winter air as she bobbed up and down, the forest embracing her. He wished the nurturing woods could help him, but he couldn't stop thinking about what might be lurking in every shadow and behind every boulder. He knew the child was aware of this as well, but innocence is an amazing brainwasher.

A staccato cackle resounded through the forest, and it was answered by a barking yelp.

Carter stopped walking and Stacey bumped into him.

"Wha—"

He spun around and put a finger to his lips.

The first call had come from behind them, Carter was fairly certain of that. The other… It echoed off the mountains to the southeast, but it was difficult to pinpoint its origin. Urgency poked him like a million ants crawling over his skin, their mandibles digging into his flesh, tiny legs scuttling and twitching.

"We need to go faster," he said. "Can you?"

The child nodded.

Carter set off at a jog, then slowly galloped to a half-run. Going faster would be dangerous. If he slipped, stumbled over a rock or a tree root, and injured himself or broke a leg, then what? Tripping ten feet before the finish line might be dramatic, but it wasn't the ending he was looking for.

A crack resounded through the forest to Carter's right. It was close, and he twisted as he raised the H&K.

Shadows gyrated next to an evergreen.

Carter fired, the pistol jerking in his hand. The bullet smacked the ground fifteen feet away, a spout of snow bursting into the air and leaving a tiny snow cloud behind.

Nothing moved.

A shadow danced beneath a tree limb.

He was losing it, his nerves frayed, and now he was seeing things. Only four shots left.

Stacey had gone ahead, but she had stopped and was staring at the ground.

There were two sets of tracks in the snow. Fresh ones. Their tracks.

"Shiiiiiiitttttttttt," Carter screamed, and he didn't care who or what heard him. If the beasts wanted him, bring it on. He'd had enough. His head filled with heat, his eyes burning, sweat dripping down his back despite the cold.

"Carter," came the cooing voice of Stacey. "Carter?" She tugged on his pantleg.

He looked down at the child, and when he saw the concern etched into her face his anger melted away. "It'll be alright. Come on," he said.

With only two options left, they took the center path. Thick oaks rose on both sides of the driveway, and Carter walked on the center bump where the snow was only six inches deep. Chickadees fluttered in and out of the trees, cooing and shrieking.

Carter froze. Did he hear the hum of a motor? He waited several minutes, trying to sift out the ambient noise. A helicopter buzzed by to the south, but it was barely visible through the trees.

"Here! Help! Here!" Stacey wailed, waving her arms in an attempt to flag down the plane's pilot.

"He can't see us, honey," he said. "Too far away and we're in the forest."

"We can find a clearing," the kid pleaded.

The rumble of the copter's rotors was already fading.

"Maybe," he said. It wasn't a bad idea, but no way he was leaving the path if he didn't have to.

When they arrived back at their starting point, the driveway leading up to the house mocking them, Carter realized they must have missed a turnoff. He had no idea how long it had been since Jed had visited civilization, and with a covering of snow on the ground there could be multiple roads worn in the hardpan that the duo couldn't see.

Carter took the southernmost path, the one Stacey had chosen originally, and the pair hurried along as fast as their weary legs would allow. When the driveway turned east in a slow arc Carter slowed, and the pair scanned the forest closely for any signs of an offshoot.

They'd been inching along for five minutes when Stacey said, "What's that?"

Off to the right, about fifty yards into the forest, an old wheel was propped against a giant white oak that still had most of its leaves, though they were brown and brittle.

Carter dropped into a catcher's crouch, trying to judge the land. There did appear to be a snow-covered hump snaking through the forest. He took several hesitant steps south, using his boot to clear away the snow.

"Bingo!" Carter said. "I think you found it."

With the end near, he remembered Jed's cash in his pocket, and dreams of food, drink, heat, and a warm bed danced in his head like sugarplums. Stacey climbed on Carter's back so they could move faster, and his knees ached as hunger pains wracked his stomach.

But it was fourth and goal on the one, one second left, down by five. It was time to leave it all in the forest.

Carter pounded through the snow, past the old car wheel, not heeding the roars, cries, and wails of the Howlers, which didn't sound close. Perhaps he and his young friend were out of the Howler's territory and had ventured too close to civilization. He felt the burn of stomach acid creeping up his throat, and imagined it was vodka settling in his stomach, a pseudo warmth oozing through him.

The driveway narrowed, thick trees boxing in the road as it cut through a thick tangled patch of pine and juniper. Shadows danced in the forest, the thinning cloud cover like pulled dirty cotton. The dark maw that led into the thicket looked like a cave entrance, and red warning lights blinked all over Carter's mental control panel. The scent of gasoline and manure wafted down the driveway, and faint grumbling leaked from the forest.

Carter looked over his shoulder, then right and left. The forest was thick, the oaks thin and spaced close together. Leaving the driveway and walking around the tunnel of pines and juniper would take time, and there was no guarantee they could blaze the trail faster than the Howlers, or that they wouldn't get lost.

A guttural growl, a roar, then gurgling bark-like laughter floated up the path behind them.

There were Ozark Howlers near.

Judging that leaving the trail and going around the evergreens was the greater of two evils, Carter gripped the VP9 tight in his hand, cinched up Stacey as he gripped her leg with his free hand, and continued down the driveway.

Stacey's short, ragged breaths were like a metronome, and Carter set a steady pace. Pine boughs laden with snow and ice drooped over the driveway, and dark pockmarks stained the pristine white where snow and ice had fallen into the snowpack. The prints of birds and squirrels crisscrossed the path, and Carter judged the pickup would just fit through the thicket of trees.

The sweet scent of the conifer's terpenes was like perfume, and it reminded him of Christmas, but as Carter stalked forward the rank stench of unwashed hair and sweaty skin overpowered the candle-like aroma.

A gurgle-growl carried on the wind and Carter froze, the echo of crackling snow hanging in the stillness. Once again, the chickadees went still, and even the wind seemed to die away, the hiss of dead leaves falling to a faint chatter.

An eruption of black fur burst from the evergreens onto the driveway. A massive Howler, teeth bared, fangs protruding over black gums. The beast surged forward on its hind legs, yellow eyes afire, its twisted horns glinting in the pale light.

Carter fired the H&K, the weapon bucking in his hand.

The Howler moved with the fluidity of air and with the stealth of darkness. Muscles heaved, snow crunched, and as the huge shapeless form bore down on him, Carter pulled the trigger two more times.

The first shot went high and wide, but the second two plunked into the Howler's chest and upper thigh. Blood leaked from the leg wound, drenching the snowpack, and the chest wound spewed an intermittent stream of crimson.

Still the Howler came on. It dropped to all fours, growling as it threw itself forward, jaws open, its front paws rising from the snowpack as the beast coiled to strike.

Preserving his last bullet Carter dodged right, but there was no space, the trees like a green snow-covered wall.

The Howler surged at Carter, claws out and swiping for his neck.

Carter went limp like he'd been taught by his surfing instructor back when he took vacations with his family. Back when he had a family. He flopped to the ground, Stacey still clinging to his back. Carter tried to shield Stacey's thin, fragile leg, but the girl still screamed in pain when they hit the snowpack in a tangle.

A foot-deep layer of snow cushioned their fall, and a blur of black fur sailed overhead, the beast's claws raking through shimmering air.

But the beast was massive, faster than Carter, and had more experience fighting.

As Carter tossed Stacey aside and pushed to a knee, the Howler stepped back, braced its massive body, and lashed out with its right paw.

Carter leaned back to avoid the blow, and it missed his face, but the curved claws ripped into his jacket and tore into his right shoulder.

Searing pain drenched Carter's vision red as he fell, tiny black starbursts appearing and disappearing, darkness creeping in around the edges of his vision, the world a whirlwind of tree trunks, snow, and black fur. He landed hard in the snow, face buried.

As he rolled onto his side, he felt an overwhelming urge to close his eyes, let go, and give it all up.

Stacey's legs darted across his field of vision as she took cover in the woods. Smart girl, Carter thought, hot blood leaking down his arm into his pants, his head ringing, weariness and hopelessness beating him down.

The beast screamed, a thick, guttural call that sounded louder than any of the Howler's screeching thus far. Was the creature calling in reinforcements? Carter only had one bullet left. His wounded arm screamed as he cycled the H&K into his good hand. For an instant he saw only the slate gray sky, clouds reaching out, then the Ozark Howler's long snout appeared above him, its mouth full of teeth, two yellow eyes filled with derision sizing him up like he was a steak hanging in the window of a meat market. The Howler leaped at him, paws out, claws distended, mouth open, blood speckled slime dripping through its fangs.

Carter aimed the H&K and the Howler's massive baseball mitt-sized paw knocked it from his hand as it swatted him.

The gun flew across the driveway, hit the ground, and disappeared in the snowpack.

Sensing its victory was near, the Howler drew itself up onto its hind legs, threw back its huge head, and roared, the air crackling with energy.

Carter crab-walked backward, ears ringing, his muscles protesting. He felt the prickle of sharp, pointy evergreen leaves scraping his neck, cold snow filtering into his ripped jacket and down its collar. The snow felt good on his wound, which was pulsating in rhythm with his heart. He grew dizzy as he backed deeper into the evergreen tree, its branches poking him and scratching his face.

The beast pivoted, turning its massive girth as it took a swipe at Carter. Branches cracked and snow sifted down onto him from above, the evergreen shaking on its frozen foundation as the Howler's paw crashed through the tree branches.

Carter had gone as far as he could, and a thick tree trunk blocked his way. Despair settled on him, and he turned to face the Howler, pain paralyzing him, the shoulder wound shrieking. He'd lost some blood, but he felt the wound tightening as it sealed itself. Carter felt no internal pain, he was breathing fine, though he was totally blown-out winded, and he hadn't heard or felt any of his ribs crack.

He wasn't done yet.

The Howler's snout poked through the evergreen leaves, the beast sniffing, searching. When it found Carter, it tore away the branch hiding him, snow swirling in the air.

There was nothing left to do except die or run, and there was nowhere to run.

Carter rocketed forward as the beast's snout plunged toward him, jaws open to take a bite. He punched the beast in the jaw with everything he had, which wasn't much. Pain raced up his arm as the blow connected, and though the blow didn't hurt the Howler, it did startle the beast.

The Howler froze mid-attack, eyes blazing as it worked things out.

Carter surged forward and tried to slip past the beast.

The Howler casually reached out a frying pan-sized paw and corralled Carter, knocking him to the ground, tree branches and snow breaking his fall. The beast howled, then laugh-gurgled as it took a step forward and pressed Carter to the ground with its massive paw. It leaned in, sniffed, and roared, blood-dappled spittle spraying Carter's face.

30

Ozark Mountains, 2:41 PM CST, March 14th, 2021

A gunshot rang out and the top of the Howler's head disappeared in a cloud of red mist, and blood, brain, and bone splattered Carter and the snow-covered pine. The beast's momentum carried it forward, and Carter rolled onto his wounded side, the beast's limp body crashing to the ground beside him. Excruciating pain leaked through him, and Carter shifted onto his back to take the pressure off the wound. To his left the Ozark Howler's body spasmed and deflated, the beast's final breath like the exhalation of an elephant.

Carter's ears rang as he searched for the source of the gunshot.

Stacey sat on her ass in the snow, her youthful face twisted into a snarl, the H&K in her hand. The kid had gotten blown off her feet, and she was still pulling the trigger, the click and tap of the empty VP9 rising above the buzz in his head. Carter inched away from the Howler, but the majestic creature had gone still.

He rolled onto his hands and knees and pressed to his feet, the gashes on his shoulder wailing, pain lancing his lower back and the tips of his fingers and toes. Blood dripped onto the snowpack. The Howler had gotten Carter good, but by all appearances his ribs had turned aside the blow, so his innards weren't spilling out.

Stacey dropped the H&K and started to cry, slow at first, then building into full-blown hysterics. She gasped for breath, her face going red, tears spattering her dirty jacket.

Carter went to the child and knelt before her, the gashes in his shoulder shrieking as the blood flow slowed and the wounds tightened as they closed. He lifted the H&K from the snow, stared at it like it was a turd, flicked his thumb and ejected the magazine, then tossed the weapon into the woods where it would most likely stay until time and the elements buried it.

"I… I…" the child stammered.

Shame washed over Carter, desperation and fear fighting to take control. The scars Stacey would be forced to carry her entire life made him feel lower than low, even though nothing that had happened in the last seventy-two hours was his fault. His wounds screamed, and it hurt to move, but move is what he needed to do.

"Come on," he said. "We're not out of this yet."

The child got to her feet, but didn't move. Her eyes were locked on the dead Howler, her face a twisted mess of angst and horror.

"You had no choice," Carter said. "It would've killed me, then you. Do you understand?"

"So what I did was good?"

Carter put his arm around the kid's shoulders, as he had with his daughter and son many times and guided her forward. When they'd gone a few hundred feet down the driveway, the dead Howler gone, he said, "Forget what you just did. Don't ever think of it again."

She looked up at him, the creases in her red windblown cheeks twisting Carter's stomach. "I thought…"

"You did what you had to do, but still…" Carter rolled his shoulders. "Sometimes we do things in life that we have to, but that doesn't make them good, or right, or even legal."

Stacey nodded, the snow crackling beneath her small feet.

"Promise me you'll do your best to forget about all of this, everything you've seen," he said.

"I don't understand, but I'll try. For you."

Carter's heart melted. "Thank you. It's not that you did anything wrong, it's just… Murder is a crime against nature," he said. "Once that line is crossed, you become the monster."

Like me.

The pair walked in silence for a time, the echo of their crunching footsteps, the gentle push of the wind, and the occasional chirp of a bird or titter of squirrels the only sounds. The driveway twisted south, and the land climbed steadily as Carter led Stacey up a gentle mountain slope, the forest thinning as they climbed. His wounds ached and throbbed, and he walked hunched over, clutching his side, pain jolting through him with each step.

A howl echoed up the slope, followed by a series of laughing barks.

Carter and Stacey halted, looking back, though the cry sounded far off. The howl was more vicious than any Ozark Howler call he'd heard. There was anger in the cry, and Carter thought perhaps the dead Howler had been discovered by its brethren.

After a mile or so the driveway angled sharply upward, and the duo's progress slowed to a crawl. The snowpack was covered in a thin coating of verglas, and maintaining solid footing required caution. When he reached the peak of the hill Carter was breathing heavy, his wounds shrieking in unison with his galloping heart. He thought he heard the rumble of cars, the whish and hum of vehicles driving on a paved road, but he said nothing.

If Stacey heard the cars she didn't let on.

A road twisted along the base of the small mountain. It didn't look paved, but it was plowed, and that meant people.

Stacey jumped up and down and clapped her gloved hands. "We did it! We did it!" the child exclaimed, but still the knot in Carter's chest didn't loosen.

The climb down to the dirt road was easier than the climb up. There were steep sections where the partners were able to sit on their butts and slide down the driveway like they were sleigh riding. Carter's shoulder wound constantly nagged at him, pulling and stabbing, but it wasn't too bad. The hunger pains were worse, and when the pair reached the road, they paused to eat snow and rest.

A metal gate blocked the way, but it was for vehicles, and Carter and Stacey walked around it. The road was indeed unpaved, but it was freshly plowed and there were tire tracks in the snow.

"Carter, look," Stacey whispered, her voice blending with the shrieking wind.

At the top of the slope they'd just climbed down an Ozark Howler sat perched atop a boulder staring down at Carter and Stacey. The beast raised its head, cried out like a dying pig, then turned away, jumped from its perch, and disappeared into the forest.

The dirt road ran east to west, and the western way ended at a regular road. Carter saw cars whizzing by in the distance. Wind gusted as the pair walked west in silence, their breaths clouding the air. When they were five hundred yards from the main road, Carter pulled Stacey into a thicket of juniper.

He had spent so much time surviving, trying to win Jed's game, that he hadn't spent much time considering what he'd do if and when he reached the last space on the gameboard. He and Stacey were steps from civilization, and Carter's real life came rushing back like the tide.

Carter had made up his mind to turn himself in, though he hadn't decided the how and when, and there were his wounds to consider. If he walked out of the woods with Stacey he'd be arrested, and she would go into the system and be forever tied to a murderer. He didn't want that, but as he looked down at the child he didn't know if he could let her go. He'd already lost one family, Aniyah was dead, and he didn't want to lose Stacey.

Then there was the scene at the farm. Jed's body, Aniyah's. There would eventually be questions, investigations, and the police would look to lay blame. He didn't want Stacey to have any part in that, and that meant he needed to let her go. He motioned for her to sit on a nearby stone, and he planted himself next to her.

"So this is where we have to say goodbye, at least for now," Carter said.

The kid's face twisted, betrayal carving lines in her freckled cheeks. Between sobs she forced out, "Why?"

Carter sighed. He couldn't tell the kid the truth… could he? No. There was no way he was unloading his guilt on a child that already needed years of therapy. He said, "I can't really explain, but when you're out of this place, and what's happened to us is examined, you may hear things about me. Bad things."

"What are you going to do?" she asked.

"I'm not really sure, but there are some things I have to do, and I may be gone for a while. But I'll find you. I promise."

She smiled.

"We're going to walk up to the road there. Someone will stop."

Stacey trumpeted, and she wiped her nose with the back of her hand.

"Tell the police the entire story, just say you didn't know my name, and that I left you on the highway. Or…" The last thing he wanted was Stacey getting put in the system, and perhaps there was a way to avoid that, at least in the short term.

"Listen, you know it's not O.K. to lie to the police, right?"

She nodded.

"But maybe this one time…"

Stacey said nothing.

"You could tell the police everything like I've said… or… You could tell them your mother is Debra Renfrow."

"Who is that?"

"My wife, actually, was my wife. But she's a good woman, and I know she'll do right by you. Tell her the whole story, everything you and I did. She'll help you decide how to deal with the police."

Stacey stayed silent.

"It's your choice, but whatever you choose, make sure you mention the farm. Tell the cops how Jed took you there. There may be animals there that need tending." What he didn't say was the Howler might get to them first like the horse, but he couldn't worry about chickens, or dead bodies. He'd won a battle, but the pulsating pain in his shoulder reminded Carter that his war continued.

Carter pulled up the kid's mask, which was still hanging around her neck, then he pulled up his gaiter.

Snow cyclones twisted down the snow-covered dirt road, and Carter's side pulsed with anger as the pair walked hand in hand, his other arm tucked against his side like a broken wing.

The murmur of the main road carried on the breeze, and when Carter was a hundred yards away from the busy thoroughfare he stopped and drew Stacey to him, hugging her, taking in her smell. He would file the memory away next to his own children, to be taken out and observed, and used to sustain his sanity.

"I don't want to leave you," Stacey wailed as Carter peeled her off.

Carter kissed the child on the head, turned, and walked down the dirt road without looking back. When Stacey's crying faded, he ducked into the cover of the forest and positioned himself so he could keep an eye on the child.

She reached the end of the dirt road and stood there, looking side to side, then over her shoulder back in his direction.

A burning sense of loss hit Carter and he forgot his pain, tears welling in his eyes.

Only six minutes melted away before a blue sedan stopped, and a man and woman got out. Stacey looked back, searching for him, but when she saw Carter was gone, she got in the car with the strangers.

Carter waited there a long time, staring at the highway. An hour slipped away, two. Then he cleaned his hands and face of dried blood using snow and turned his jacket inside out to hide the gore before hiking to the bustling road and setting out along its shoulder, thumb out.

31

Borderland Pass, I-49, Ozark Mountains, 9:19 AM CST, July 2nd, 2021

The hum of vehicles racing down I-49 carried through the forest to where a female Howler sat on her haunches in the shade of a white oak, the tree's green leaves singing in the breeze. The beast's yellow eyes were focused on the interstate, the bright metal colors flashing by and cutting through her home. The beast grumbled, the baby in its belly kicking and thrashing.

Tree branches cracked as a huge Ozark Howler sauntered through the forest, its muscles relaxed, skin covered in black fur hanging from its arms, legs, and torso. The beast huffed and chuffed as it walked, its head bobbing up and down, yellow eyes locked on the female. One of the male Howler's horns was broken, a product of the beast's fight to win his mate.

The female roared as the male got closer, and the alpha eased to a halt and dropped to the hardpan, rear legs tucked beneath his belly, front paws out like a dog.

A horn blared from up on the interstate, and both beasts turned their heads toward the noise.

Birds sprayed from a patch of evergreens as a third Howler joined the party, another male, but this one was much smaller.

The female made no sign when her son sat next to her, it was his father she had a problem with.

The three beasts sat there, the sun arcing toward noon, the buzz of the highway filling the forest. Shadows danced beneath the tree canopy, rays of sunlight breaking through the thick cover of leaves like spotlights. Gnats filled the air, and the beasts constantly swiped and slapped at flies, tics, and mosquitoes that continually harassed the animals as they tried to hide from the midday heat.

The screech of tires, a racing engine, then the pop of a backfiring exhaust. An old flatbed truck carrying a crushed car glided to a stop on the shoulder of the interstate. A car door slammed and a big man wearing jeans and a red shirt got out and buried his head under the hood.

The young Howler sniffed and pushed to his feet, drool dripping from his half open mouth, the youngling's fangs not fully developed, its horns just nubs beneath its thick hair which made the beast look more like his mother than his father. The beast took two strides toward the highway and the female growled; a powerful, low, steady rumble that made the youngster freeze in his tracks.

The alpha appeared uninterested. He stared into the forest, tracking a chipmunk as it darted in and out of the trees.

A few seconds dripped away before the young Howler jerked into motion, faster than before, like if he was quick enough his mother wouldn't see him. Like most children when trying to outthink their parents, the young Howler was wrong.

The female roared, a dinosaur-like shriek that echoed through the forest and made every living thing within earshot pause and take note. All except the youngster. Like a petulant human child, the young Howler ignored its mother and continued toward the interstate and the truck stopped on its shoulder.

With a quickness that defied her size, the female surged to her feet, muscles rippling beneath black fur, yellow eyes on fire, jaws open, teeth bared. The creature's ears jerked around as if searching for a signal, then went still, her snout moving in small circles as she leveled her head and gave her son the dirty eyeball.

Still the young Howler didn't stop advancing toward the highway.

Mom looked to Dad, who was still focused on the chipmunk. She growled, a low gurgle that turned into a clicking cadence.

The alpha turned his head and saw the youngster striding toward the interstate.

Wind pushed leaves across the hardpan, and a cloud of gnats filled the air. The alpha got up slowly, like it was a hassle, cleared its throat, and let loose with a string of hyena-like laughing barks.

Youngster didn't look back.

Like fathers everywhere, the poppa Howler had only so much patience. The beast closed the distance between itself and its son in six large steps. Muscles flexed, and the alpha pushed up onto its hind legs and roared, then lunged forward onto the smaller Howler, its paws raking his son's back. Dad's claws didn't dig in because the alpha didn't want them to, but junior got the picture.

The young Howler squeaked, then tried to bark like its father, failed, and ran whimpering into the forest.

The alpha gurgled and huffed as it stalked back to its spot and sat down.

Up on the interstate the flatbed was running again and pulling away.

The two Howlers sat in silence, watching I-49, birds flitting around them, the hum of the highway carrying through the forest as they waited.

The End

Other Severed Press novels by Edward J. McFadden III: Predators & Prey, Wolves of the Sea, Fortune's Cypher, Crimson Falls, Hell Creek, Barracuda Swarm, The Cryptid Club, Dinosaur Red, Drop Off, Jurassic Ark, Keepers of the Flame, Throwback, Sea Tremors, Primeval Valley, Shadow of the Abyss (#1 Amazon Bestseller Tag), Awake, and The Breach (#1 Amazon Bestseller Tag, Amazon #1 Hot New Audio Release Tag). His other novels include: Terror Peak (#1 Amazon Bestseller Tag), the Theo Ramage Thriller series: Quick Sands, Sandbagged, and Too Much Grit, Dogs Get Ten Lives, The Black Death of Babylon, and HOAXERS. Ed lives on Long Island with his wife Dawn, and their daughter Samantha.

CHECK OUT OTHER GREAT CRYPTID NOVELS

BIGFOOT WAR
by Eric S. Brown

Now a feature film from Origin Releasing. For the first time ever, all three core books of the Bigfoot War series have been collected into a single tome of Sasquatch Apocalypse horror. Remastered and reedited this book chronicles the original war between man and beast from the initial battles in Babblecreek through the apocalypse to the wastelands of a dark future world where Sasquatch reigns supreme and mankind struggles to survive. If you think you've experienced Bigfoot Horror before, think again. Bigfoot War sets the bar for the genre and will leave you praying that you never have to go into the woods again.

CRYPTID ZOO
by Gerry Griffiths

As a child, rare and unusual animals, especially cryptid creatures, always fascinated Carter Wilde.

Now that he's an eccentric billionaire and runs the largest conglomerate of high-tech companies all over the world, he can finally achieve his wildest dream of building the most incredible theme park ever conceived on the planet...CRYPTID ZOO.

Even though there have been apparent problems with the project, Wilde still decides to send some of his marketing employees and their families on a forced vacation to assess the theme park in preparation for Opening Day.

Nick Wells and his family are some of those chosen and are about to embark on what will become the most terror-filled weekend of their lives—praying they survive.

STEP RIGHT UP AND GET YOUR FREE PASS...

TO CRYPTID ZOO

SEVEREDPRESS

facebook.com/severedpress
🐦 twitter.com/severedpress

CHECK OUT OTHER GREAT CRYPTID NOVELS

SWAMP MONSTER MASSACRE
by **Hunter Shea**

The swamp belongs to them. Humans are only prey. Deep in the overgrown swamps of Florida, where humans rarely dare to enter, lives a race of creatures long thought to be only the stuff of legend. They walk upright but are stronger, taller and more brutal than any man. And when a small boat of tourists, held captive by a fleeing criminal, accidentally kills one of the swamp dwellers' young, the creatures are filled with a terrifyingly human emotion—a merciless lust for vengeance that will paint the trees red with blood.

TERROR MOUNTAIN
by **Gerry Griffiths**

When Marcus Pike inherits his grandfather's farm and moves his family out to the country, he has no idea there's an unholy terror running rampant about the mountainous farming community. Sheriff Avery Anderson has seen the heinous carnage and the mutilated bodies. He's also seen the giant footprints left in the snow—Bigfoot tracks. Meanwhile, Cole Wagner, and his wife, Kate, are prospecting their gold claim farther up the valley, unaware of the impending dangers lurking in the woods as an early winter storm sets in. Soon the snowy countryside will run red with blood on TERROR MOUNTAIN.

CHECK OUT OTHER GREAT CRYPTID NOVELS

RETURN TO DYATLOV PASS
by J.H. Moncrieff

In 1959, nine Russian students set off on a skiing expedition in the Ural Mountains. Their mutilated bodies were discovered weeks later. Their bizarre and unexplained deaths are one of the most enduring true mysteries of our time. Nearly sixty years later, podcast host Nat McPherson ventures into the same mountains with her team, determined to finally solve the mystery of the Dyatlov Pass incident. Her plans are thwarted on the first night, when two trackers from her group are brutally slaughtered. The team's guide, a superstitious man from a neighboring village, blames the killings on yetis, but no one believes him. As members of Nat's team die one by one, she must figure out if there's a murderer in their midst—or something even worse—before history repeats itself and her group becomes another casualty of the infamous Dead Mountain.

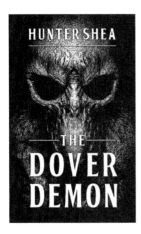

DOVER DEMON
by Hunter Shea

The Dover Demon is real...and it has returned. In 1977, Sam Brogna and his friends came upon a terrifying, alien creature on a deserted country road. What they witnessed was so bizarre, so chilling, they swore their silence. But their lives were changed forever. Decades later, the town of Dover has been hit by a massive blizzard. Sam's son, Nicky, is drawn to search for the infamous cryptid, only to disappear into the bowels of a secret underground lair. The Dover Demon is far deadlier than anyone could have believed. And there are many of them. Can Sam and his reunited friends rescue Nicky and battle a race of creatures so powerful, so sinister, that history itself has been shaped by their secretive presence?

CHECK OUT OTHER GREAT BIGFOOT NOVELS

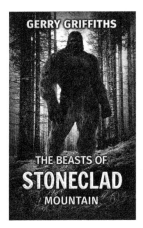

THE BEASTS OF STONECLAD MOUNTAIN
by **Gerry Griffiths**

Clay Morgan is overjoyed when he is offered a place to live in a remote wilderness at the base of a notorious mountain. Locals say there are Bigfoot living high up in the dense mountainous forest. Clay is skeptic at first and thinks it's nothing more than tall tales.

But soon Clay becomes a believer when giant creatures invade his new home and snatch his baby boy, Casey.

Now, Clay and his wife, Mia, must rescue their son with the help of Clay's uncle and his dog, a journey up the foreboding mountain that will take them into an unimaginable world...straight into hell!

BIGFOOT AWAKENED
by **Alex Laybourne**

A weekend away with friends was supposed to be fun. One last chance for Jamie to blow off some steam before she leaves for college, but when the group make a wrong turn, fun is the last thing they find.

From the moment they pass through a small rural town they are being hunted by whatever abominations live in the woods.

Yet, as the beasts attack and the truth is revealed, they learn that despite everything, man still remains the most terrifying evil of them all.

Printed in Great Britain
by Amazon

42783985R00099